MW00876990

Wind

Keep living out loud!

[signature]

Russell Stuart Irwin

Order this book online at www.trafford.com
or email orders@trafford.com

Most Trafford titles are also available at major online book retailers.

© Copyright 2011 Russell Stuart Irwin.
All rights reserved. No part of this publication may be reproduced, stored in a retrieval
system, or transmitted, in any form or by any means, electronic, mechanical, photocopying,
recording, or otherwise, without the written prior permission of the author.

Cover art: Russell Stuart Irwin
Cover design: Kevin Williamson

Print information available on the last page.

ISBN: 978-1-4669-7162-2 (sc)
ISBN: 978-1-4669-7164-6 (hc)
ISBN: 978-1-4669-7163-9 (e)

Library of Congress Control Number: 2012922895

Trafford rev. 06/21/2017

 www.trafford.com

North America & international
toll-free: 1 888 232 4444 (USA & Canada)
fax: 812 355 4082

Acknowledgments

THANKS to Elizabeth for the fine wine of you, you and me . . . our journey; to Ryan and Dana, Ashley, Michael, and Jonathan for being so uniquely you and so wonderfully us; to "the three bright lights" for all you have added to the we in *famiwe*; to Will Brunk for ping pong and for praying (for thirty years), Bernadette Randle for insisting, Steve Heald for cussing, Kevin and Matt for advising and encouragement, Dan and Dana for listening, Kyle Sullivan for "getting" *Payāma*, Don and Sue for a table to sit at and write, and friends and immigrants (too many to name) for your authentic contributions to the road home.
And:

> Blessed art Thou O Lord, Our God,
> King of the Universe
> Creator of the fruit of the vine.

Dedicated to Ron Cowan—for believing.

Prologue

"A king has a vineyard. It is the Royal Vineyard right in the middle of the Royal Garden."

The visitor and his expected oration had not yet been formally introduced; nor had he made any opening remark. As lunch was being cleared, he just stood up and began telling the story, voice strong and arresting, though, *a little on the high side for a famous speaker*, Māya thought. After hearing of his coming, she had waited for it expectantly. Several people made mention that he would be traveling a great distance and visiting other villages along the way. "*That's* all he does, travel and talk?" she had asked her mother. Such a thing was an appealing revelation to a girl moved from long days of sun-baked field labor to long days of tedious labor because of her extraordinary weaving skills.

The day had finally arrived, and the whole thing seemed such a hullabaloo, even after weeks of anticipatory chatter running through the village. Her own excitement was most surprising.

Everyone swiveled toward him on their benches. Strolling between the tables, his hands helped themselves to shoulders and the tops of the children's heads.

"Walking through the Royal Garden," he continued, "its beauty and life please the King greatly. It constantly changes because the King enjoys surprises. Endless varieties of flowering marvels adorn every new day as myriads of garden scents welcome his presence. Springs are hidden by sculpted hills of moss-covered boulders, trees, shrubs and ivy. Their splashing sounds tease his anticipation until the passing of a great rock or entering of a nook through a veil of hanging vines exposes the falling waters like doors flung open and a bride revealed to song."

The storyteller paused long enough to let the last phrase or two sink in.

Māya enjoyed surprises also, more then anything else. They were the wonder of the day-to-day. And the bride reference, though just allusion, was a delightful surprise in the story. Swept away, she quite naturally pictured herself as the bride. It was her common fancy, but on this occasion, introduced with some choreographed trickery, like the waterfalls in the "Royal Garden." Māya *lived* somewhat swept-away, not usually needing any help from a story teller. Effortlessly, her mind supplied the smells of a King's garden and the floral wonders of the bridal procession.

Māya was blind. This was her gift. Scenes she imagined were far more colorful and majestic than anyone else pictured, unhindered by limitations imposed by visual experience. She dreamed wedded dreams with abandon, safe in her certainty such things would never grace her days. What enchanting power was there to break the spell of blindness, but in dreams? Otherwise, would any prince forgive unseeing eyes when choosing his princess? Her dream world was a neat resolve, and all too safe.

"Not only is the vineyard at the center of the garden . . ." The speaker was in no hurry, walking through the modest gathering, his story measured, a full range of engaging dynamics in play. He was drawing nearer. "It is made of a single vine topping the rounded hill at the center of the garden." Passing, he hesitated. "As in long flowing locks, its fruitful strands spread, covering the entire hill."

Retracing steps, he came and stood before Māya. She felt her hair lifted from her left shoulder and visualized it black and shiny in his hand. As if *in* the story, she too was paused . . . breath, thought, movement, all but her pounding heart frozen. Even Māya's normally busy eyelids were incapable of blinking. He placed his hand on her head. A *blessing* . . . all was quiet. She felt his eyes upon hers. Unexpected and unfamiliar feelings of destiny produced tears in those wide but unseeing eyes. He moved on.

"Ripe clusters of fat fruit in every color by which grapes have ever been known . . ." His voice was far more distant than the few steps taken as he walked away. "They bow the branches, hanging lower than leafy shadows and sparkling in the light of the sun, causing what we all would expect . . . desire!"

Māya was momentarily unable to listen, distracted. There it was, the long-awaited moment come and gone. If ever an enchanting moment was capable of breaking the spell . . . . She sighed. It was just as she had always imagined—the eye to eye magical deliverance . . . tears, finally a couple of fluttery blinks and . . . "Yes!" . . . release from the spell! But, no, it had passed with no effect.

"But the fruit is more than just desirable," the storyteller assured his listeners, "its taste more than satisfying. It is lifegiving!"

Māya's chin had been high, indicating expectance. The posture was not realized until it lowered, suddenly signifying something deflated . . . defeated. That very moment the habitual dreaming stopped and the safe certainty left. This darkness was her reality, here to stay. She stared, blank and stunned, unprepared for the unwanted epiphany. *This is my situation,* she silently resolved. *It's not going to change.* She was thirteen and the thought had never before occurred.

"From the point at the peak of the hill in the center of the garden at which the vine comes out of the ground . . . the whole kingdom can be seen, its deep mysteries and glorious treasures revealed. The point is not only an exact place . . ." There was a long pause. Māya looked up, dim, yet back with the story being told. ". . . but a fixed and precise time from which all time flows. The outer walls of the kingdom can be seen from there."

He sounded very young for a *priest*. But Māya was not an expert on these things. There was no reference point in her community experience and he was the first missionary to come through the village during her thirteen years. She had heard of priests in other villages, but her impression was that they were always old. A priest with a young man's voice made no sense to her. In fact, she was bugged by it and by the attraction she felt. Chatter had revealed he arrived on a spunky Criollo pony, which Māya associated with cowboys. In her world, cowboys were Criollo-bound transients with lots of stories. She heard a comment about him being dressed all in black. A man of God dressed in black, like some kind of religion outlaw . . . to her, he was a cowboy.

Father Bellingham, she was told to call him. She might not know priests so well, but she knew fathers. The village was full of them, run by them. And she knew voices. She could evaluate much with impressive accuracy just by hearing one. In no way was *this* voice the voice of anyone's father. She sat puzzled by the title, and aware of the visitor's restless Criollo, tied to a tree just a few feet away.

Interested in Greek and Latin, the youthful Bellingham had originally been dismayed by his assignment: circuit missionary—Chile, South America. It seemed a thoughtless dispatch, a meaningless and undeserved exile for the self-proclaimed "scholar." But it had grown on him, or he had grown into it. This was helped by discovering possession of a remarkable gift with the Mapuche languages of the broad region of his service. An equally peculiar love for the people who spoke them supplied motivation for perfecting their use. In just a handful of years he had come to be more fluent than many of the villagers, holding audiences such as this one captive with the delicacies of their own tongue, even exacting the nuances of different dialects. It was like sport, hobby, profession and romantic devotion all rolled into one.

Some creativity was required. He learned early on there was no use in implementing the preaching techniques taught in seminary. Anything technical in nature was discovered to be "impossible." But he had enjoyed some success with stories. Stories connected. This had become Bellingham's way. Determined to preach the scriptures, he set out to turn every preachable section of text into parable form, occasionally finding a way to slip in some Latin or Greek. Sometime later, after the parable had time to mature, he would return for a longer stay to shine more light on the details. LETTER CARRIER was ornately stamped into the leather of his saddle bags for personal enjoyment of a self-designation he took seriously. But the official look did make its impression on others. Some wished to touch the beautifully crafted bags, but no one ever had. Nor had he invited anyone to do so. It was as if the leather carvings were sacred representations of the parable he crafted from the Scriptures with equal care, usually drawn from New Testament letters. Deliveries were made with recipient-sensitive modifications.

"There is another vineyard outside the Kingdom walls," the cowboy missionary's audience was informed. His voice turned suddenly stern and sobering, *more like a father*, Māya thought. "The vines in *that* vineyard are dead," he explained, "though they carry on in some mysterious *state* of deadness . . . death diseased . . . under some spell introduced by a local sorcerer jealous specifically of the King's vineyard."

Māya's chin was again high. She had not expected the story to include spells and sorcerers. She felt tingly, as if the sorcerer in the story might be the very one responsible for her "situation."

"Just as mysterious as the ongoing deadness is their location outside the kingdom walls. Intended and prepared for the Royal Garden, they are rebel branches." He took off his black cowboy hat, turned it upside down and ran the index finger of his right hand around the rim, thoughtful, staring inside. He did this so naturally no one suspected there were notes in there. Finally, he looked up.

"Now, some of you, being expert farmers, maybe even vineyard keepers, might want to get smart with me and demand an explanation for how a branch detaches from the vine, runs off, self-tosses up over a great wall and plants itself elsewhere." After running fingers through his long hat-matted hair, he put the handsome hat back on his head. "I am telling you right frank, I am not that smart in the area of great mysteries, nor have I been privy to the planning meetings of the King's gardeners so as to get any inside scoop." Without realizing it, he had left the formal tone of his practiced presentation. "But I don't think there is any detaching, per se. Best guess on my part . . . it would appear a rebel *will* is at work in these branches, a want in each for being their own royal vines—the death-disease I mentioned.

So, when they spring up, they do so outside the kingdom. At any rate, it is a sad sight beyond the walls, all those death-diseased vines with no fruit on them, but trying to cover up the fact with shriveled brown leaves and look as royally fancy as possible to each other . . . awkward too, you can imagine."

Māya was feeling distressed. Eager for the identity of the sorcerer and some answers about his craft and punishment, she had been intently focussed on the details. Yet, she felt the story had turned on her. Disturbingly, the sorcerer seemed to have escaped from view and responsibility. She keenly sensed the same agitation in the village members immediately around her and was thinking it might be best for the cowboy, Bellingham, to get on his Criollo and go. This far along though, there was nothing to do but continue hoping the evil sorcerer issue would soon be dealt with in the story.

"Wondrously," the oblivious offender proceeded, "though they are dead in their diseased state, the King loves the displaced branches and made a way for them to be grafted back into the Royal Vine. Whenever one of the branches has *had it* with the whole pretending aliveness business, it simply looks up beyond the walls to the hilltop in the Royal Garden and takes heart in the King's Vine."

Father Bellingham's horse was starting to cause untimely distractions. Walking over to the tree and releasing it, he handed the reins to Māya. "Would you please hold on to him for just a few minutes?" he asked. After walking back to the center of the seated gathering, he stood for a silent moment, arms folded.

"Another great mystery . . . somehow, by the special favor of the King and the taking-heart I mentioned, a branch that was not there before just appears, connected right to the Vine. If you were to ever visit the Royal Vineyard and look closely, you would notice something different from what you are accustomed to in your vineyards . . . evidence of grafting rather than sprouting where the branches are connected to the Vine. They all get there that way. It's the only way."

The preacher looked over at Māya. The reins had fallen to the ground, but the horse remained at her side. Her hands had found the leather artistry on a saddlebag.

"The King has a name for these precious branches. He calls them 'Poiēma' . . . his personal creative master-works, intended all along for the fruitful work of the Royal Vine at the center of the Royal Garden."

There, he had slipped it in, a bit of Greek, albeit just one word in the story. He usually liked to work in two or three for the sake of staying sharp. Māya heard the inversion of her own name in the word and saw the name Poyāma in her mind. She dearly enjoyed its connection to the vines in the story, its association with the King's favor, the Royal Garden and good fruit. But the sound of it is what would stay with her long after the story was forgotten.

Bellingham walked over and took hold of his horse's reins, which Māya was mortified to realize she was no longer holding. A consoling pat of a shoulder assured all was well.

"What does it mean?" she asked, her softly spoken Mapuche arresting Bellingham's attention.

All eyes were suddenly on Māya.

"Poyāma . . . all names have a meaning. What does it mean?"

"Poiēma," Bellingham corrected, delighted someone cared to ask. "God-made," he answered. After a lengthy pause, he looked around at the others, whose eyes were again fixed on him, and added, "God-made for generous goodness of everlasting value."

He turned and continued walking his horse around the outside of the gathering.

"The King has revealed one other mystery about this 'grafting' of Vine and branches. It is a profound mystery, maybe the greatest mystery of all. Yet, you may have already guessed it."

No one actually had any guesses at all.

Arriving at the spot where he had originally dismounted, the young priest stopped.

"This grafting . . . in his kingdom it is regarded as marriage. *This* is the story of the Royal Union!" He paused and one last time looked around, making sure to meet each set of eyes with his own. "The King has planned a grand wedding feast, the Royal Celebration . . ."

Turning, he put a foot in a stirrup and was quickly seated in the saddle. "It is not far off. I hope to see you all there." A fancy revolution—the kind for which Criollos are known—ended with a lunge forward that brought front legs high off the ground, and he was gone.

"Take heart in the King's favor!" was yelled over shoulder.

No one had expected such an odd ending, *or* the invitation. Five minutes passed. As some stood to leave, Māya remained seated, pondering a lot of new unsafe ideas and feelings. Something about "the King's favor" had gotten through. She pointed her face toward the blue sky above. "Poyāma will be the name of my first child." Hearing her own name called, she rose and made her way back to interrupted weaving as others returned to the fields, many feeling somewhat cheated by the brief event and its abrupt conclusion.

Poyāma's Tongue

Creole—a sauce, a dish . . . tomatoes, peppers, seasonings, rice—for some, this word is loaded with delicious implications of tastes and scents resulting from applied orders of scientific facts commonly called recipes—ingredients blended and cooked.

Where language is concerned, this savory blending of ingredient "facts" may serve an understanding of a *spoken Creole*. In both cases the tongue is messenger, its report pregnant with unique consequences of cultural interactions and the movements of peoples and nations within intimacies of the family abode. But spoken Creole presents evidences of such movements far more complex and revealing than even the most dynamic recipes.

Take, for example, speech within a winegrowing village in a valley in central Chile, under Spanish political rule but local French dominion, in the early to mid nineteenth century. There, the imperial languages of Spanish, French and English converged and infused affect, but the indigenous Mapuche and the Hindi dialect of indentured laborers transplanted from East India (by way of British Guiana) ruled the character of the community tongue. However prominent or subtle, blended epochs were present in the strategic negotiations between French merchants and Spanish governing officials, and no less in the vineyard conversation and chatter within homes of the locals, where Creole reigned.

Beyond the Chilean mountains and coastline that cradled the village, English made its ascent to the status of universal language, nearly unhindered by national boundaries. But the native language of an adopted son is more resistant. Such was the case with Poyāma. The tip of his tongue was trained under the influence of his father's Hindi to maintain contact with the ridge joining hard and soft palates in the roof of his mouth. The result in English was an elimination of the *th* sound: the—de, another—anoter, brother/broter, nothing/

noting, think/tink, etc . . . The strong tonal delivery of Mapuche—primarily his mother's influence—left its lasting mark in ending consonants opposing connection: fast—fass, it's—i's, exist—exis, act—ac, can't—can' and so on.

Of course, we know that language is not merely tonal with various intermittent constrictions, but grammatical and directional as well. Some products of mixture expressed in a common tongue may be "cooked-up" with proper words but served in arrangements which are incoherent or humorous to the hearer. Others may present as oddly identical meanings, like, "your face is knowing" and "you look familiar," or, "time for a smoke" and "jus now we knock a blow." And somehow, if even by humor, confusion in the exchange concerning what is meant reveals *meaning* in the higher sense: origin, history, journey . . . things that matter personally and interpersonally. Word is not merely a vehicle for conveyance of a specifically defined meaning, but is inseparable from the existence, experience and expression of all that is meaning*ful*. Whether speaking of it intentionally or not, Poyāma's journey was ever on his tongue.

I

The Vineyard

A TASTE

"Gloria . . ."

Everyone stared, waiting, knowing that Gloria was never in a hurry. Tasteful sensibilities were not to be rushed or ordered like cattle across the land and into a corral, swiftly processed for consumption. Light was soft. Lanterns—one on the wall near both doors at opposite ends of the room—were low. Their illumination spread like a caramel coating over polished knotty pine, gently reflecting the dance of a dozen flickering flames in candelabra above the tasting table at center. Wine bottles and glasses on the table also sparkled with their reflections. Like a resonating note suspended in the silence between symphonic passages, the spoken name held a composed moment expectant of its owner's voice. It was a wine tasting *event*, requiring words as much as wine.

"Paradoxical . . . ," she announced, "plump and plain, yet exotic and luxuriant . . ." Pausing, Gloria was as the cluster of grapes in her hands, which she drew upward and pressed around her plump nose and against full rosy cheeks. "Basic and magnificent," she continued, "one and many, meager and plentiful, simple and complex . . . round . . ." Fingers delicately traveled bulging contours as if the descriptive words were being read from brail on the skin of the fruit. "Abundantly classic . . . deep and enduring." A few short sniffs, a deep breath and the cluster was returned to the table's centerpiece. After a playful gesture, she folded her hands and added for cliché, "Quite difficult to describe in a few words or phrases really."

"The wine, Gloria dear . . . we are all familiar with the grapes," answered Claudia LaRue, wife of Richard LaRue, Gloria's brother, who was rolling his eyes. The two lifelong friends smiled at one another, indulging the humor testing Richard's patience.

"Gloria . . ." he said again, nodding toward a glass in front of her.

Others standing around the table, eighteen in all, were anxious for the sensual report from the one they considered queen of taste, master of aromatic detection and vocabulary. Never eager to take a turn, modesty was her skill and stealth. Embellishment was as foreign as veneer to soil. Expertise was worn with a generosity of inclusion leaving all in her presence elevated as artists, noble peers with that rare power of communal dignity universally coveted. The anticipated appraisal would, as always, be simple and brief, understood and easily owned, not imposing, but evoking nuances of the shared experience.

The fanciful commentary on the grapes seemed to all uncharacteristic. But it was not alone in departure from her norm. "Unusually pensive and melancholy," one observer had mentioned to another earlier in the evening. Claudia, a person faithful in the direct approach, had asked her about "peculiar sensitivity," further questioning if there was any need to talk about anything. A subtle shake of her head was Gloria's response.

Poyāma was especially attentive—dry-mouthed, actually. And as he listened to Gloria's comments on the grapes, he noted curiously that they matched his own thoughts of *her*. He stared, studied her, savored every detail as if his eyes had taste buds and licked with delight the most delicious sight in which they had ever indulged. He wanted her, imagined her in his life every day, felt a quality and depth of "missing" never before inspired.

Thick brown hair was pulled back, gathered into a long, wavy tail, a dozen or so uncooperative strands dangling free. The ungathered were loosely coiled and bounced to the slightest movement. Like family and friends of his homeland, her eyes were dark, yet their own distinction of deep layered browns touched with green. Unlike his kin back in Chile, her skin was fair, her lips rosy. He had always pictured his bride olive-bronze, dark eyes without the green, shiny black hair and shorter—the girls in the village of his youth were generally petite. *Surprise* more than anything else made him think she was *the one*.

It was their third meeting. The first had been on the occasion of another wine tasting at the LaRue's, mostly to show off LaRue wines and recently awarded medals. The second had been inspired by the first. Having never been so delighted or taken aback, Poyāma had extended Gloria an invitation to picnic. At the time, he wondered if the long planning and difficult journey from South America was all for this—meeting her. And indeed, her acceptance had pronounced *Worthy!* upon every expense, tedium and trial of immigration.

The picnic was a celebration of mutual interests. They had talked entirely of wine—of its extraordinary capacities of resilience and resistance to opposition; how, when expertly cared for, its years move slowly and age characterizes magnificence; and yet, how very fragile its constitution, how ugly its reaction to hasty and imprecise tending, how countless minute perils lie between vine and the satisfying late winter's glass beside the fire. They shared views on the troublesome, yet elegant aesthetic of its three taste dimensions: sweetness, bitterness and acidity.

Poyāma learned of Gloria's training in France, the cause of her absence during his first four years as a neighbor to the LaRues. He was pleased by her amazement when discovering they held the acquaintance of several prominent French wine masters in common. Gloria found the origins of the Chilean winegrowing activities under which Poyāma gained his experience most intriguing. It was 1848 and the French-run vineyard co-op in which he was raised and trained had been established more than thirty years earlier. Its owners were deeply invested in the French industry. Such uncanny connections to correlative concerns and shared welfare astonished both picnicers.

There were a few moments at the picnic of an ordinary nature possessing extraordinary power. Gloria was sitting to Poyāma's left, reclined on her right side, propped by her right arm, legs folded back behind her, black boots crossed at the ankles. Around the base of her neck was a closed white collar overlaid with lace, ornamented with shiny spots of gold thread within its stitching. Between the collar and the boots, a long cotton dress lay flowingly upon her curvy form. The dress and its movement were complimented by a vest that wrapped her shoulders and from them fell formless. A well-worn straw cowboy hat—what one might call full of character—rested lightly on her head, wavy locks and random braids gathered and pulled back loosely beneath it.

Gloria's face was mostly in shadow cast by the tattered hat. But torn holes and openings in the straw weave allowed spots of light through. Most were small. They dappled her skin when she was still, mimicking the lace in her collar. One caught Poyāma's attention. It tipped her nose and followed the contours of her lips, rolled over her chin and onto her neck. He stared. Gloria moved and they all appeared awaken for dance. He watched. Becoming still again, one touched the corner of her mouth. She was smiling, blushed, staring back. Suddenly realizing it, as if startled from a dream, he blinked and turned away.

Was dat OK? he wondered. He had always been told staring is rude. *How come she smile back at me when I do it?*

Gloria reached up with her left hand and took hold of her hat. Poyāma looked over. As she lifted it from her head, Strands of hair clung to fibers of straw and rose until letting go, appearing to catch fire in the sunlight while falling back tangled. Her head was back as she enjoyed the sun's touch upon her face and neck, though no more than Poyāma's eyes did.

Thirsty, he reached to his right where a container held clusters of grapes. He broke off a small branch and consumed a handful of the freshly picked fruit. Intention to offer them to Gloria was fleeting and forgotten—his mind all aflutter. A moment later, she leaned across him to reach for the grapes and her hair caressed his nose in passing. The touch was light, the smell intoxicating.

A silent, internal marvel of craziness ensued, destabilizing Poyāma's universe. His heart rate instantly doubled, his skin tingled and his hands itched under tension of conflicting commands rushing into them from a mind seeming deranged. Force of will kept his hands where they were: behind him, pressed against the ground and supporting his reclining body, fists clenching the blanket spread beneath them. When Gloria reached across him a second time to return the container of grapes to its original resting place, it was more than Poyāma could take.

"Excuse me," he said, sounding short, but only because he was short of breath and afraid his heart could be heard pounding like a drum in his chest.

"Oh, I'm sorry . . . ," Gloria answered, returning to her former repose. "How rude . . , I should have just asked."

But Poyāma was actually excusing himself and getting to his feet. "No, no, no problem wit dat. You OK," he assured, walking away and heading toward the horse-drawn carriage he had delivered from dust-covered inactivity for the occasion. "Time for we take a long ride togeter."

Gloria thought it a rather abrupt transition. But, by the time her picnic companion returned leading two horses pulling the fancy surrey, all of his chemical settings were returning to norms and the long ride idea appeared quite natural. It was hours before they arrived back at the picnic spot to gather food, wine and blanket and call it a day.

Delight motivated the promise to meet again—a promise, like many, more easily made than kept. The picnic took place only days before the beginning of harvest. Though highly anticipated on both sides, the third interaction would suffer delay by two and a half months of sunup to bedtime harvest hustle. It was not as each had imagined: just the two of them. Nor did it come about as they had expected: initiated by Poyāma. But, a second wine tasting event would have to do for the time being.

Finally in her presence again, Poyāma's full capacity of consciousness was held captive by Gloria's beauty and gracefulness. More than just personally admirable, her professional stature was somewhat heroic in his mind. Having begun with visions of belonging among the renowned wine tasters, his was a clumsy tongue exposed to too many languages. The home-made Creole of formative years especially retained influence over English often drawing laughter and mimicking humor. Wine tasting was for refined expressions, not crudely articulated ones. Those boyhood dreams of a place at the tasting table turned into an art of decline and focus on the production and distribution side.

A one-time gesture of neighborly politeness was the thought behind acceptance of the first invitation to wine tasting at the LaRues'. This second one was only accepted for the opportunity to see and listen to Gloria. Whose wine she was about to taste was almost forgotten amid the excitement of being in her presence.

Poyāma was gazing at the brown eyes across the table when they closed. The sip was drawn in. The rim was lowered. Behind wet lips the wine was rolled on her tongue as it was also swirled in a glass releasing scented riches. Unknown to anyone at the table but the two winemaking neighbors, Richard LaRue and Poyāma Vishnu, this was a product of Vishnu Vineyards—Poyāma's wine. A proud, competitive man, LaRue secretly hoped to use the authority of his sister's French training to make a point of the foreigner's inferior craft. But Gloria smiled and her smile was as a conductor's baton commencing a silent sonata of rejoicing in the faces around the table.

"Bouquet rises from this glass like luster from a fine diamond . . . ." She frowned a thinking kind of frown. "Intricate and multifaceted, yet elegant, a concentrated nose, muscat-like, black currant, wild cherry . . . lively tannin, young and firm . . . ."

Eyes open, she pulled back from the glass as if astonished and watched the wine roll around its interior, again frowning, this time a disturbed, distracted kind of frown. Rim beneath her nose, she added thoughtfully, almost dreamily, "Yet, old-fashioned, even ancient qualities . . . woody . . . blackened smoky-burnt-woody with a slight hint of tobacco . . . windy, as if the winds of an Indian summer swept long and strong . . . late harvest, browning leaves, snowy whiteness . . . unusual, enjoyable. It will age nicely toward a maturity to be relished." Staring into the glass, she whispered, "A maturity for which my heart will yearn."

Everyone but Gloria and Poyāma began swirling, sniffing and tasting the wine in their glasses, suspending composure for the moment, having heard things never before conveyed about a wine. All were eager but stumped, unable to detect any of the second set of elements described by the acclaimed taster. Still, each deferred to her judgment and enjoyed every whiff and every drop, emoting ambiguously all the while.

The disturbed frown remained on Gloria's face as she stared downward at nothing, a great distance between her physical and mental locations. Wine tasting was command of senses, precise, scientific. Something unexpected, something outside control of her own senses had asserted influence over disciplines proudly connected to personal responsibility.

"Well," Richard LaRue finally blurted, "even a beginner's gotta get lucky once in awhile." He tipped his glass toward Poyāma, forgetting that no one else was yet clued in to the secret that the wine was a Vishnu vintage. Bursting into laughter at the comment, all but Gloria and Poyāma missed the indication in the tip of the glass.

Emotional reactions to Gloria's description had filled Poyāma's eyes prior to LaRue's sarcasm and were dangling on eyelashes, threatening to fall. When everyone burst into laughter, he flinched and they did fall. Due to preoccupation, no one saw them. Yet, flustered, he nodded and excused himself from the event, unaware that Gloria set her glass down and exited in the other direction. For both, the experience was profound, inclusive of premonition, as if the report had been invaded, something mysterious inserted, something working in the opposite direction of deja vu.

A few of the people present had laughed out of sheer habit of laughing at LaRue's frequently offered humor. Others, thinking the wine to be his creation, interpreted the comic remark as unusually self-effacing for the outspoken, award winning winemaker. All were left puzzled by the abrupt departures. LaRue set down his glass and followed Poyāma to the door.

"De dirt a man trow is de dirty him get," he was scolded by his offended neighbor. It made him laugh, which only worsened offense.

"You know, Richard, friendship hang by a tread dat easily get break."

LaRue chuckled. "In my opinion, friendship that hangs by a thread ain't worth havin'."

"Maybe so," Poyama answered while mounting his horse, "but a wise man take care for such ting."

Put off by the implications and unaware of any reason for such severe reactions, LaRue thought his neighbor was taking things a bit far. All amusement was gone from his tone when letting him know it, which included the suggestion the "foreigner" get over himself, and the announcement, "We're all immigrants here!" as Poyāma rode away. Though angry, neither man thought the words exchanged in parting would have lasting effect.

EATING THE SUN

"Gloria, Gloria, perfec again, what a shame! No wrinkle, no tussle, not a one of you silk tread out of place. A-ah-h, look here! You bed perfec made. Dese fellow no coming to you again? Two night in a row now, I am right? Two morning now I find you like dis. Two night now you going wit no victim blood in you fang."

Poyāma hung his wagging head and turned away. "Time for smoke," he said, drawing a cigar from a vest pocket. His normally low gravelly voice was even lower and almost a rasp. He liked it. Two fingers slid into the pocket and snagged a matchstick. He chuckled. After clipping the end, the tapping on an open palm began—ritual.

"Maybe i's you dresssss. Maybe black and yellow velvet is not de looking dey like any more. Style changing, you know." He stared at her. "Gloria, Gloria . . . number tirty-two . . . I never tink I get so lucky for have so many."

Shaking his head while Walking to the far end of the porch, each slow stride was punctuated by the clomp of a boot on wood plank. The smell of morning dew reached Poyāma's nostrils as subtle hints of a new day's near arrival revealed a thick cloud hovering three to five feet above ground. Surrounding the porch, it spread outward until merging into fog and dark gradations of grayness. Bushes, trees, fence posts, out buildings and a nearby well pump showed themselves shyly as if peeking out at the tarrying dawn from behind the lingering veil of night. The well pump was one of two on his property, but they among only a handful in the entire region. Poyāma was a man of rare privilege, "the man among men" kind, not only standing out, but drawing admiration and envy. He enjoyed that.

Vine covered hills and normally eminent barn and stable were yet invisible. Their invisibility gave him pause. It had never happened before. By virtue of their monumental greatness, it seemed impossible. *Fog so tick as dat?* He wondered. For a moment he was captured like a shadow in a dark corner of a painting, blended into the perfect stillness of the morning. He had awoken bothered, keenly aware it had been ten years to the day since the painful conclusion of the wine tasting event at the LaRue's.

Never have I see a day so still like dis one, he thought, sure of it. *Maybe because all my worker leave me for California gold?*

Just a week ago he had been informed that the six brothers he had employed for more than eight years were preparing to leave. They had been the most loyal and were the last of a staff of more than fifty to move on during the past year. A third year of brutal drought proved too much for their reservedly rewarded allegiance and provided too little defense against tempting stories about fertile lands ripe with opportunities westward and prospecting successes on the opposite coast. This was the second day without their help.

No, he decided, *de stillness have noting to do wit dat. Dis hour never active for nobody but me. I am always firs to rise.*

Blank regarding the unusual stillness, his thoughts turned to guarded hope in the fog, the first of any form of moisture in months. Even the well had failed him. It stood near, between porch and vines, like an old friend, faithful until recent days. Always it had answered with just a crank, maybe two, gushing water. It supplied the individual filling of hand dug troughs around the base of each vine, getting them through two and a half years of severe drought. Just weeks ago the unresponsiveness began, the sputtering, then nothing. He silently chastised himself for procrastinating on the new well. But the well by the cellar was strong. Who would have thought it could start sputtering so suddenly also. It still produced, but with a lot of work and patience.

Strange time, he thought, staring at the well. "Maybe de dew will give helping for de vine and forgiving for de sky dat become so long of stingy." He glanced toward the heavens above the vineyards. "Dis wretched drought."

These were the first negative words about a three year drought from a man trained under French vineyard masters to value confidence in the rebounding and balancing nature of seasons as if this confidence was the key ingredient in an ancient recipe for success. The rest of the recipe was instructive of patience, observation, trust and all labors applicable to such ingredients and activities. But the negativity was not related to the drought, or day two of being alone and without help, or lacking need for help at a time of year normally demanding extra help, except that these left a vacuum filled by a haunting memory.

"Ten year, Gloria . . . ," he whispered, not to his resident Gloria, Gloria Thirty-two, but to a woman in his mind, a memory. "Dat number make a hard word to believe. How ten year pass so fass?"

How he knew it had been ten years since the night of the second wine tasting event at the LaRue's was a matter of practice. Not a day went by in which it did not cross his mind. He had left the event a tangle of conflicting thoughts and feelings all churned by an ever-active "foreigner" consciousness—an *outsider* sensitivity too often allowed to rule over interpretation of social interactions. Partly humiliated by tears no one else noticed, partly feeling belittled by the words "lucky" and "beginner," and greatly angered by misunderstood laughter, all boiled together like ingredients in a pot, stirred by uncertainty about intentions, words and meanings. Combined, all made him feel the focus of a joke he did not get, part of some *insider* humor for which he had no appreciation.

And there was the added mystery of Gloria's describing something not in a glass containing the wine he had supplied. While traveling home the evening of the event, the thrill of her high praise had disintegrated quickly under scrutiny of each word that could not be connected to contents poured from a bottle labeled Vishnu Vineyards. They were words that became confusion with sounds of laughter in the background. They were words to which he had awakened earlier than usual on this particular morning—laying in bed as if staring at them in the dark—words accompanied eerily by the thought, *prophetic,* for the first time in the ten years since they were spoken.

There had always been an unsettling tension of significance connected to the details of Gloria's critique. From the earliest reflections on that ride home from the event, expectation was a profound sensation that could not be dismissed. And still, ten years later it was strong—in fact, stronger than ever. Yet, the question, "Expectation of what?" had never been answered.

In the comfort of his own bed in his fine home, gazing into the dark early hours of that morning, deeper memories had followed the introduction of the word prophetic. It occurred to him that no other *Poyāma* had ever crossed his path. He had wondered about his name. Those thoughts ushered in many others about his childhood—events, people, beliefs and values. All were strangely near.

Holding the cigar in his left hand, the LaRue wine tasting event and the *expectation* were presently near. Pinching fingers put match to flint. But the flame did not make it to the tobacco.

"Today . . . ," he whispered ". . . today, what I expec for ten year finally come . . . I feel it."

He stared out into the early morning. Out there . . . amid the stillness . . . orderly, precise in earth covering procession, were the vineyards that grew wealth and sustained status—actual and imagined. Countless rows were invisible, yet visible by the intimate overseeing heart of their keeper, every one. In the ten years since the event, he had enjoyed the kind of success that reduces a decade to a moment, the proverbial blink of an eye.

"Dis is Saturday coming? Yes, I believe dat word is true. It look to me like Saturday. It feel like de same."

Poyāma's thumb complained of the closeness of heat and the flame was out with a quick shake. Smoke was its obituary. Watching, he leaned and drew in the burnt scent of the slim opaque vapor as it rose perfectly straight, undisturbed in the slightest.

"A-a-a-ah, caught you dis time," he said to the vanquished flame. "You ancestor, dey escape me . . . le's see, one, two, tree, four . . . dis Saturday? Yes, four generation. Monday I las capture de soul of a light before it slip away beyond dis hungry nose."

He chuckled and paused the preparations for lighting another match. Like a boy playing alone, calling the details of a competition with championship implications, he loved this game. It was the smoker versus the smoke—not the smoke drawn through the cigar, but the smoke that was vanishing essence of vanquished flame, fleeting and shifty, normally a challenging capture. The game owed its inspiration to the tasting table and the challenges of capturing the subtleties of bouquet, which he had learned early-on were "slippery as wraiths of smoke." The game had rules—strict rules. match stick could be held no higher than his belt buckle when the flame was put out. Smoke "caught" could not merely be faint whiff of smoke, but was required to contain perfume of match flame in three distinct qualities of distillation: light, heat and consumed resin. The recent catch was unusually satisfying.

"Yes, I know, i's no breezing today," he said thoughtfully, as if answering a protest from the defensive consciousness of the extinguished flame. "A-a-a-h . . . why so stingy? Like de sky you getting too?" He glanced upward. "De sky what give no rain for tree year you want to be like? A-a-ah! Four generation is a long time. Should you be always winning? No, today I have a ve-e-ectory!"

Poyāma was keenly aware of olfactory disciplines responsible for his game's technical qualities—those necessary for scorekeeping. But his favorite contributors were dearly personal: a philosophical bent inherited from his father and a rare "perfect-pitch" sensitivity to smell genetically acquired through his mother. Both parents felt near when he played the game. Loneliness was also a major factor. Responsible for habitual conversing with himself, it was a constant companion. Yet, only occasionally was loneliness identified as one of the causes of his game's invention. This was one of those occasions. He was unusually conscious of *alone*.

The second match was lit. Left hand gripping the railing at his side, flame was held to cigar with the right.

The fat cigar was mounted between his teeth as he watched the smoke. "No, no bweezing tchoday," he mumbled around the obstacle pressed against his tongue.

After numerous deep drags the flame grew and engulfed an orange glow at the end of the leafy morning custom. Holding the match at buckle height, he turned its tip upward. The starved flame quickly shrunk without a flicker. Below it was the long, dry pine stick, food a plenty. But its nature was to rise, only rise, and it disappeared. A new stream of smoke rose as reaching for the excellence of invisibility. Perfectly straight it rose without waver. He wondered about wind, gone on Monday, again today, but constant the four days between. Yet, Monday was not still like this. Again, he thought surely no day he had ever seen was as still as this one.

"OK, perfec stillness. So, maybe too much advantage today," he admitted, resisting the desire to capture a second victory on this fine, exceptionally still Saturday morning. *Charity* and *turning from greed*—he sensed proudly the influence of his mother's South American Catholicism. "See, I am a true gentleman, noble and fair. One veectory is enough. My nose, like de owner, is not for greedy. We have enough wit de one happiness."

The pass was a missed opportunity to gain another point on the leader with the end of the year just a couple of months away. In the nine years since its beginning, the match lighter's nostrils had never won the competition. *Contentment in the benevolence of the gods*—he smiled, reminiscent of the distant Hindu influence of his father, who never missed an opportunity for conveying traditions of wisdom and philosophy.

Bent brows became one at the top of his satisfied nose. He turned, looked toward the other end of the porch and began walking, ponderous and certain this was a day different from all prior days. Another deep drag on the cigar and he stood again before Gloria Thirty-two, who he thought looked pitiable.

"Gloria, have we ever talk about eating de sun? Maybe I find back my religion, because de memory of dat word from Pa come to me dis morning. Pa always tell me for dat idea. I can' believe I forget it until now. From de time I was a little boy he tell me, 'Poyāma, everyting muss eat de sun for live. All de living eat de sun. Plant eat de sun, bug eat de plant, bird eat de bug, man eat de bird, all get energy for live from eating de sun. Look around you and you see.'

"Now Ma come behind and say, 'You listen to you Pa, Poyāma. You listen to dat word of he and find always you way for live. Dat word will guide you to forever live.' Now, I know she mean someting differen from he, because she don' tink de far off way of Hindu like Pa. But Ma never speak a word agains my Pa. She only find way always for honor his word.

"One day de missionary preacher come trough and pass de snack when he done wit what he talk. We kid always wait for de snack like prize. He pass de snack . . . noting really, jus some wee bit wine and bread, but we ac like he giving candy. Ma lean to me and say, 'Poyāma, you remember what you Pa say. De good Lord always find way for make de living by get dem to eat de sun. How he do it is none of we business, but he make always a way.'

"Now, Gloria, dat word puzzle me from Ma like you can' believe. Firs, Pa never say noting about de good Lord. Dat word always belong for Ma only. But today I wake wit de memory dat haunt me for ten year . . . memory of de Gloria for what I name you and all de oter Gloria . . ." He paused a pause that grew long. "I never stop for tink about her constant," he muttered. A quick, hard shake of his head and the former thought was resumed. "Anyway, dis morning after I wake, dat word from Ma come right behind dat memory of Gloria loud in my head. I wake up tinking hard so early I don' know if I get some sleep pass two or tree. More den dat, I have strong feeling I believe dat word of Ma. But, for what do it mean, I have no strong noting . . . feeling *or* tink."

He moved close and stared at Gloria.

"You looking hungry," he said. "Two day is long time to go witout." He studied her. "You know, Gloria, when I was young, yes, I could do it . . . once, almos tree day I forget to eat for so busy. Now, six hour de limit . . . *maybe*. But I have becoming relax, a domestic man for comfort. Relax has way of demand de striving of yout are tame. Why resis?" He patted his stomach and made a sweeping gesture encompassing land and possessions. "Look what dose day have provide me. A-a-ah, no more strive. Time for satisfy."

Gloria's long legs and dark eyes never failed to make a fearful impression upon her landlord. He looked down at the hot coal on the end of the cigar.

"It may be dat you crouching is too low dese day . . . you know, giving youself away. A predator muss avoid looking like one."

Drawing in a mouthful of smoke and popping his jaw, a thick, white, spinning circle moved slowly toward Gloria. Closing one eye, he looked at her through the ring of smoke.

"Forgive me advising you concerning dis proud old profession of yours. You know you craf far better dan me, a humble keeper of vineyard. But it seem to me dat de advantage is in de desperation of you victim. Could it be you are show dem two much of your own? Maybe like me, some more relax, someting not for announce deir get destroy?"

He looked closely, studying with admiring eyes. "I's not dis beautiful necklace da's de problem." Beads of dew upon Gloria's web was one of Poyāma's favorite sights in all the world. In fact, there was no wonder amid endless beauties in the numerous square miles of his ranch that compelled him to stare longer or study more often.

Gloria Tirty-two, he thought, amused. Each of his substitute Glorias had numbered last names. Though most often they were not spoken, always they were thought of in this way, connected to a long, proud order.

"You jus need de fat bug to find dis web and bring you morning meal . . . de fat bug what jus eat de fat leaf, what all summer eat de sun." It occurred to him that the drought had greatly reduced the number of green leaves for bugs to eat. For a moment he stood silent, pondering the problem of shortage Gloria was facing. "Maybe you jus soak in de sun when it rise and dat good enough."

Leaning outward over the rail he looked east. "O, jus a few second now, Gloria."

Standing and again facing the web, but shifting focus, he looked out into darkness and fog, beneath which he knew were hills covered with vineyards.

"Watch," he whispered. "Twenty five second I say, and you? You say Ten? OK, one, two, tree, four, five, six, seven, eight, nine . . . Ah-ah-ah, look, you on it today, girl!" He gazed, reverent for the punctual tint of light upon the darkness, a sliver giving first-definition to the eastern horizon, a subtle but profound moment he had come to enjoy as introduction of a new day. Though, on this day, because of the fog, it had to be imagined.

"Like usual, I was off jus a little my nimble friend."

Staring up at the hills, the thought came that the family vineyard across two continents on the coast of another sea will eat the same sun on this day. He stared, as still as the morning for a moment. Suddenly inspired, he yelled out, "Drink up all you tirsty vine! Plenty of time for eat de sun all day. Now you muss drink! Dat firs light leak across de horizon jus enough for we see and know de sun coming. When it fill de sky dis fog and de dew go away quick. So drink! Drink you fill!"

Sensing a movement in Gloria's web, Poyāma drew his focus back to the sparkling droplets hanging upon silken strands. Some had fallen. *Muss be my loud voice*, he thought, knowing it was not Gloria's light steps. He watched as she retreated to the top of the web where a wood beam met the ceiling at the corner of the porch.

"Sorry for yell so close, girl. But dose vine need for wake and drink. Dose branch what bend wit heaven fruit are my life," he whispered, moving his attention again to the southern facing slope, swept away in memories. "And what a life it has been."

Nearness of those recollections was momentarily disabling, as laughter and song of the local festivals and picking and stomping grapes with family and friends brought a smile. As a boy he watched his father teach others who came from far and wide seeking the master's advice in arts of vine. Who could forget such generous beginnings? The depth of pride remained a constant through the years.

A thought of the Casablanca Valley Wine House on its mountain perch in the Andes foothills was a thought of family honor, but only because of his father's favored status. "The House," as everyone called it, was lord of vine and soil. As a boy, it had never set well with

Poyāma that all of the vineyards and the locals who tended them were servants of The House. His parents, on the other hand, spoke only in gratitude of The House for providing training and a good living in such a noble craft. Secrets of The House, sworn to stay in the family, were employed here in his own vineyards, significant contributors to their bounty and his success.

Poyāma's father, Vishnu Harricharran, had been moved from his home in Bihar, East India as a young man. Transplanted in British Guiana, he was an indentured laborer working sugar cane fields, an East Indian expertise. A restless youth, he found his way to a French merchant ship, working cargo at stops along the northern coast of South America in exchange for food and board. All was progressing well, and hopes of travel to Europe and from there back to India looked promising. Even an altercation with French crewmen ended in his swift-fisted favor. But that is where things turned.

Saddled with several false but serious accusations (one man's word against that of four Frenchmen on a French ship), he spent two years on Devils Island off the coast of French Guiana. A strange name for an island nestled amid a cluster named Salvation Islands, yet, an appropriate name, given the abominable treatment of the residents of that penal island—mostly political prisoners.

Upon release, things turned again in the favor of the young misplaced Indian. The first man he met was Jean Pierre Chauvet, part owner of the Casablanca Wine House project in the Valparaiso region of central Chile. He happened to be there on that day overseeing shipment of Terra Petra ("black earth"), soil product of a pre-Columbian civilization extracted form the Tumuk Humak Mountains of southern French Guiana. Its coveted use was Experimentation at the Chilean project.

Chauvet was a generous man with an unusual confidence in the virtue of a second chance. He made Vishnu Harricharran the first hire of The House and his personal winemaking apprentice. Restlessness and toughness converted to loyalty and focused determination, the eager pupil wasted little time rewarding his mentor's goodwill. Attracting friends and relatives from the sugarcane fields of British

Guiana and creating a trophy workforce, he became manager of the project and an exceptional winegrower.

An errand was the cause of meeting a young woman to his liking. Her name was Māya. She had also been recently introduced to the Valparaiso region. But she had not come from quite so far away; nor had she come to work vineyards. Māya had moved from a Chilean village further south, just beyond the Bio-Bio River. She had come to attend Saavedra School for the Blind in Santiago, supporting herself by weaving, which is what she was doing when they met in a busy market place. Vishnu was shopping textiles for his bosses.

Conversing was easy enough for both to dismiss the word *stranger* within five minutes. Though blind, Māya blended in with the bustling environment so naturally it was more than an hour before Vishnu noticed anything different about her. When he finally did ask, it was in the vein of clarification regarding one of those *details* about the woman he already knew would be his wife. They married shortly thereafter and the two young lovers planted themselves like grafted rootstock in a Casablanca Valley beneath The House. Poyāma Harricarran arrived at first harvest.

Some background on The House may be of interest: Where a wine comes from is, of course, the most important factor in wine making. Old world wines only state where the wine is from on their labels, nothing about the grape. While it is likely most are aware of this fact, it might be that some lack appreciation of the reasons behind it. The quality of a vineyard is bound to a complex combination of physical properties: drainage, micro-climate, chemical and mineral make up of the soil, diurnal temperature swing (high day temp for ripening and sugar build up, low night temp for acidity increase), slope location for sun control of mildew and disease . . . this humble beginning to an extensive list will suffice, and one gets the idea.

If we can further contemplate the similarities between a cluster of grapes and the discrete cluster of atoms making up every molecule in a universe of infinite material variety, we draw nearer an appreciation of the absolute uniqueness of each vineyard. The French word for this is *terroir*, and the French phrase describing it is *voix des pierres*— voice of the stones. The French regard the winegrower as steward of the *terrior*.

In light of the importance of location, one might wonder why a French wine house would locate itself in South America, train locals to keep the vineyards and use such vineyards for production of wines to be exported from that location. There is a simple answer. The concern of The House, for which the Harricharrans and other families worked, was primarily scientific. But it was not the scientific confirmation and fine tuning of long-standing French tradition and practice, as one might think, but scientific experimentation.

More specifically, though not entirely, the product focus of The House was not French, but German wine. Popular German winemaking techniques at the time were based on manipulation of biodynamics—an affront to *terroir*—and were seeing significant gains in consumer response. (Note: Some have claimed that the German concern merely gave strength and backing to a project begun by French rogues who felt stifled by strict and confining disciplines ruling the French wine industry.)

While it is true that the French wine growers regard their products as elite and their traditions as supremely proven, and while it is equally valid to qualify their regard for German traditions and techniques as overly industrial (polite for *too* German), it would not be correct to assume the French have no cause to keep an eye on *what those Germans are up to* and where and why they are having success. It is, after all, an international wine industry. And the fastest way to lose top spot in any industry is to ignore the advances of your top competitors and deny their attributes. These must be acknowledged, certainly not for adaptation, but for precise understanding of how they are flawed and how to accurately convince the international wine purchasers of the signs of inferiority. Yet, there is a universal *bad form* problem with front-runners exhibiting anything more than the casual glance over the shoulder at trailers for the sake of a hard earned and well deserved smirk. Anything remotely like competition concern, not to mention obsessing, must be handled remotely—that is . . . out of sight.

Two primary factors played into the choice of this particular "out of sight" location. The first was the cover of Spanish politics ruling the territory. The second was ideal vineyard conditions. Nestled between the Andes Mountains to the east and the Pacific coastline to the west, the extremely dry Atacama Desert in the north and Antarctica south, Central Chile enjoys a moderate, dry, Mediterranean quality climate served by cool coastal breezes and lots of sunshine. The Casablanca valley was chosen for the added uniqueness of its extended summer season. Typical harvest in the southern hemisphere runs between February and April. But vineyards in the valley overseen by The House profited by the added month of May.

So it was that The House came to be located high in the foothills of the Andes, lording over vineyards in the Casablanca Valley to the west, making use of pre-Columbian agricultural ingenuity, practicing German biodynamicism, employing native Chileans and Indian immigrants brought over by the English to work sugar cane in British Guiana, and exporting under various Spanish names throughout Eastern Europe, Asia, South, Central and North America, and rightfully (though vaguely) labeled: Made in South America. It was transcultural globalization before its time.

As a consequence, numerous Indian and Chilean vineyard keepers, proudly believing themselves to be learning French wine making from the masters at The Wine House, actually came to be experts in experimental German wine growing techniques. Poyāma's father was first and most advanced among these. Poyāma had been *his* most devoted pupil.

A thought tugged at the corners of Poyāma's mouth, gradually lifting it into a smile. So savory, this thought, it deserved a long satisfying drag on the cigar and several celebratory smoke rings. *It was destiny.* Born amid the stresses and joys of harvest, son of Vishnu the wine master—chosen first pupil of French masters at The House—and of Māya the renouned weaver . . . mastery in this art of vine was Poyāma's destiny. Attaching export destination labels to boxes of wine was his first job—the greater the distance the greater the romance. "De whole worl have love for wine!" he often announced proudly upon arrival at home after a day of work. When the time came to be promoted to his father's side in the vineyards and cellars he felt as though he had become Vise President of the universe.

Yet, visions of personal vineyards somewhere across the sea had begun with personal tragedy—the death of Poyāma's little brother, Vishwaas, for which he felt responsible. Until then, he would have gladly spent all his days a resident of the village in which he was raised, servant of The House or not. But from that day, a preoccupation to leave for somewhere, almost anywhere, was kindled. It was encouraged by stories of India told around the family dinner table, and those of merchant travels heard at The House. When the decision was made to leave his home and make a life on the wild and seemingly endless continent to the north, it lacked all of the usual drama, though not the pain. Some thought it overdue, a mere matter of logistics. Māya expressed encouragement of her son's decision between bouts of weeping and absorption in her weaving. His father, confident of his son's imminent success, shouted final instructions from a dock in a harbor on the Pacific as Poyāma floated away on a steamship. Even so, it was a decision to be rewarded far beyond any anticipation.

Upon arrival in the United States, there were legal papers to fill out. When asked his name, the answer, "Poyāma Harricharran," was given.

"That'll never do here," he was told. "We gotta have a first, middle 'n last name, and they all gotta be somethin' a commoner can say in English. The last name's most important here, so let's get it decided first. What's your father's name?"

"Vishnu Harricharran."

"The first part'll do. Folks'll probly call ya 'Mr. Vish,' or just 'Vish' . . . dependin'on who, where they're from, whether or not they like ya . . . ." He shrugged. "Now we need a middle name."

Under pressure of the moment, with a lump in his throat and heart rate elevating, he answered "Vishwaas." The clerk frowned and wrote Was on the paper in front of him. "We already got the Vish part. No sense repeatin'."

"Two A in Vishwaas," Poyāma corrected, looking at the paper. And following a shrug, the second A was added to the new middle name—Waas.

Poyāma had traveled from central Chile, up the west coast of South America, all the way to the east coast of North America to get away from a particular hurt and there it was that quickly, his little brother's name, part of his new permanent name. He was allowed to keep Poyāma, the name his mother decided would belong to her first child after listening to a story told by a circuit missionary years before meeting her husband. Even she did not remember what it meant or the context of the traveling priest's message by which it was inspired. She only recalled enjoying the sound of it. Once attached to her first child, it insured all subsequent naming was done by the children's father and only good Indian names were given. The allowance to keep it was made by the immigration official based on a projected common use of the shortened version, "Poy," thereafter disallowed by the newly named immigrant. The name on the paper he was handed read: Poyama Waas Vishnu.

It might seem that a trip to the United States by boat from Chile would naturally take a person to the west coast, a winemaker to California. But Poyāma's travels included some sight seeing along the north rim of South America inspired by stories of his father's adventures as a young man. A lengthy stop in British Guiana to visit relatives was followed by a brief visit to French Guiana and launch from there to a U.S. destination: North Carolina and the foothills of the Blue Ridge Mountains. Within six months he bought land near Morisa, a little town in Surry County, just south of the Yadkin River. Standing on his porch in the peculiar stillness of that morning, smoking a homegrown cigar, he was fifteen years removed from the initial land purchase. The property size and value had increased exponentially.

Yet, disappointment cast a shadow upon inventory of prosperity. There was one way in which Poyāma had not followed in his father's footsteps—the finding of a bride. This was not for lack of longing or intension, preoccupations that only seemed to be increasing. A comfortable arrangement as producer for a wine house was never formed. Lacking that, it became necessary to take on many unexpected responsibilities—landowner, vinedresser, wine producer, employer and exporter among others. No matter how sincere his intentions to pursue Gloria, demands of success would not let up. Then there was the silence about the wine tasting event, which grew a spoiling awkwardness like mold inside a wine barrel. Strained relations with her brother also encouraged the passing of lonely years by collecting fine horses, entertaining himself with such things as the smoke game and talking to pet spiders bearing the name of his beloved.

A morning of first-thoughts, yet another occurred to him: even his success and great wealth were somehow owed in part to Gloria. Beginning as murky as the morning, the thought quickly gained clarity. Clueless as to how to proceed forward in pursuit of his first love, Poyāma's work became the beneficiary of misplaced passions. An oft muttered tribute expressing motivation for efforts and drive came to mind: *Dis make for a good life for her someday soon. She will enjoy dis.*

REJOICE!

I am De House!
The thought was pleasing and worthy of a fresh array of smoke rings. It also fended off, for the moment, concerns about lost opportunities for pursuit of Gloria, and perhaps fading chances for marital partnership in general. More smoke rings were called for on this excellent morning of such a fine realization: *Yes, yes, I am de House!* It was a thrilling moment, his mind occupied with a worthy distraction. A dozen or so unusually round dancing smoke rings were sent spinning and tumbling about expressing their creator's pleasure.

"'Time for knock a blow,'" he said, further waxing nostalgic, misty eyed. He chuckled. "Long, long time since I hear Pa speak dat word. How I forget a word so perfec? Much better word for introduce de fine pleasure of leaf dan 'time for smoke.'"

More smoke rings followed—perfect, too perfect. Stopping, he stared, as if having heard the once familiar voice of his father commanding an end to foolery (something they had enjoyed plenty of together) and a return to work. *How strange de moving of dese ring,* he thought. Looking down at the cigar, a similar impression was made by the perfectly straight rise of smoke from its tip. Elevated between two fingers, it came to eye-level. Poyāma tilted his head and blew. Smoke from the end of the cigar moved and soon two perfectly straight lines of smoke ascended and disappeared. "Never have I see a day so still as dis," he muttered, glancing around.

Reaching, he attempted to flick a large clump of ash over the porch rail onto the dirt below. It landed on the rail, unnoticed. The cigar rose to meet his lips and he puffed on it thoughtfully, as one would a pipe.

"Ambition of yout, Gloria . . . noting to explain dem. And who could have imagine? Who would have dream de god would show dis favor to a foreign lad wit noting but a few piece of cloting on his back and de tradition of family in his mind? But de heart is hard for reckon, my dear. De heart full for believe is a man not stopping."

Poyāma surveyed fog dressed surroundings gushing like a darling flattered by the peeking attention of morning sun.

"O, if Pa and Ma can see me now, and my two broter, my many cousin, and dose Seeram twin. Ah, de ting we leave behind," he said with a sigh, reaching out and flicking more ash from the cigar. "But here . . . here . . . I am De House!" he yelled into the new day. "And who would have tought a young man can travel so far for provide such a fine home for a girl like you, my dear Gloria Tirty-two?"

Both hands on the rail and leaning out, he yelled again, "*I* am De House!"

Thinking about row upon row of dry failing vine brought to mind another boyhood memory. The circuit missionary with the "snack" always preached from a pulpit in a small one room church on a nearby hill whenever he came through. The Harricharran family, like numerous others, always attended. Once concluded, not a word was ever spoken about the message. The young Poyāma had always assumed the other congregants to be like him, lacking understanding of what had been said and disliking the tunes to what had been sung. He tried to recall one, but soon gave up, stumped.

Ah, de song of dose hill were wine, not church, he decided, punctuating the thought with a shrug.

Suddenly, the first few rows of vine, barely visible beneath the hovering fog and spread across the base of the southern face of the hill before him, looked like pews and Poyāma felt inspired. Leaving the porch, he strode out to the nearest vineyard and stopped little more than ten feet from the first row.

"Listen here everyone! Here I stand before you, belove. Yes, it is my knowing face you see—take comfort! Here in dese two hand . . ." He stopped and quickly transferred the cigar to his teeth and held two cupped hands outstretched. The cigar bounced as its obstruction distorted the words that followed.

"In dese hams I hol out por you diss heart. Noting too musch por *you* my sschildren!"

Quickly becoming slobbery, the opening remarks were shortened. Pinching cigar between thumb and forefinger, the minister of the vines removed the soggy end from between his teeth, thoughtlessly shifting it to the "Vishnu hold" between ring-finger and pinky. Both hands rose high over head and outward.

"I am Poyāma!"

Remembering the original declaration, "I am De House," only after he had spoken, it was easily dismissed in favor of the more gratifying replacement. Quick steps passed before the Steuben in the front row and did not stop until ten rows up the hill. Again, hands were raised, fingers spread.

"I am Poyāma! Here me what I have for say, belove." Arms lowered slowly. "Dis is de day of you and me laughing. Dis is de day of you and me rejoice! You know dat word, rejoice? Wine is about rejoice. Sometime we forget dis. But dis we muss never forget. You are de grape, de fruit for de vine. Vine make for wine. Wine make for rejoice!"

The preacher ran down the hill, across the front row, turned the opposite corner and faced an adjacent assembly of Sauvignon, his hands again raised.

"I am Poyāma, and I remind you: Rejoice! Rejoice! Rejoice! If not for rejoice, what we doing? If not for de song, who care for we make de wine?"

Climbing the hill as he preached, Poyāma stopped and perused the absent and the dying. He stopped before a pitiful showing of Villard Noir and took a thoughtful smoke. Blowing the smoke straight over head, he was reminded of the rare stillness of the morning. A long gray glob of hot ash hung from the half gone cigar. It was not noticed when it fell.

"You was my firs," he said in a fatherly tone. "Remember? How many harvest we celebrate togeter, huh? I remember de firs . . . tree-and-a-half year I wait for dat one after I baptize you in de eart. Look at you. You disappointing and hurting you master. How can you look like dat? You muss be inspire for de ress of de vineyard. See over dere, de Merlot, and down dere, de Sauvignon, over dere de Chamberlin and over dere de Vignole." Poyāma turned and pointed in the direction of each vineyard, all unseen, most far away on distant hills. "Labruska, Traminette!" He looked up and westward. In his mind's eye, seeing across many hundreds of hilly acres, he spotted the Muscat of Alexandria, inexplicably the one vineyard that was thriving. "Hey, Muscat, you still looking good today?" he yelled.

Pausing, he recalled having imported and planted the Egyptian Muscat solely because of the descriptive inclusion by Gloria the night of the event a decade in the past. *Dere she is again . . . she everywhere,* he thought, and for an instant stared into her beautiful eyes. "Glory!" he whispered, as if Gloria had stepped through the fog and appeared before him. "Das how come she receive dat name."

Turning and looking down the hill where he began and gazing upon rows of Steuben, he sighed. Across the isle were the suffering Sauvignon, and he marched up the hill shaking off sadness.

A loud voice rang out from the stable. It was that of Xerxes, Poyāma's prized stallion. Nothing he had ever accomplished or owned made him feel prouder. Somehow that one horse was symbol of all. The fact was arresting in the moment. Stopping the climb, he stared into the fog toward the stable.

"Pride of a man life and lus of he flesh," he murmured, as if reciting a well known poetic declaration of reward. Without any recollection of where the saying originated, he related to it as complimentary, and had always done so. Evoking it was inspired by sentimentality and romance. Xerxes was its embodiment.

Xerxes called out again.

"See!" Poyāma shouted to the vines, "De king hear dis sermon and send up some encourage! 'Amen, broter . . . you preach it!'"

The hike up the hill was resumed. Reaching the top and looking down the opposite slope, the preacher remembered his sermon: Rejoice! Though dark, the valley below was clearer, something he noted as strange. Large carriages could faintly be seen lining the exterior of the packaging plant laden with cargo he had personally loaded the day before. Inside the lower stables, three young Thoroughbreds awaited training. Others grazed the northwestern hills. Morgan moved upon slopes to the northeast. Only a few were perceptible through the blanket of fog. They appeared as phantoms. Yet, familiarity filled in all details. A series of great maple and glass doors appeared as amber gems hung from a necklace—the road following the base of the adjacent hill. Inside that hill and behind the doors were the wine cellars, vats, press and all things to do with processing wine.

A sound rose up from the valley, normally recognizable as the squeaking up-and-down crank of the lower well pump. But with the hired help gone, he dismissed it with a shrug and the thought, *nobody should be down dere.* Moved by the mysterious beauty of the fog and reminders of wealth in the dark valley underneath it, a question emerged in his mind like a response: *Why I never bring Ma and Pa here for see all dis?* The squeaking was forgotten.

He knew he was blessed. Everything about the property turned out to be ideal in ways he could never have anticipated. Just one hill over, erosion left bare spots revealing rock ledges and dry, cracking soil. *Fine for de hill holding a cellar, but a nightmare for a vineyard,* he thought. Only a slight spoilage of near perfect property management came to mind: the periodic disappearance among the Thoroughbred and Morgan over the past year or two. It was always a single loss, suggesting a hungry animal, something he could accept as Nature's way. But it was always a healthy young adult, never a foal and never the aged. No animal he knew of was capable of out racing one of his horses or taking one down without a messy fight, of which there was never any evidence.

This was loss due to rustlers. He was being pilfered, taken advantage of by someone. It was an unbearable, deplorable aggravation, like a missed stitch in a new boot, a damaged button on a custom made vest. Yet, the losses were far enough apart they never stirred vengeance worthy of interruption to the daily work schedule, not enough to take necessary actions to catch a thief, exact due punishment and squeeze out of him full recompense. It was only enough aggravation to arouse oft expressed threats of such and poison a mood.

He consciously switched his thoughts to the abundance of wine still being processed underground and took a deep breath of the still air. *Even if dis year crop should fail . . .* Another switch was needed. Turning back to the hillside he had ascended, Poyāma slammed the door of his mind to the consoling thought. Cause for rejoicing was before him. Failure of the crop was not. Standing atop the hill, hands outstretched, his voice rose.

"Here me unhappy vine! Even unhappy vine have right for rejoice. I am Poyāma. You belong for me, so shout for we: *We* are Poyāma!"

Running across the crest of the hill between two last rows of Merlot, the revival leader was enthused, believing his own message. Reaching the end of the Merlot, he stood like a steeple crowning the hill with outstretched arms.

"I hear tu-u-u-u-nder-r-r! Who need rain for tunder? I hear tunder of rejoicing. I hear tunder under dis soil, tunder dat cry out to me from you root! Poyāma vine are awake for joy!" He spun and leaped his way down the hill, arms flailing. "Joy! Joy! Joy!" Arriving at the place where the sermon began, he turned and faced the awakened congregation. "I, Poyāma, came to dis great country from a differen America, from many hill for why I chose dese, from a differen country still pleasing me to call 'home.' But only half what you looking at today is Sout American. Anoter half coming here from India, for why dis native people here wrongly name . . . de far away land of my Pa I never see.

"Listen to me, you hear someting, all you Traminette! You, like Poyāma, coming to here from half a dis and half dat. Listen Muscat!"

he yelled. "Like India, you coming to us from far away ancien land, ancien worl you never see. You hear dis word, Egyp? I love for dream of dat word."

Poyāma's quick feet made many steps as he delivered his plea. Bent before the Sauvignon, his hips were brushing dry leaves as he leaned over the first row as at a pulpit.

"Listen to de story of *you* . . . Wine come to de Italiano from Egyp, maybe Babylon too. Italiano strike up de rejoice for wine very loud like dey do for everyting. De Italiano rejoice for wine come to de French. De French say tank you very much, den claim wine like it deir own . . . only little bit Italian, but more dey own . . . like wine begin dere!" The preacher laughed. "So, de German say tank you to bot, but now, time to remake de wine differen—German wine! From dere de English say tank you to dem all and send winemaking to Nort America where everyone seem to tink everyting begin in *dis* place. Nobody even know Chile have a place on de map!"

He laughed again, a bit harder. "O-o-o-o-h boy, we someting, we! Everybody forgetting for read de Bible . . . lots a wine in dere long before it discover any of we! De Hebrew, de Babylon, de wedding . . ." He lowered smiling eyes, enjoying a passing thought. *Ma would be happy for know I listen so good for dat preacher who visit us.*

"But what is loss?" he yelled, looking up and scanning the invisible hills. "De rejoice is loss! We forget for keeping rejoice in de *vine* for de rejoicing stay in de *wine*. Today is up to we! We are Poyāma and Poyāma is rejoice! New land, ancien land . . . some of we, some of dey . . . here, all we coming togeter for rejoice! Children, you muss love to dream of *dat* word. If we forget from where de vine come, we lose de rejoice."

Previously gesturing arms settled for the moment. The preacher chuckled to himself. *I like dat . . . a good sermon should end wit something like dat,* he thought, smiling, the sound of "de vine" ringing like a bell in his mind. Looking up, he gazed out over his vines and lifted his hands as in benediction.

"If we forget *divine*, we leaving behind de rejoice! Wake up children of divine, wake up! Let all God create rejoice!"

Turning, the steps back to the porch were slower than those leaving it. Back where he began, hands on hips, Poyāma stared out into the morning wondering where the spontaneous sermon had come from, but pleased with the result.

"You know, Gloria, a long time back . . . up until today . . . I tink dat belief noting but color of de chameleon. Not anymore, no way, girl. Belief de real true ting. Believe dat word and you be a happy Gloria."

Raising his gaze, he saw that Gloria Thirty-two had retreated to her little silk home.

"A little early for give up and quit for de day. De dark still cover de barn. De night still fall on de vine. You should stay like always until shadow of de barn fall on de vine before you giving up." He shrugged.

The unspoiled design of Gloria's web still sparkled with dew drops. The stillness was again making itself known, unsettling. *Maybe she know someting. Maybe she know no food coming dis day. Maybe today is not de day for believe.* The preacher, not liking these thoughts, tried to recall a few of the finer points of the recent sermon.

"O, you miss a good one dere, girl. If dat man preach like dat when I was a yout, we all would got save."

LARUE

There was a subtle movement upon Gloria's web and several dew drops fell to the railing beneath. Poyāma stared, engrossed. Gloria was tucked away. She did not cause them to fall.

A throat clearing sound came from the other side of the porch. He spun, startled.

"You have a knowing face! Where you coming from, LaRue?" It took only a few riled steps to reach the opposite porch rail, upon which his neighbor was leaning. "Why you coming here at surprise so early? You never do noting like dat before!"

LaRue laughed. He always laughed at the first hearing of the immigrant's speech, as if surprise was ever new. Poyāma's low vocal tone was nature's contribution. The grovelly texture was product of home-grown cigars—ten years of Casablanca Valley, Chile variety and fifteen years Yadkin Valley, North Carolina make. But it was the "wrong" articulation of English that caused the American to respond as if to a punch line, however serious the spoken words. The greater error was assumed simplicity. Had he known common English was the lesser of four languages his neighbor spoke, the inclination would have been to take him more seriously.

Poyāma tilted his head, thoughtful. "How long you are standing dere?"

"I posted my horse in the front maybe a minute ago and caught the last part of you talkin' to yourself here just now, if that's what you're concerned about." The answer relieved the concern until followed by, "That's not to say anything about sittin' on him right over there listening to you rant like a preacher before walkin' him to the front to tie up." The part left out was how attentive the listener was to the sermon. Delivered mysteriously, from LaRue's perspective, by the shadowy figure of his neighbor darting around under cover of fog and darkness, it took some effort to shake the impression and ignore the content.

"Well, dat not good what you do me like dat . . . A-a-a-h-h, sneak up on a man. A broter have it coming how him do, you know."

Slapping the rail, LaRue broke into more laughter. "OK . . . well, I'll be lookin' forward to that. If I remember right, it's been about ten years since you last made it over our way." The fellow winemaker laughed again, removed his hat and gave it a good swat across his thigh. "What was that other one . . . that was my favorite."

"Oter one . . . oter one what?"

LaRue drew his head back and squinted. "'De dirt a man trow is de dirty him get.'" A howl and more thigh slapping with the hat displayed his enjoyment. "O, my, my . . . grandma's puddin's got nothin' on that one. That's the best. I've used that a few times."

"Dat what I say when you spoil de good word of you sister for de wine I create," Poyāma responded, quite serious.

"Oh, yeah . . . well, that was a missunderstandin'."

"No, dat was you being not nice for me."

Beating his leg with the hat again, chuckling and shaking his head, LaRue turned and looked up toward the hills. "I don't know how you didn't notice me ridin' in. I could hear you from all the way back at your entry. You must've been engrossed."

"You bring up someting my mind find curious too. Dis morning is still, like no oter. It have no sound but my voice. So, you come here quiet, like a hunter dat slip under my sharp hearing. You muss have walk you horse from de entry . . . in de dark." Poyāma paused, thoughtful. "De morning short of six yet."

With a chuckle and a tug on a chain, the early visitor flipped open a pocket watch. "So it is. I must a been feelin' ambitious this mornin'. Say, I know you've told me before, but remind me again why you talk to your vines."

Thoughtfulness delayed the answer. "Dey kind of people like we," Poyāma finally said matter-of-factly. He sat on the rail and leaned against the house. Watching his visitor's bemused reaction, he laughed. "Oh, my, I wish I have a hat."

They looked at one another, suspended, then laughed together. LaRue spun on the heel of one boot and stylishly ended the revolution pointing at his neighbor with his hat. "That was good. You got me on that one . . . that was good."

A chipmunk ran out from under the porch and scampered toward an outbuilding. Three shocking bangs followed an impressively quick draw and it was obliterated.

"Guess my reputation hasn't gotten this far. Varmints around my place know better."

Poyāma's ears rang as he dismissed the boast but noted the error in past thoughts of strapping on his guns and heading to LaRue's for a showdown. He was especially impressed by the fact that somehow, in the lightening fast draw, LaRue's hat found his head.

"Really," he said, getting back to the question LaRue had asked, "de reason is de living like to hear de knowing voice."

Thinking about that for a moment, LaRue stared, then responded. "Yeah, well, my vineyards know my voice well enough, 'cause they've been hearin' me hollerin' at God for three years now. I can't imagine it matters much in this heat and drought. My dog is about the only one that seems to be respondin' to my voice lately, and if it keeps goin' like this I'm gonna be fryin' him soon."

He walked over to the front of the porch and sat down on the corner of the step. Ordinarily, he was a proud, hard, successful man, if otherwise unextraordinary. But recently, pride had come to show some cracks. He was ten years the senior of his immigrant neighbor, whose handsome features and dark, smooth complexion seemed to cancel out another decade or so. The only thing that spoiled LaRue's enjoyment of his own wealth was how diminished it seemed in comparison to that which he presently looked out upon. The tall magnificent barn a hundred yards to their right and no-expense-spared stable fifty yards up the hill from it especially made him grind his teeth. Both were just beginning to display a ghostly hint of their size and similar shapes. He gawked jealously. Knowing the stable was full of rare horses from around the world made his stomach turn.

"I heard you've got a new Japanese horse in there. How in the world does a guy get a Japanese horse over here?"

"Das easy. You send for it."

"O, right, you just send for it . . . how silly of me!"

Some measure of this kind of torment was always his experience when coming to the Vishnu Ranch. Consequently, he did not often pay his neighbor a visit, let alone an early one. Early visits were the practice of close friends. And, while the two vineyard keepers were capable of putting differences aside and finding ways to get along with one another, it would be more than a stretch to call them friends.

Poyāma looked out toward the barn. All was quiet, but there was an unusual tension in Xerxes. He sensed it as if his own. Leaving the railing perch, he walked over and took a seat up a step and down a few feet from his guest, whom he thought more cowboy than wine grower. Though this was a land teaming of "foreigners," he had always sensed a bias against his particular type when with the confident LaRue. Occasional interactions in social settings left him feeling as second-class as LaRue was presently. Slender and strong, rough-faced and socially nimble, the elder vinesman fit a stereotype of "American" in the mind of his Indian-Chilean counterpart.

Silent and immense, the greatest barrier to their relationship moving beyond acquaintance was lack of trust. LaRue had a sly, agile shrewdness in his business practices, something he always assumed others to be matching him on. Never missing an opportunity to call unsecured property "a find" or deceptive gain "advantage", his eyes were always open for both, here too, assuming a justifying common law of human nature. Poyāma's success baffled him, even if he could not help admiring the legendary capacity for hard work and diligence. And to LaRue, baffling implied slight-of-hand from the other side, something of which Poyāma was always keenly aware. Thus, their conversations tended to be sluggish interactions between examination and its resistance. This one seemed to have a purpose, but even its initiator was momentarily forgetful of what it was.

While thinking of something else to say, LaRue stared out toward the vineyards, remembering the different names called out during the sermon. "Who would even plant such combinations of grapes?" he mulled, barely audible.

"Wha's dat?" Poyāma asked.

"O, nothin', I just . . . I've never seen this technique employed, this interspersing of so many varieties of grapes. Some of them shouldn't be able to grow in this area at all."

"Dis five acre of hill by de house jus what I call de garden, what I use for my own enjoy, for keep an eye on everyone right here . . . maybe try some new ting. De usual vineyard are out dere across many tousand of acre." Lavish gestures with both arms, seemingly encompassing the world, demonstrated enjoyment of stating rightful claim to "many tousand of acre."

"I tell you dis a long time ago already, when you come here once. How you let someting keep up for annoy you so long?"

Good question, LaRue thought, more annoyed than he was letting on. Ignoring it, he turned and looked upward over his shoulder. "Well, Vishnu, knowin' how early you get goin', I thought I'd try and catch ya before you got out into your day." He chuckled. "Ya know, I wish I could get it through your head that this is not French viticulture you're practicin' here, all this yackin' at the vines, sprinkling indigenous organic materials on the soil, mixing minerals for washing the leaves, and on and on . . ."

"How you know what I practice?"

LaRue was quiet, feeling caught. "I'm a snoop, I admit."

"You come here dis early to tell me what you already complain before?"

"Well, no, no I didn't . . . but it bothers me. It bothers me that . . . ."

Just then, a loud, shrill horse cry rose from the stable. Alarming, it bent into a low kind of growl.

"Xerxes," the proud owner said with a smile masking concern.

"I know who it is. I've been around horses my whole life. That's the first one I've met that's truly scary."

Poyāma hopped up and started for the stable, knowing LaRue would follow for the rare opportunity to tour the horse stalls.

"He hear my voice and expec me fetch him some grain and give him a brushing. Some farm wake to rooster, dis one wake to voice of a king . . . king Xerxes." Poyāma laughed, gloating.

"Where'd you come up with a name like Xerxes?"

"O-o-o-o-o, I never forget dat name from time I was a boy. A preacher man come visit de valley and we village once in awhile. Sometime he get all de youngster around him and tell de Bible story. One time I hear dat word, 'Xerxes,' and raise my hand quick and ask him for spell. Den I right it in de dirt beside me. When I get home I make blood from grape and right it on my hand like tattoo and wear it for tree or four day. I always go by dat name when I play wit all de oter boy."

Xerxes let out another announcement of his agitation.

"What was the story about?"

"You kidding me? Xerxes was de king who give a contess for how he pick he favorite girl to be queen over all his oter favorite. After dat I can' remember noting from so far back when I was a boy."

"I see. So, South American kids remember their Bible stories about like North American kids."

Poyāma stopped. "We can talk about dis cause no lady around. But you know what Xerxes say backward?"

His guest frowned before slapping him on the head with his hat.

"Hey, no lie, de French boy who know English equal to French, son of one of the de vineyard owner, he teach me. I make tattoo for dat one also, only like you name wit two capital . . . SexRex." He turned and continued walking. "I tell you broter, I get spank for dat one so hard I move on from dere more quick dan you shoot de little stripe rat. Ma not up for hearing noting about it coming from de

Bible story by de missionary. Dat only make her more mad when I explain. But I never move on from de name Xerxes. When I lay eyes on dis horse I say to myself, Xerxes, dat him!"

Striking the air with his hat, LaRue laughed. "'Dat him,' he mimicked, "de king! Speaking of which, how much do you get for that big boy in stud fees?"

Knowing the clever LaRue to use conversation for extracting business information, the suspicious Poyāma answered in his usual misleading way.

"You know, dat horse make me see dere no money in wine like dere is in horse, not in dis area. California maybe, France maybe, Italy, Germany . . . but not here. Dat horse make me forget making wine for money, I make so much money on him from de foal he create here and de stud fee . . . I jus make wine anymore for love doing it."

Turning away with a scowl on his face, LaRue was unimpressed with the transparency of his neighbor's lying. "That must be why you're doing so well in the wine business," he said, playing along. "Wine is about love, right."

"Muss be, 'cause it keep breaking my heart wit dis drought."

This, too, LaRue new to be false. It would take many years of failure to have any impact on the wealth brought to this ranch through wine production. He realized something other than the conversation was annoying him. *The air,* he thought, *I distinctly remember thinking this was a bit of a windy day when I was saddling my horse.* He tried to recall when it began to change but could only conclude, "What a strange morning."

As they reached the gate to the corral, Xerxes bellowed a demand so loudly it made the early ones seem like polite requests. The tone and inflection of the vocalization was nothing Poyāma had ever heard from his horse.

"I better get him feed pretty soon," he said, though certain breakfast was not the issue.

"Yeah, you better," LaRue answered, amused by his neighbor's evident anxiety and the discovery of who was actually owner and who was owned.

Staring at tall double doors as Poyāma slid them apart, LaRue studied a hand carved scene spread across both of them. It depicted vineyards, buildings and mountains he did not recognize, though the buildings were similar in architectural style to the stable itself and all others on Poyāma's property. *Doors,* he thought with a shake of his head and a smirk, trying to think of any other stable he had seen that was not designed open at both ends. *Pomp! That's all that's about,* he concluded, jealous.

As soon as they stepped inside the stable he too sensed the tension of animal wrath in the air. Awe of the interior stable complex equally had his attention. As LaRue gawkingly strolled, Poyāma raced around lighting lanterns before heading to King Xerxes' fine stall. A wide distance developed between the two men, which made the owner of the stable uncomfortable.

There were fifty-six extra large stalls in the massive enclosure, two isles separating rows of fourteen, and the isles themselves separated by a spacious training ring at center. A man knowledgeable in lumber, LaRue recognized the polished wood as imported, by virtue of the fact he had never seen anything like it. Finished throughout in polished brass, the craftsmanship was exquisite to the detail.

Some quick calculations based on estimations of vineyard acreage, wine processing and distribution, mucking and all forms of horse care for so many animals, buildings and grounds upkeep led to a guess of no less than thirty laborers needed to maintain such a place as Vishnu Vineyard and Ranch. *Where are they?* he wondered. The rumor mill had informed that almost all had left. By all reports, he knew Poyāma to be a hard man, expecting those he employed to share his drive and dedication, though not especially generous in sharing compensations resulting from such labors.

This alone is a full time job for two or three men, he thought. *Why is he out preaching to vines if he has no one to help with harvest even if his imploring produced a miracle?* Then it occurred to him: *This fella is living in denial of a major predicament.* "He can't possibly manage . . . or even keep track of all this alone," he muttered aloud to himself in astonishment.

"What was dat?" Poyāma called from Xerxes' stall.

"O, nothing," LaRue responded, "I was just doing a little square footage math and trying to decide if this is actually a stable or if it should be registered as a cavern?"

So taken by the stable, he almost forgot there were horses in it. He walked up to the nearest stall and peered in. A beautiful dappled gray and white mare with striped hooves stared back. It walked toward him inviting personal attention.

Poyāma poked his head out of the stall well more than fifty feet away, where he continued to brush and calm Xerxes as he ate.

"She call 'Tom-Tom,'" he announced. "Appaloosa . . . She come to me from far away out wes."

The brushing, feeding and assurances of his master were claiming a calming effect on Xerxes. but he was not yet his norm, which made Poyāma nervously convinced LaRue's presence was the agitation. He continually looked over the wooden wall of the stall to keep an eye on his visitor.

"Pura Raza Espanola, favorite of de Roman soldier. De Spanish breed dem. One of de firs I get introduce wit back in my home country. I call him Felix, what mean lucky, because he make me feel lucky for grow up in a country of Spanish occupy, learn vineyard from de French and live in de United State. Da's a big life dere broter!"

Each time LaRue was spotted at the stall of a different horse, information was supplied. Stroking the bushy white main of a reddish roan colored horse, he was informed: "Ardennais, very hard working, strong like you never believe. I get him from a man in Louisiana, but all de ancestor go far, far back in ancient time of Europe." A few minutes later, stepping into the stall of an enormous horse with an amber coat, LaRue heard: "Belgian. I name him Zeus! Maybe de very firs working horse. Powerful like locomotive. Dis one make however hard work you can imagine come to be easy like sleep."

And so it continued: "Arabian, he Find a way here from de beduin. Dis horse treat a man so good, I tell you for sure, day make up de word 'friend' to suit him . . . . Comtois. I name him Napoleon. Have you ever hear of dis man Napoleon Bonaparte? You should know him, I tink he French like you. De man who send dis one for me as a gif tell me dis horse come down from de one dat great General always ride into war . . . . Canadian. I hear from someone dat only a few of dese exis any more in de whole worl."

In this way Poyāma kept his eye on LaRue and also made sure LaRue knew he was being watched. Finally, the Frenchman came around to Xerxes' stall. When he looked in his jaw fell open. He had never seen the horse so close and had never seen an animal so imposingly tall, nor so equally wild and majestic in appearance. Poyāma looked terrified, and indeed, held his breath, knowing the moment was explosive.

"No-no-no-no-no-o-o-o . . . nobody give you no problem Xerx. evryting Ok." the stallion and the cowboy stared at one another until LaRue could take it no longer.

"I don't like the look in his eyes," he muttered.

And Like a thunderbolt Xerxes bellowed and lunged, whirled around and kicked the wooden wall separating them with shocking force. The collision of hooves and wood was so violent LaRue backed up thirty feet quicker than he had ever sprinted the same distance. Instinctively he had drawn his gun and was standing thoughtless, pointing it in the direction of the stall, from which Poyāma had slipped out, latching it behind him. Turning and seeing the gun-drawn LaRue, he charged without the slightest hesitation. In an instant LaRue's shoulders were pressed against an adjacent wall and the gun was on the ground several inches below his dangling feet. He could have kicked, swung, cursed, spat or reacted in any number of ways running through his mind. But the surprise of the vise-like grips holding him there discouraged resistance and protest. He just stared down into eyes glassy with insane rage.

"You ever point a gun at one of my horse again I for sure kill you like a cockroach under my boot!"

Poyāma's early morning guest was lowered to his feet, but a grip was maintained on one shoulder as LaRue's hat and gun were picked up. The grip was not released nor the items returned until after both men had left the stable and passed through the corral gate.

For a moment they stood silent, just staring at one another, both men catching their breath.

"It was an accident, a reflex . . . self-defense," LaRue finally said. "I wasn't gonna shoot anyone, horse or man. I can promise you that. Otherwise it would've been done."

"You show me already dat reflex is how a gun get fire. A man learn self-control over reflex and keep back from 'acciden.'"

"Your horse is every bit as dangerous as my reflex. You should try teaching *him* some control."

"I apologize for dat. I never see him behave in such a way before."

"Apologize? You just threatened to kill me over a horse. There's no reason to pretend politeness. I see what kind of hateful man you actually are. Thank God the whole thing with you and Gloria came to a quick end."

These words were merely spoken as another kind of reflex, one of gamesmanship. LaRue had been in many intense situations and knew how to keep his head and how to rebound. In fact, he was already mostly recovered. Able to read a situation and read a man *in a* situation, he was more easily bothered than offended. Adept at surface banter, what served his advantage was most on his mind. What he did not know was how to recognize, aim at and hit a target deep inside another man. So the blow he had just landed was completely accidental and unnoticed by him.

Poyāma, on the other hand, was disarmed. It was as if he had been stabbed. He liked to think of himself in the noblest of terms. But the indictment was so starkly, unavoidably true. He had lost his head and exposed something of his character he could not reconcile with the person he believed himself to be. Hate indeed was a close follower of the contempt he had for LaRue. Invoking Gloria's name was salt in the wound.

"Well," LaRue said with a sigh, turning and walking toward the house, "I better get my horse and get out of here before all your hired laborers show up and I'm out numbered even with my *reflex*."

Once more, he proved to be accidental genius. This was more banter, just a calculated guess to slip in a jab, sarcasm, a petty insult highlighting shortfall. No brilliant psychological warfare was intended.

It hit the mark nonetheless. Poyāma was defenseless against the realization of his own responsibility for the loss of fifty-plus employees over the course of a couple of years. Following behind LaRue, he wondered how it was possible that he had convinced himself otherwise. He had always had difficulty keeping staff. The whole situation melted into morbid contemplation just as suddenly as the violence had flared up.

Never before had anyone called him out on his errors so directly and accurately. His life was managed safety by use of tireless modulation of relational distance and masterful positioning for the upper hand. Success and wealth were like impenetrable walls built of awe in the common acquaintance. Toughness and intellectual superiority were gate and gatekeeper. Somehow LaRue had snuck in some crack somewhere and discovered soft spots in the armor of greatness. It had taken years, but exposure was as a marauder and the blows were landed.

Specifics relating to the difficulties of keeping staff were like strands of a rope tied into a noose that was tightening. Regrettable epiphany that it was, he knew the reason for the difficulties and felt hanged.

He knew that not only was it because his way was always right, but by its outcome he was always favored. Prior to that very moment this never represented any kind of moral or ethical failure to Poyāma, just the natural results of rightness, albeit within the universe of his view. More than once or twice in the past he had mused over the regularity of "right" favoring him. Muse then produced two offspring: confirmation that right and his way were indeed the same, and mild regret on behalf of others, that their ways were not the proper basis for similar favor. Alas, how could a man be faulted for such virtue? It was up to others to raise their standards if they wanted a share of such privilege. Yet, in a moment, all those years of unchallenged conviction proved surprisingly fragile.

Noticing how far thoughtfulness had caused him to lag behind, Poyāma increased his pace to catch up with LaRue. It was such a very strange day. Everything about its beginning was odd. And he knew that somehow the very oddness of it contributed to LaRue's comments striking so deep. No, this was not just an unusual day. Something was happening. He did not know what it was, but sensed something intentional, though quite apart from his own intentions.

Nearing the porch, both men were feeling very strange about the whole incident in the stable. Both, also, were aware they did not enjoy disliking the other. In each case it was a revelation. Yet, LaRue's pride was bruised and he was want for reaction that would reestablish his strong-man stride. Having been manhandled left a foolish impression, as did the confirmation of his neighbor's legendary strength.

Still mortified by his actions, Poyāma just wanted to be pardoned. But asking was the hurdle. He decided to jump it.

"LaRue, please . . . you de better man. I speak de word about self-control and look how I lose it so crazy myself. De gun scare me and I lose myself in dat minute. You could have shoot me. But you hold back and let it go. You de better man. I beg you ignore what I . . . I whish you can forget what I . . . ." He stopped and stood staring at the back of his neighbor who continued to walk. "Please forgive me for how I speak and ac rough. I never kill nobody. It was crazy what I say for you."

Just like that, upper hand was handed over. LaRue stopped and turned. The first words that came to mind were spoken.

"Tell me again, Vishnu . . . I know you've explained it before. Why is it you don't brand the horses in that stable like you do your Thoroughbreds?"

Indeed, this question had been asked before and each time drew suspicion. So, Poyāma, whose resumed steps closed the distance between them, gave a typically short answer. "Fine art get add noting by nobody but de maker." Uneasy about the subject, he quickly and awkwardly changed it. "Earlier, you say someting botering you."

"I did?"

"Yes, when you firs arrive . . . before we visit de stable."

"O yeah." LaRue looked over shoulder up into the fog-dressed hills. His interpretation of the apology as opportune moment to pry about the horse collection resulted in both men forgetting—or dismissing—the forgiveness request.

"That was quite a while ago," he said, recalling the original interactions and still sensing opportunity. "I was . . . look, I'm a proud man, I admit it. And, like any proud man, I think my way is right. So, it bothers me, Vishnu, that you . . . that you're doing so much better than me at this vineyard keeping thing I've devoted my life to. So, I watch you, I admit. Every true professional wants to be the best. So, ya watch the best. But I only get bothered more by watchin' you."

"You get boter for my success? Dat strange. I enjoy for see you success."

"Only because it's so much less than yours!"

"Yes, true, I enjoy dat too. But I also enjoy for see you do well."

LaRue looked up at the sky. "Are you laughing!" he yelled.

"Who you talking too?"

"The big man up there. We have a runnin' joke about me providing plenty of humor for him lately."

"Is dat French?"

LaRue looked over his shoulder again and chuckled. "No, I don't think so." He lifted his right boot and planted on the stair to the porch and leaned toward Poyāma. "Look . . . think of it from my point of view. I know I'm a Frenchman that's never set foot on French soil. But I'm the real thing nonetheless, 100% French. We might've spent a displaced generation or two in England before my grandparents came here, but we've been LaRues all along, French to the core, and winemaking has been in our family all the while. It's my right to be king of wine country . . . at least of my own county.

"And here it just so happens that an Indian man from South America who can hardly speak a sentence without making me laugh, who thinks he was trained by French wine masters but practices what everyone in my family and in the industry confirm to be the techniques of German mystics, who misses the basics of vine keeping—hoping for a harvest in October from vines that should have matured in September—and stands on a porch having deep conversations with himself about it, and . . . he just moves right next to *me*, of all places, doing something he don't know what it is and kickin' my rear end doin' it! You think God's got a sense of humor?"

Poyāma's eyes were closed beneath a frown as if contemplating a riddle. "Well, I have no easy time following all dat. Give it to me once more and I get it. Den I give you de correc answer."

Bursting with uproarious laughter, LaRue spun on his left heel, Poyāma peering at him through one eye, its brow raised and a subtle smile on his face.

"Gosh, I like chattin' with you!" LaRue declared. "I don't know why we've never done business together?"

"I do," Poyāma replied, suspicious of the whole conversation and assuming LaRue's external manner was cloaking internal conditions not so easily passed offences and tensions.

"Right . . . well, just a beer or something . . . how is it we've never even had a beer together?"

"How it is a man could ever be tirsty enough for put beer in he mout? Da's not de drink for de man wit tase. You, a refine Frenchman, should know dat."

After putting his hat on, LaRue stared, a big smile across his face. "Yeah, OK . . . You're a funny one Vishnu," he said, walking back toward the front of the house to get his horse.

"Das all you came here for . . . to find out if I tink God has humor for you?" Poyāma stepped onto the porch and walked to the rail.

Stopping, LaRue looked up at him. "No, that wasn't it either. To be completely honest with you . . ." he paused for gathering the right words.

"Why would you be anyting else?"

"What's that?"

"Anyting but completely honess wit me . . . why?"

"Anyway," LaRue said, rolling his eyes, "the last two years were agony, watching you figure out ways to keep producin' bumper crops while mine kept turnin' into compost and fire starter. I've been avoidin' your place for two months, hating the idea that you might be 'rejoicing' for some fabulous harvest again."

Disappearing around the front of the house for a moment, he reappeared pulling a tall, handsome Thoroughbred.

"But rumor got to me that you're not doin' any rejoicin' lately. So, I decided to see for myself how you're doin' this year. Now, after listening to your desperate preaching and watching your calm temperament unravel, I can see you're in the same shape I'm in, maybe worse this time. So, I'm feelin' much better, thank you."

Grabbing hold of the saddle and putting his foot in the stirrup, LaRue mounted his ride. "Yeah.., something bothers me alright. It bothers me to see you up there coaxing vines to produce, when any novice could identify they have obviously failed. Stunted stubbles... raisins! All the while you're runnin' around proudly thinkin' of yourself as an expert practicing French winemaking. And bein' so wildly rewarded for it, who could tell ya different?

"Vignoles... last week of August, Vishnu... that's first harvest, not October! Traminette and Seyval—first week of September, Merlot—second week... Sauvignon, St. Vincent and Chamberlin— third week... you get the picture? The Villard Noir you were talking to up there... mid September. This is late October, in case you're not good with the northern hemisphere's calendar either. Your dear Steuben—which no French winemaker would plant, let alone make wine out of—first week of October harvest, and *they* should be last. This is October twenty and you're still waiting for things to get started. This is nothing any French winemaker would want the proud name French associated with. It's time you admit it, Vishnu, it's over. Please be logical. There's no harvest even for you this year. And your claim to French training is a ruse."

Logical, Poyāma thought, glaring. *De man who like for argue have got to love dat word. A word like dat cover a lot of ting it victim have no way for disagree. He take me like de fool what have no logic for pick up on how he cheat like dat for argue.*

"You with me Vish, or did I lose you? O, I know . . . I'm probably stretching your vocabulary. Logical means the way you put together . . ." LaRue stopped cold, distracted by the smile transforming his neighbor's face.

"If I let you in on a secret, will you believe me?" Poyāma asked. His visitor nodded and leaned forward, listening. "I am working lately for exis someting new."

"You're working on an invention . . . we're talkin' about experimentation?"

"Mmmhm. I notice de season been changing and not go back. Dese long summer keep happening. So I learn some ting and find dis long summer likely stay dis way . . . at leas a couple year more. So, I begin experimen for pushing de harvest time back a mot or so . . . maybe two mot. We do a lot of experimen under de French where I learn from. We learn science and hard work make all new ting exis."

LaRue leaned forward. "What's a mot?"

"A mot? Why you ask me dat? You know what is a mot."

"No I don't. What is it?" LaRue insisted.

"A mot! You know . . . a day, a week, a mot . . . like, de mot we in now, October. Why you play . . . ?"

LaRue interrupted with a boisterous outburst of laughter. "A month? It's pronounced month, thank you!" He laughed some more before adding, "I'll give you ten dollars right now if you can properly say mon-n-th-th-th!"

The laughing stopped and silence hung in the air while Poyāma considered whether or not he could say the word as his neighbor had pronounced it, not that he cared about ten dollars or believed it would actually be paid by the challenger.

LaRue again leaned forward. "Allow me to let *you* in on a little secret. The French don't do experimentation with keeping vineyards. We choose the right land, plant the vines, apply proven practice and stay out of nature's way."

"So, right dere you speak to my professional knowledge and experience. If you, a Frenchman expert, come to here and recognize dis land to be perfec for vineyard, you muss see dat I am expert too for choose dis land and dis climate so perfec. Maybe it boter you dat you here firs and you make mistake of choose *your* land instead of dis."

"That . . ." LaRue paused and chuckled, feeling he was the one who missed a connection of some curious logic somewhere. "That, or you learned of my success, saddled up next to me and had a mighty run of good luck since." Sitting up tall in his saddle, he added, "But I do thank you for the information. At least I know my neighbor is not crazy, just confused." Looking up into the hills, he laughed. "And a bit over ambitious. Move the season . . . ," he mumbled, shaking his head and chuckling.

They stared at one another, both amazed at the other, that a man of such success could be so wrong in his thinking about their shared science and craft. Yet, a hint of admiration for his counterpart's faith and the audacity to be a visionary surprised LaRue. And a measure of jealousy for the Frenchman's confident tie to a standard of a land, a people, tradition and identity from which he was several generations removed gave Poyāma pause. That they were speaking at all after the earlier tussle made a fleeting impression on both.

"Your king Xerxes is having a royal fit over there."

"You right. Time for go back and serve de master."

LaRue looked like he wanted to leave but not without some kind of resolve or satisfaction. "Can we agree that this year is a bust . . . over . . . done?"

Poyāma smiled. "I can' do dat."

The Frenchman looked surprised. "Really . . . we have an agreement?"

"No. Why you ask again? I jus answer you once already."

"You just said you can . . ." LaRue frowned, tipped his hat and rode off.

Walking back to the other side of the porch, Poyāma found himself disturbed. Just prior to the last exchange he had noticed foam residue in the gentle morning light that caused him to give Larue's horse a look-over. It was still sweating from an evidently hard run. The realization further caused him to wonder why a man out for a morning ride takes one of his finest Thoroughbreds, an animal made for speed, not casual visits to the neighbors'.

He start out wit no intend for come here. He chase someting and happen to come here, he ponderously decided. *Dat explain why he put de problem we have so quick behind. He have someting else what weigh on his tought . . . someting else he sneak around for discover.*

A feeling of having been robbed, used or otherwise taken advantage of was converting Poyāma's thoughts to gloom. Scanning every detail of the troubling interactions with LaRue for evidence of loss, the gloom spread until merging with those former thoughts of personal error. There the gloom turned to dismay. Perhaps all he had thought of as "right" was, after all, *not*. insecurity welled up from some previously unknown depths, as if everything were in question, all the way back to the foundational institution of his youth: The House.

Maybe my worker only say dey leave for California. Maybe dey jus leave to catch a break from me. Maybe de people who teach Pa and me was not really French. He stared for a moment. *Na-a-a-h-h, dey talk like French!* Still as a statue in the pervading stillness of the morning, a more serious possibility came to mind. *Maybe LaRue is de one who is right. Maybe his sister stay better off for . . . .* The statue blinked. *Maybe I never find in me de love Gloria deserve.*

Poyāma felt a need to recall the theme of his recent preaching, but it seemed lost and forgotten, far away among different hills. Gloria Thirty-two remained tucked in for the day. "No wonder I make success so fass in dis country," he said to her. "A man like dis LaRue have no mind of rejoice. He should have listen for what I preach earlier. Den him tink differen."

Xerxes was making as much noise as he had been at his worst point earlier. Staring out at the stable, Poyāma was baffled and worried. Then, something else demanded his attention.

Directing his gaze back to the silken masterpiece of his eight-legged pet, tremors were moving upon its surface. He had assumed the earlier movement in the web was due somehow to LaRue leaning on the opposite rail. This time, as it unloaded many more droplets, his mouth went dry. The web fluttered and waved slowly back and forth. Bulging slightly outward toward the vine covered hills, the appearance was that of someone blowing directly into the woven center. It sprang back. For a few seconds it was still. Then it bulged outward again until a lower strand snapped.

Poyāma's eyes grew wide as he drew back. The dryness went to his throat. He had seen large moths hit and struggle in Gloria's web and not break one of the strands holding it in place. Looking in the direction of her retreat, he whispered, "On a morning such as dis . . . so still as dis . . . you web break as in de strong wind?"

He glanced around. *What time is dis?* he thought, staring at long, fog-softened shadows as if at the hands of an ancient clock. Mortality and fleeting opportunity were on his mind, not connected to any previous thought.

"Like shadow on de eart . . . ." he whispered, before all mental activity froze.

The length of the shadows indeed declared the dawn and their lie upon the earth indicated west. And out of the east arose a thunder like no other Poyāma had ever heard. Staring at Gloria's web flapping freely on the breezless air, he listened. The speed at which it grew nearer forced his mouth open, even as his breathing stopped. With a sudden turn, he placed his hands upon the porch rail and thrust outward to see beyond the front of his house. Framed in the distant entry to the ranch, but two hundred yards nearer and growing by the second, was what appeared to be a blazing white flame.

II

A Holy Devastation

WIND

"Glo-o-o-ori-i-i-a-a-h-h!"

Glancing up in the direction of his sleeping pet, Poyāma sighed. "No, not you girl. *Him.* But you should come out and see. I promise, you eye never fall upon glory like dis!"

There it stood facing him, stern and great, no more than ten feet from the porch, a horse more magnificent than the finest prize of his fertile imagination. Only able to stare, he had not moved since the moment the horse had whirled around and come to a stop, gleaming, unnaturally white. The animal stood tall, drew its head back and thrust it forward as if punctuating its arrival with an emphatic "Yes! I am here!"

Hello, Poyāma thought as he continued to gaze, still as the stillness on the air of the unusually still morning. Images played and replayed in his mind—riding into town, arriving at the LaRues, turning heads at the annual harvest festival, he and Gloria riding as one toward a long delayed second picnic. Wealth had come so quickly and grown so lavishly he enjoyed the luxury of taking it for granted. But before him stood splendor of a kind for which he had never dreamed. Want for its possession was like none he had consciously known, yet, familiar as his own name. It was a big problem for a man accustomed to thinking in terms of capability to earn. And it had arrived unannounced almost on his own porch.

Round, rippling muscles were accentuated like the lining of clouds by the sun. And as if lightning was dancing through those same clouds, fluxing, twitching illumination played upon the horse's form with its every breath and every expression of exuberance. So awe inspiring the impression, Poyāma was tempted to wonder what kind of animal was standing before him. The horse lowered its head and a vigorous shaking began from its shoulders, lifting high its mane and ending with several swats of a long white tail and a flapping sound from the floppy flesh of its mouth. Breathing hard through flaring nostrils, the great beast rose up on hind legs and let out a loud whinny that made his audience step back and lean against the house.

Impulses to step forward were continually aroused in Poyāma's mind. He remained still. It was not the kind of still he held for the deer that frequented his morning talks with Gloria, wanting to avoid scaring them off. He was anchored in place by the weight of amazement. The startling approach of thunderous hooves and the speed with which they covered the three-quarters of a mile from the front entrance of the ranch to the house was an impression still growing. And as he responded with disbelief to the constant reports of his eyes, he feared the possibility that the glorious animal might leave just as quickly as it had arrived.

Someone must have belonging to dis animal!

The thought leaped upon him like a bandit.

"Dey will come for him!"

He had not heard from Xerxes in a while and it would be very unusual for the demanding stallion to calm down on his own. When the visitor stole a quick glance back toward the stable, the knowledgeable horseman was informed of tension in Xerxes' silence. Gloria's web hung loosely. Catching his attention, focus moved back and forth between the intruder and the web. It seemed strange that Gloria had not left her daytime shroud to see what the commotion was all about. Of course, she never did so for any other commotion, but this warranted special attention.

"And what knowing do have about all dis," he whispered in her direction, reaching out his right hand and feeling for the railing.

The hand found the rail, and something odd also. He looked down. There between his fingers was a clump of ash, fallen from the cigar he had been smoking earlier. It was still slightly warm at the center. A worry came to mind. *Where is de cigar?* He stared, trying to remember the last drag taken. *Some time during de preaching . . .* The conclusion left him shaking his head. Carelessly tossing away the burning stump of nearly consumed cigars was a habit he often thought ought to change. It haunted him now. *Probably in de dirt somewhere*, he hoped. The dryness of the past three years encouraged a personal rule that lit cigars never be taken beyond the porch, which was surrounded by dirt and ideal for their discard.

But if not in de dirt, wherever it land is dry, he worried. Glancing up at the hills while taking stealthy crossing steps to the middle of the porch, the recollection of how much ground he had covered during his speech put an end to any temptation to go out and look for the burning stubble of cigar. *Dat silly sermon.* His head shook in disbelief of the impulsive carrying-on.

I muss look in on Xerxes, he thought, with a look toward the stable. *But where can I put dis beautiful animal for keep him stay.*

The wild white steed walked toward him and stopped at the center of the porch step. Its breathing was relaxed, seemingly recovered from flight across the ranch. The same could not be said of the man in its gaze.

Infamously alone, and near professional at deflecting the fact, Poyāma had numerous "Glorias" with whom he shared his solitary wealth . . . front porch, back porch, barn, stable. But such a momentous occasion ought to be shared with someone and those would not do. He would certainly write his family the details, but a letter would take months to reach them and never carry the experience justly. Nor was it relevant to the present longing for shared experience. He could hop on the horse and track down LaRue . . . *not him, of all people*, he thought.

The horse tilted its head in a way that Poyāma instinctively interpreted as, "I am here, share it with me." A wordless introduction had been made, confirmed by a look in the horse's eyes and a "Welcome!", conveyed in its posture. *I have live here for fifteen year*, the ranch owner thought in response to the odd feeling that it was his porch but the horse's land.

Stepping from the porch, cracked soles of favored boots made veiny prints in the thin surface of moist earth. They were "first boots," purchased when the land was, taking as many steps upon it and bending as often as their owner to work it. Yet, what made them his sentimental favorites was the memory of having worn them the day of the picnic with Gloria. More than comfortable, they were worn as unconsciously as skin, unfashionably as greasy hair and bad breath. The pair's aging was identically rough due to near continuous use. In earlier years, removal was sometimes forgotten when the body they supported collapsed onto a couch or bed at the end of long, hard days in the sun.

Poyāma stopped less than an arm's length from the most awe inspiring animal he had ever seen and stared down at its hooves, broad, scarred and hard as petrified tree stumps in appearance. Thoughtless, his right hand reached out to pet the silvery white mane and in an instant it was reaching instead to catch his fall. Seated on the ground and feeling like an insect in the shadow of a silo, he watched flailing front legs, fierce eyes and a gaping mouth declare the objection to uninvited handling. The horse lowered back to all-fours.

Ten minutes passed, eyes of the rebuked moving slowly, admiringly. "Like alpine-glow!" he said aloud, in response to the colors of dawn upon the rolling contours of the snow white muscularity.

On his feet again, Poyāma took a few paces back when the horse moved toward him. Bumping into the porch, his raised right hand betrayed trembling, but received a soft-nosed caress in its palm. The horse turned and stood diagonal to the porch. Interpreting this as invitation, he reached out again. Stopping an inch or two from the surface of the horse's coat, his hand opened and closed several times and then hovered over bulging masses above its right shoulder joint.

When contact was finally made, the horseman's eyes were filled with wonder.

A noise in the house shattered his captivation, and he jerked around as if to catch someone in the act of something. An object had dropped or fallen over. He wanted to investigate the disturbance, but could not leave the horse's side.

A competing distraction was equally upsetting: not a sound was coming from the stable. A quiet stable of hungry animals meant silent brooding. He pictured the horses inside restlessly pacing, turning in their stalls, reacting to Xerxes standing tense, twitching, listening for any sound reporting the activities of the intruding stallion, territorial fury building. Directing his gaze to the stable, a thin, white pillar of smoke on the eastern edge of the vineyard commanded attention. Scanning to the left of it, another was spotted higher up the hill, barely visible through the fog . . . then another in the isle between the Steuben and Sauvignon.

Earlier fears were confirmed. The cigar butt and two burning coals flicked from it had started small fires in the grass where they landed. Natural reaction would ordinarily be an immediate dash to the three spots to stomp, smother with dirt, whatever it took to put out the small blazes. But preoccupation with the creature more splendid than all other possessions combined overruled nature. Nervous eyes ricocheted between horse, stable and vineyards. All but Poyāma's heart and mind was strangely still and quiet. And in the fear-filled silence, distant sounds of a trotting horse reached his ears, faint but unquestionably a horse.

Somebody coming for you!

Under seizure of terror, he ran up onto the porch and, reaching the side railing beside the loosly hanging web, flung himself outward to locate the visitor. The scene was as lifeless as a painting. It also lacked fog. *Dat strange,* he thought, recognizing the fact for the first time. Looking back at the vineyard, he saw that the fog, though thinned, was still there. A sprint across the porch to the opposite rail and the view was like a visual echo—void of any movement. Yet, the sound of hooves drew nearer.

"De house is hiding someone coming," Poyāma whispered. Leaning a little further, almost losing balance and falling over the rail, he exclaimed, "LaRue!" as if cursing. "Why he come twice more dan he come any oter morning?"

The most appalling thought imaginable attacked his frantic mind. Body retracted from the outward scouting, he ran from the porch and stood before the horse. At once the fortunes of the two men had been reversed and Poyāma was filled with envy of his neighbor's splendorous wealth.

"How de Frenchman come upon dis horse so perfec? He jus come early for pretend like he jealous of all my expensive horse. I see how he tink dis one trough. Now he look to make *me* de joke of God!"

Looking into the eyes of the horse he became flushed with the miserable feeling of being the object of devilish humor.

"A-a-a-ah-h-h-h! OK, we walk out and return you straight away," he said, attempting a recovery of dignity. He took four steps and turned around. The horse had not moved. "OK, I lie, but you know me too good already . . . no way we can do dat."

Looking from side to side he devised a plan to watch LaRue until he showed the side of the house on which he would approach. Then, the horse would be rushed to a hiding place in one of the outbuildings on the opposite side, using the house for cover.

"No time for dat," he declared, running onto the porch in a panic, opening the door and scrambling around inside looking for a piece of fruit with which to lure the animal in. He stopped and stared at a basket containing just a few apples and pears, sure it had been full.

Maybe de six broter empty it before dey leave for take on dey trip. No, I have a piece las night after dinner and it was full den.

Thunderous thuds snatched his attention, causing a startled whirl. And there, to his amazement, the horse was standing in the house, massive, seeming as though it should not have fit through the door.

LaRue was coming around the corner of the house as Poyāma closed the door and stepped out onto the porch. The two men stared at one another.

"I know, Vish, I know, I'm surprising you again." LaRue looked as though he might dismount but changed his mind and stayed seated. "Forgive me, please."

Poyāma shrugged.

"Look, I had something to say earlier that I never got around to. I know I have created some ornery interference between you and Gloria over the years that has . . . well . . . What I want to say is . . ." LaRue looked at the ground as if wanting for assistance. What he got was distraction. "Those are huge!" he said, referring to the hoof prints around the porch.

Poyāma walked to the edge of the porch and looked at the prints. "Xerxes," he said.

"You had Xerxes out already?" his neighbor asked. "That beast is even bigger than he looks. Whata ya feedin' him?"

Poyāma stared back, his blank silence making things difficult for LaRue.

"Well, anyway, I was wrong . . . that's what I wanted to say. I won't do it anymore. So the way is clear for you to give things between you and Gloria another try."

It was a stunning message in its lack of connection to the horse, its unexpected invitation and tone of humility. But if ever there was a man to make masterful use of weakness in another man's defenses, it was LaRue. He tipped his hat and directed his horse in a circular exit away from the house before stopping.

"O, I almost forgot," he said, shifting in his saddle. "You haven't seen a white horse running wild have you?"

He had actually not forgotten, but could no longer contain the question. Unsure of what he had actually seen and wanting to avoid tipping off his neighbor of any potential free-ranging treasure, the restraint was over *how* to ask.

"No, noting like dat," Poyāma answered.

"I can't be sure I saw one, it was gone from view so quickly. Somethin' white and fast anyway, was out 'n about early this morning . . . seemed to be headin' this way. It was probably nothin'."

Poyāma gave another shrug and said, "Good luck wit dat."

Looking over his shoulder, LaRue wanted to express something of concern about the fires, but figured some technique unknown to him was being employed. Thinking he had already spoken too critically of such things, he held his tongue to avoid further insult. Eyes darting, Poyāma was becoming alarmed at the growth of the fires and wanted to request help putting them out. The plea nearly burst out of him.

As LaRue rode away for the second time, he contemplated the disingenuous interaction, embarrassed even in the company of himself to have used Gloria as cover for his real reason for going back. But he was glad to accidentally leave behind an apology long over due. He also hoped the suggestion concerning his sister would be heeded. These were unmistakable alterations to his typical attitude. He could not help noticing them, or wondering how they happened.

Poyāma was watching, making sure LaRue actually left. "So . . . he give away de reason for why he visit so early," he muttered to himself. "And why he come back again and pretend for talk to me about Gloria."

He watched until horse and rider sped through the ranch entry. Then he turned and gasped, seeing the flames in his "garden" vineyard that were continuing to grow. On impulse, he ran off the porch and several strides toward the hill before stopping. Xerxes' anger was creating pandemonium among the horses in the stable. Worried about him, Poyāma stood still, staring at the stable. Spinning around and rushing onto the porch, he opened the back door of his house, partly expecting the great horse of seemingly magical qualities to have vanished. But it stood right where it had been left, calm, noble and bright.

Burning vines were instantly forgotten. Rough, labor chiseled hands rose slowly, cautiously, by the guidance of a desire also responsible for his accelerated heartbeat and held breath. Invitation was again in the animal's eyes.

"So . . . , you have no belonging for LaRue."

Holding the horse's face, scheming thoughts came to mind, mostly to do with ownership. But only words from his heart were spoken.

"Dat man who visit have a sister so beautiful no man ever exis a new word for describe. I start for collec horse when I see she too high for me. Still, I always hope for she stand right here in dis house beside me some day. I always wish for anyting it take for make dat happen. But always de year jus keep going pass."

To this the horse had an evident response. It reached out and gave Poyāma a shove with its nose, causing him to back up as it walked forward.

"I like for LaRue use dat word 'wild,' what mean no stable and no corral have a name carve for you on de door. Today I make you one, for you enjoy a home here wit my oter horse in de beautiful stable." Still backing up, halfway across the porch, a name was in his head as if deposited. "Wind," he said. "De name Wind fit you perfec."

DILEMMAS

S tepping from the porch, Wind leaned left and whirled, leaped and kicked acrobatically before charging northward up the smoking slope recently used for the sermon, "Rejoice!" The three white pillars had grown in diameter by four and five times their size at the time of LaRue's most recent visit. Fire could be seen spreading along the ground at the base of each. Bending southeastward from high on the hill, Wind headed straight for the distant stable looking like a locomotive ablaze.

Poyāma immediately realized the error in opening the door and freeing Wind. The former containment was ideal for focusing on putting out the fires and feeding the other horses. That opportunity was lost.

He watched as the four-legged inferno leaped the fence, raced across the corral and circled the large building housing the collection of exotic steeds as if it were a chicken coop. Leaving the corral opposite the end it was entered, a wide tour of the land around the house was made before coming to a stop in the exact spot from which he had launched. A great sigh, a vigorous shake, and the long hair of Wind's mane appeared to throw light into the air in every direction.

When his hooves stopped pounding the earth, pounding noises continued. In fact, sounds of many hooves slamming against stable walls and many vocal horses trumpeting the imminence of a breakout were chaotic as a train wreck. Swirling winds played upon the hill, fanning three flaming patches. The blackening pillars of smoke rose from each and joined above the vineyard as one, which continued the ascent until meeting low clouds that had moved in from the northwestern hills and were filling the sky overhead. The former stillness of the morning was a forgotten novelty.

How can I make de horse don' leave while I take care of de vineyard fire and all de horse in de stable? Poyāma agonized. Thumbs found one another at the back of his neck and locked, something they had done only one other time in his life. Engulfed by shock and confusion, forearms were pressed against their respective sides of his head and both elbows pointed outward while wagging back and forth. Wind stood relaxed, a lone picture of calm amid conspiring dilemmas.

"Beautiful . . . wonderful horse . . . You stay here for I fetch you some sweet feed."

Sprinting toward the stable, what Poyāma really had on his mind was fetching a rope for tying the horse to the porch so he could focus on the other problems. But the idea felt both wrong and ridiculous. A third of the way to the stable and nearing the barn, a look over his left shoulder made him stop, unable to bear the sight of flames spreading and growing taller so close to the vines. The well was dry. The wind was picking up. If the flames were to be put out before getting out of control there could be no delay. Still, he hesitated.

A dash toward the flames was abandoned thirty strides up the hill with the realization that opportunity for stomping out insignificant fires was long gone. Two old boots would have little effect competing with the wind.

A blanket . . . In de stable . . . A sprint toward the stable was halted after about fifty yards. *No, de stable is far, de house is close . . .* Actually, they were nearly the same distance from that point. Turning and bolting for the house, he saw that Wind was no longer there. He stopped again, spinning and frantic, fear whipping up thoughts like the swirling air fanning the flames.

For several critical minutes the triangle of twenty to fifty yard sprints and stop-and-start scurrying continued. Finally, the white horse appeared from behind the far side of the barn, cantering along the outside of the corral toward the stable. Poyāma ambled for seventy-five yards in that direction, making it to the corral. But after hopping the fence, no amount of urgency could will a rush to the large stable doors, given the number of idle sprints he had already run. Leaning against the fence, he tried to catch some air before plodding the remainder of the distance across the corral. Upon reaching the doors, he bounced off of them clumsily and fell to the ground gasping for breath. Dark clouds racing to cover the sky seemed to mock the stunted movement at ground level.

Never have a rain storm find so much welcome as dis! he thought, pleadingly.

Rolling to the left and getting to his feet, one large door was pushed open. The calamity of noise inside the stable was frightening and violent crashes of hooves against wooden stall interiors were startling. All the horses were in an uproar, as if the rage of Xerxes were a contagion spread throughout the entire stable. Looking into the cavernous building, it was the first time Poyāma wished it were smaller—much smaller—and that it contained far fewer horses. Overwhelmed with the size of the problem and not wanting Wind to come in and make things worse, he stepped inside and closed the door behind him.

Xerxes was like a crazed Brahma Bull trying to toss a rider at a rodeo. His bucking, kicking and whirling consumed every inch of space in the large stall rattling under duress of a tempest it was not made to contain. His owner watched in amazement as head and tail alternately made rotating appearances above the stable wall and splinters of wood continually flew out over it.

"I's de white horse . . . he cause all dis!"

Yet, irrationally, even as the words were leaving his mouth, Poyāma ran and grabbed the front pull of a feed cart and took hold of a shovel. Hoping to leverage the horses' food-driven nature against the general revolt, he pulled the wagon to the center of the long isle between adjacent stalls 3 and 26—Zeus and Napoleon. From there,

Scoops of grain were tossed over the doors of the first ten stalls as he part stumbled and part raced down the corridor. Not the neat and pampered individual treatment the horses were accustomed to, but in a matter of minutes he was moving the wagon to a new spot along the wall across from stall 21—that of Xerxes.

Hitting the back end of the great beast as he whipped around, nearly the entire shovel full of grain shot right back over the wall. Undeterred, Poyāma tossed another in. Soon, stalls 1 to 10 on the left and 28 to 19 on the right had received grain. When The feed wagon arrived at its next stop between stalls 12 and 16, the owner turned stable boy rested against the end of his shovel, trying to catch his breath.

Noise and banging had not subside in the least and not a single horse had been appeased. In fact, sounding more like countless rampaging coyotes, it was evident the grain had gone unnoticed. The whole exercise only confirmed the commotion was over the visiting stallion outside. The horses wanted one thing: they wanted out! Abruptly, Poyāma scooped up a shovel of grain, hurled it aimlessly, and, letting go of the handle, took off running to the sound of the shovel clanging off the brass fixtures on stall 13.

No way I can let dese horse out right now, thought the desperate, devoted collector. His charge through the gauntlet was for a visual update on what was going on outside. Realizing it would have been much closer to just go out the doors at the north end, he stopped and looked over shoulder. By then he had passed the halfway point. Turning to resume the mission, an exhausted stumble to the right left him panting against the wall of stall 7.

If I let dem out Dey only get more upset by de fire. And Xerxes will chase away de white horse for sure.

As if on cue, almost directly across from him, a hoof crashed through the door to the angry horse's stall, punching out a large piece of wood and sending splinters flying. Some landed at his feet as a thunderous thud from behind sent him to the ground in the middle of the isle. Scrambling to his feet, Poyāma was again on the move. Huffing and puffing his way toward the front entrance at the south end of the stable—a mixture of trot, waddle and shuffle—he tried to ignore the deafening drama all around. Other doors were being violently abused and cracking sounds were adding to the mayhem.

Finally, rattled nerves compelled a sudden change of mind. For about three limping strides the new mission was to reach the front to open the doors then go back and begin letting the horses out. That mission, too, was aborted when Felix kicked his stall so hard the latch sprung and the door opened, freeing its occupant to nearly trample Poyāma on the way out.

A spontaneous and furious opening of all stall doors resulted. Poyāma had been seized by panic. Barely coherent enough to be Aware of the dangers, he kept to the side, staying clear of rampaging beasts and free from wood slabs flung open with the force of wild bursts from powerful bodies. It could not have been a worse reaction. Stumbling from side to side down the corridor of quivering containments, an indoor stampede was loosed.

Reaching Xerxe's stall as more than a dozen animals ran by, surviving the ordeal had become doubtful. They, too, were in a panic, senselessly sprinting laps, four and five abreast. the new mission was to make it to the doors at the north end and open them to let everyone out. Fear of all out bedlam was the primary contributor to a thought of moving on and freeing Xerxes last. It was overruled by concern that the prized stallion was going to hurt himself.

Poyāma reached for the latch. As he did, another kick busted open the door and Xerxes let himself out. Diving from harm's way and scrambling on his belly to safety, the owner narrowly avoided being trampled while the stable interior was punished with a kicking tantrum before the midnight black menace raced by to join his cohorts' in the derby.

With the stable interior turned into a dustbowl, breathable air was only to be found in the back corners of the stalls. Door to door was the default approach—freeing a horse, stepping inside a vacated stall, getting some oxygen, and moving on to the next stall. It made for a long mission to the doors at the north end of the stable. But he finally made it. Accounting for getting out of the way, he timed his opening of the doors for when the horses were mostly on the front side of the stable. Yet, after opening them, he fell out sprawled on the ground, lungs burning and helpless against the high probability of being trampled.

One horse leaped over him. Soon, another ran by to the left, then another to the right. Hearing the approaching rumble of many hooves, feeling the ground tremble beneath them, he drew up his legs and wrapped his head in his arms. When they had all passed, not one had come closer than a few feet of him. He looked up to see Xerxes standing tall and proud before turning to bolt away. He had leaped, then stood guard, forcing all others to split right or left around his master.

With the freed horses running the corral somewhere outside the stable, Poyāma was immediately aware that the ruckus inside was reduced by only half. Amid the panic, the isle on the eastern side of the training ring had been forgotten. It was still shaking with riotous protests. He rolled over onto his back in the dirt, muttering, "No, no, no, no, no," in response to the realization that the task was yet ahead.

The morning had dramatically changed. It was much lighter, no longer enveloped in fog, but smoke, and the clouds above were lower, weighty with rain. And it was windy.

"A-a-ah-h! Where is Wind?" he shouted, rolling over and getting to his knees. It was then that he noticed how much smoke there was. White smoke was as thick as the earlier fog and consumed everything in sight. The fence around the corral was a faint suggestion of boundary. Outside that boundary, appearing through the smoke, Wind stood, staring.

Poyāma got to his feet and took one step forward before twenty-eight horses, led by Xerxes, rumbled around the Stable and stood between him and Wind. All were like soldiers at attention for long seconds. Xerxes turned and looked back at his master with a lingering gaze. Then, back at the intruder. He walked toward Wind until the two were separated by only the fence. Angry horses inside the stable pounded away at their stalls, like an intensifying background of drumming.

A shrill cry of furry shattered the tension as the jealous black stallion rose and turned on his hind legs. He looked down at his master with fire in his eyes. When all four hooves were again on the ground, they covered a hundred yards of corral in a few seconds and leaped the opposite fence, twenty-seven horses following. A few others also leaped the fence before it was obliterated by three of the larger beasts, who hit it together without breaking stride.

Poyāma dashed to the side of the stable yelling for Xerxes. But he and all that followed had disappeared into the smoke. Compulsion to go after him was instantaneously absorbed into a scene that was a shock to his eyes. Many vines were ablaze. The wind was driving flames horizontally at ground level so the sparse grass patches nearing the barn continually lit their distant neighbors.

His mind was swirling like the wind: *I muss fight back de fire! . . . No way can I let Xerxes jus leave like dat!* He was shaking. *If de barn catch, de stable is soon nex.* His wide eyes were darting around wildly.

Wind appeared, standing beside the broken out section of fence, having watched Xerxes lead the other horses on a rush to who-knows-where. Poyāma looked at him with disdain.

"I muss keep de flame back from de barn!" he mumbled, turning and running back into the stable. Dazed, he grabbed blankets to beat back and suffocate the flames. Yet, even while hobbling through the stable, heading toward the front entry doors, the desire to throw them down, dash for one of the other horses and go after Xerxes required repeated resistance.

"A-a-a-a-a-h-h!" he emoted, opening one of the doors at the front of the stable, running with blankets and saddle pads and seeing fire rising up the southwest corner of the barn. After racing more than seventy-five yards to the growing blaze, pads and blankets were flung to the ground at the corner of the building and wild stomping ensued. One of the smaller blankets was employed for a few breathless swipes at the climbing flames. It was abandoned for a saddle pad. When Flames took hold of the pad, burning the hands swinging it, another blanket was grabbed and made useful until the heat on Poyāma's face was too great. All demonstrated only the futility of his efforts.

When the blankets and pads were consumed in flames the focus of rescue became Poyāma's own flesh. He ran. Away from the path of hungry flames, the defeated firefighter crumbled to the ground, once again gasping for breath. Saving the stable and the house became the new concern.

A thunder clap crashed through the roaring sound of wind-driven fire and a rain drop hit him on the forehead. "Dat all you got . . . for all you big talk!" he yelled between breaths at the clouds above. As in response, bone-rattling thunder made him recoil. He studied the gray canopy, tumbling and rumbling and lowering ever closer to the earth.

An image of Xerxes racing away came to mind and in that instant not even the house mattered. "Maybe . . . maybe you could find . . . it in you heart . . . . to go fetch him for me." he whispered, no longer talking to the clouds.

"Please," he added, getting to his knees. The white horse was running through the corral near the stable. It stopped and they stared at one another. "De oter horse!" Poyāma exclaimed, horrified. And once more, weary legs carried him to the corral, where he stopped for a breather against the fence before continuing on to the stable.

It took fifteen minutes to free the horses, all the while pushing past the pain of lungs that felt as though they would soon explode. Emerging from the stable as if from a bar brawl, the scene in the corral was disorienting. Having assumed all twenty-eight horses fled to find the others, he expected to meet only smoke and flames. What he saw was ghostly movements of horses in and out of varying densities of smoke.

Behind them, like a backdrop—mostly white, with intermittent patches of gray and black—spots of dancing fire flickered in the whiteness, in one place climbing high like a pillar, seemingly attached to nothing. There was no white smoke above the pillar, where all appeared to merge into billowing darkness. Beyond the horses, he was unable to perceive the height or distance between the spots of flames. The objects to which all were connected were invisible, as only brightness of flame pierced through the opacity of smoke.

Unknowingly, Poyāma had continued stumbling forward while trying to make some sense of the scene, which, in other circumstances would have been magical. Turning, eyes following a few of the horses, he soon recognized that they were circling him. He stopped and began counting. "Twenty-eight," he reported aloud to himself a moment later. "Dey all here . . . Why?" He began turning again, yelling as he watched them. "Hey, you brain full of smoke? Why you stay here? Go! Go away . . . Run far for de fire have no reach to get you! Go!"

Had anyone been watching, they would have been convinced, at least for those few moments, that a ring master was putting on a dazzling show, complete with theatrical smoke and fire effects. But the horse master figured out that the horses were scared and confused. Abruptly he began charging at them, randomly, this way and that, breaking the ring, yelling and dispersing them until all had disappeared into the smoky distance. Coughing, he bumped into the fence and held on, staring at the pillar of fire, seeing from the new perspective that the surface it climbed was the front façade of his barn.

"Now what?" Poyāma demanded of himself, desperate. "De town is far . . . and de whole town have no help for stop dis."

LaRue! The appalling thought of going to his neighbor for help again slipped through normally impenetrable defenses. Wind would make quick coverage of the miles between his ranch and LaRue's, but the thought of riding him was right there with wishing to fly. The fact that he had already told LaRue he had not seen a white horse made the consideration that much more unattractive. One of his own horses was needed. He got to his feet and began plodding his way up the hill, where he could see better to try and spot one. Zigzagging between patches of burning dead grass and leaping over others, he stopped for a breath of clean air three-quarters of the way up. Turning to the right, he saw long ribbons of flame blowing horizontally from an engulfed barn toward the stable. Part of the southernmost corral fence was ablaze. Glancing over his left shoulder, heat and the sight of fires continuing to spread through the vineyards motivated more movement up the hill.

He reached the top and looked into the valley and toward the hills layered northwesterly. There they were, Vishnu Ranch

Thoroughbred and Morgan, all too far away to catch and saddle as quickly as needed. But three young horses had been stabled the previous night in preparation of morning training. Any of them would be perfect for racing to find LaRue.

Turning and looking down again at the barn, a horror met Poyāma's eyes. Several of the second group of horses released from the stable had never left. He counted as they raced through the corral and into the stable—"Seven, eight, maybe more." Tempted to run down and save them and choose one to ride to LaRue's, intense heat blowing up the hill relieved temptation. In only a matter of moments the stable would be ablaze. He turned away, knowing those horses would likely not leave the stable again.

"A-a-a-a-ah . . . run back in to de place dey tink of as safe," he lamented. "Da's jus de way of some horse."

Redirecting his attention to the valley on the other side of the hill, the three young horses in the lower stable were his only hope. But no sooner had he taken a step, when an odd movement caught his attention. Five hundred yards or more to the northwest, three horses were walking closely side by side, heading due north.

"Only horse dat somebody lead behave like dat," he muttered aloud.

Squinting aided detection of details suggesting they all were saddled. *Tree!* He thought, alarmed. One at a time was bad enough, but three was cause for a chase, and momentary forgetfulness of a raging fire.

"Hey!" He yelled, instantaneously crazed. Charging downward on wobbly legs, the other grazing Thoroughbreds suddenly seemed near enough to race for one, hop on and chase down the criminal helping himself to Vishnu Ranch property. Halfway down the hill, an insignificant fraction of the way there, reality interrupted craze with a headlong tumble to a sprawled stop. Not one to concede reality a hindrance to justice, he turned and attempted heavy steps up the hill, envisioning a speedy flight on the white horse to overtake a shocked thief. When oxygen no longer supplied the vision, a dizzy fall to one knee halted progress altogether. Justice would have to wait for its champion to catch his breath.

As red blood cells again started making it to his brain, bitter, muddled thoughts were its product. That anyone could steal from another man was unconscionable. That one could be taken advantage of while fighting fires threatening all he owned was beyond any merciful response. Feelings of hateful vengeance assembled in mental images of gunfire, flying fists and feet swaying at the end of a corpse hanging from erected gallows. These were dramatically encouraged by thunder claps, flashes of lightning and dark clouds receiving billowing black smoke rising from the catastrophe on the other side of the hill. The villain would pay for all.

Of course, the rustler had been busy well before the day began and was evidently taking advantage of the absence of the normal ranch staff, not the fire. The fire, a responsibility belonging to Poyāma alone, was unrelated to those activities, even if it happened to provide an unexpected distraction assisting the evildoer's escape. But pieces relating to these facts did not enter the rancher's frayed considerations. Looking over his shoulder in time to see the three horses vanish over the distant hill, he caught a fleeting glimpse of a person half the height of the animals.

A man dat short provide a narrow search, he noted for future pursuit, which would have to wait until the fire was put out.

A strong and sudden gust of wind nearly pushed him over and a roar like that of a tornado blew away the righteous rage of vengeance. Cramping leg muscles barely mobilized him to the top of the hill where, stunned but not surprised, his eyes met the sight of both barn and stable engulfed in flames flying like flags, thirty feet or more from their wooden food sources. Turning away and ducking from hot gushes rolling over the hilltop, Poyāma's left arm rose as if bearing a shield.

The white horse was spotted. Having followed him at a distance to that side of the hill, Wind was standing near but low enough on the decline to avoid the heat and suggest an invitation. To Poyāma, he looked no less dangerous than flames.

Pressed to the ground and momentarily out of the way of the fire's breath, reflex claimed Poyāma's harried mind: *I never ride any horse what have no training from me or belonging to me . . . dat is stric forbid! My broter die like dat. I never break dat rule from my yout to now . . .* He stared. *And dat horse no good. He de one who bring all dis trouble.*

As a gust of hot air came over the hill, it swept away a haunting, painful memory along with the interference of "stric forbid." Out of desperation, he chose trust. Pushing from the ground and running, he leaped to the back of Wind. Expecting the great beast to instantaneously bolt in response to a thrust driving heels in its ribs, a slide off the other side of the unmoved stallion, a splat on the ground and a tumble thirty feet down the hill was the shocking result. Pounding the ground with his fist, he winced in pain and cursed a rock that happened to be in exactly the wrong place. A half minute of quaking and eyes closed agony were needed for recovery from the sharp pain.

Opening his eyes, he saw Wind positioned as before, twenty feet or so down the hill and turned at a sixty degree angle away from him.

"So, he make de nex invitation for make me de fool some more?"

Poyāma lay back against the hill, ready to give up and accept that he was ruined, his body feeling all but dead. Waking up early to thoughts of Gloria seemed a year in the past. *Maybe I make her a new place,* he thought, assuming the house would not survive. *Maybe I bring her to a new place like I never accomplish at dis one.* Gloria was never far from his heart or mind. Even disaster only revealed the fact.

The original stillness of the morning, the sermon, "Rejoice!", and the visits by LaRue felt not only distant but surreal. Rolling his head to the right, leaping flames could be seen rising high in the air beyond the top of the hill.

De barn and stable gone. De house too before long. No worker remain for help me wit noting. How all dis happen?

The moments of rest were turning into a paralysis of fatigue he knew must be resisted. Yet, the feeling of being spent was as a heavy weight pressing him to the ground. There was no response from any muscles to an initial command to move. He clenched his teeth and closed his eyes to concentrate the command on certain places.

Xerxes gone. His eyes opened wide. "Xerxes!" he exclaimed, pleased by the thought that he had heroically freed the great stallion and he was out there for him to go find and bring back. All was not lost. Xerxes was running free somewhere.

He lifted his head and looked at Wind. "No, dat horse make Xerxes upset for why he run off. No way he help me fetch him."

As raindrops fell sparsely, he thought about invitation. He thought about his last attempt to ride Wind. *Nobody own or control him,* he pondered. Rolling over and pushing up off the ground, he stood and stared. *Dat horse somehow have demand for relationship.*

"You take me for fetch Xerxes?" he asked. There was no apparent response.

"I need help. You take me for find help?"

Wind Shook his main and stomped as if eager to get going.

After a few running, then lunging steps, Poyāma threw himself into the air yelling, "Please take me for find de help I need!" Wind's acceleration was so perfectly timed to the landing, it was barely felt. They sped down the hill, looped west around the lower stable and underground cellars, then headed southeast toward the entry of the ranch as a light but steady rain began to fall.

Clinging to thick white mane, Poyāma watched as the familiar terrain in front of his house passed quickly. The hill on the back side of the house was streaked with fire, gathering into two large balls of flame on the eastern side. The wind continued to blow northward, keeping the heat and fires moving in that direction, away from the house.

Soon they were through the Vishnu Vineyard and Ranch entryway and heading east, presumably to find LaRue. But the rain was already providing more help than could be summoned by a small army of people. It pelted horse and rider in the face as they moved at great speed. Because of the speed at which they traveled and a route taking them through unrecognized areas and across broad open spaces, it became impossible for Poyāma to tell where they were actually headed.

What help LaRue or anyone else can give anyway? He wondered. Trusting the firefighting to the timely rain, activities of Xerxes and the other horses took over top spot among his concerns.

"How 'bout we find de oter horse what get away!" he hollered. "I like for you to meet dem all and make friend."

The charge became a walk so abruptly that Poyāma found himself scooting backward in order to return to the middle of Wind's back from the base of his neck. The walking pace steadily slowed until the distressed rider was conscious only of it and the rain. Yet, it was not so slow as to tempt hopping down, certain his own two feet could not carry him any faster and uncertain of just about everything else.

Finally, his last suggestion broke through the thought monopoly and was analyzed in every possible aspect for the next fifteen minutes. A lot of unbranded expense and prestige was running around free with the renegade, Xerxes, at the lead. Getting the horses back before they scattered, got too far away or someone else got their hands on them was a *control and retrieve what's mine* issue, not a friendly one. Wind's speed and fearlessness was the key.

Poyāma leaned forward. "I like for you help me catch back all my horse. We do it togeter."

Sitting up, he tried but could not resist the added thought, *den I add you to dem.* Accompanying images were lavish. A new, bigger and better stable, the architecture designed around two fabulous stall suites, Xerxes at one end of the complex, Wind at the other. Something about it felt devilish. So, mental intervention was needed. He turned to Gloria, the only subject in his mental inventory compelling enough to overthrow old habits. Recalling their picnic, her voice was never sweeter, her eyes never brighter, and his want never greater.

Horse and rider were as before, like lightning upon the wet landscape. The thrill was so consuming no consideration was given to the connection between the revised request and the result. Thunder announced a harder rain and the clouds did not disappoint. It was a deluge!

"Tank you! Tank you!" Poyāma yelled, emotional with relief and gratitude. "Tank you rain! Perfec timing! Exac what I need!"

Raindrops appeared horizontal as they flew by. Torso low and forward, legs squeezing the horse's sides, forehead between the two-fisted grip like a jockey in the home stretch, his face was turned northward and eyes squinting when they began passing escapee horses. One by one, they appeared and disappeared in the dense streaks of precipitation.

Twenty two was the count when Xerxes came into view. Knowing he was the lead horse, Poyāma wondered why there were only twenty-two. Then, realizing he had passed only a couple of the wide-bodied draft horses, it was assumed the others could not keep up and dropped off somewhere along the way. It was a worrisome thought, as each had a special place of high value to their owner. And he knew they would be considered so to anyone else who might find them running free. LaRue came to mind.

Soon they were matching strides with Xerxes. Side by side, there he was, close enough to reach out and touch. Poyāma wanted to yell an apology or an explanation, something to make things right, something to assure the great stallion he was still "King," something to get him to accept Wind as just another newcomer, not a threat, not a rival to his supremacy. No words came. As Wind nudged ahead, Poyāma drew even with his prize runaway and looked him right in the eye.

Xerxes bent to the left, leading the others off in a northeasterly direction. And with that, Wind looped right and slowed to a trot in the driving rain. His rider had the distinct feeling they had accomplished a mission, but had no idea what it was.

The rain was too thick to see beyond forty or fifty feet to spot landmarks. Where the sun was in the sky and how far they were from any particular location were curiosities unaided by clues. These factors conspired to make any judgment of direction a challenge.

If Xerxes drive de oter horse dat hard from de time dey escape, we come a far way from de ranch, he surmised. *And if Wind follow after LaRue in de beginning like I say, and not veer too far off when he steer de oter horse somewhere to de lef . . .* He thought for a moment. *We probably near de LaRue property, maybe even on it.* But the big loop around to the right resulted in a feeling of heading back from whence they set out. The feeling was erased by a silent admission of perplexity punctuated by a shrug.

He thought of Gloria seeing him riding high at the command of the spectacular Wind. *I have de prize of all horse . . . time for add de beautiful lady.* He smiled, imagining the added pleasure of seeing LaRue's jealous expression.

De rain save de day. For sure it have de fire under control by now, he assured himself.

Leaning forward, Poyāma was hesitant before speaking. "I tink it might be nice for stop by de LaRue place and see dat de cowboy make it back OK in dis storm."

Initially, there was no change to their course or pace. Then Wind stopped, his head swung low and expulsions of those throat clearing and sneeze-like sounds for which horses are famous preceded vigorous shaking of his wet mane. If ever a man saw a horse guffaw, it was during the meandering, whinnying, flinging of the mane spectacle of the following moments. After the comic behavior stopped, the meandering continued for quite a while, silent in the rain.

Poyāma's thoughts vacillated between going to see Gloria, worrying about unattended flames, going back for Xerxes and feeling like Wind's hostage. It occurred to him that back at the ranch it was only raining lightly when they left. He cringed. *It might jus still be a light rain way back dere—or worse . . . , maybe it stop and not rain at all.* A shudder ushered away the unpleasant thoughts.

Finally, annoyance caused him to blurt out, "OK, I have no care if LaRue drown in de rain. I jus like to show you off to Gloria, and make de Frenchman fill wit envy like when she speak good of my wine."

A sweeping turn to the right straightened out and became resumption of the previous course. After some consideration the maneuver was interpreted as an agreeable response to an authentic statement. Poyāma had something new to ponder, and ponder he did. When every moment and every interaction since meeting were evaluated, he reached down and patted Wind's neck.

"OK, so . . . , you make de invite or don' get touch . . . , nobody make you dey own possess . . . , you expec relationship, have a demand for communicate . . . , a-a-and, respond only for what is true. I tink I get it now. You have a way like a person and rejec all oter way."

Heading in the direction of the LaRue ranch, Poyāma began to wonder whether he actually wanted to continue all the way to the LaRue homestead. Recalling the recent outburst, he decided it had been primarily confession. Then, part of the confession became a reminder diverting his attention:

'Like he did when she speak good of my wine.'

A distance of years evaporated and the clear memory of words spoken by Gloria a decade ago was as a treasure held in hand, adoringly reexamined.

'Yet, old fashioned, even ancient qualities . . .' He had always thought "old fashioned" suited him. But the use of the descriptive words "ancient qualities" had remained a mystery until that moment. He reached forward and patted Wind, thoughtful.

' . . . woody . . . blackened smoky-burnt-woody with a slight hint of tobacco . . .'

"'Time for knock a blow,'" he muttered, thinking of the fire and its beginning. His mouth went dry. *windy as if the winds of an Indian summer swept long and strong . . . late harvest, browning leaves, snowy whiteness . . . .'*

Wind's "snowy whiteness" received more patting and strokes until a terrible realization pushed the memory to the side. Riding up to the LaRue's soaking wet in the pouring rain likely would not inspire Gloria's awe *or* her brother's envy.

Everyting I hope for when I meet dis horse go de opposite. What if he make harm and show me for look de fool in front of Gloria?

Jolted, all thoughts focused back on the current calamities. The rain was coming down hard. But, because of questions regarding location and the distance they had covered, uncertainties about it being equally heavy back at the ranch returned. This time, no shudder whisked them away.

"What if de rain take no power over de fire?" he yelled, regretting the panic stricken, abrupt decision to leave the ranch at such a critical time. Astonishment at riding around in the rain chasing horses and interests in making impressions quickly turned to self-disgust.

"Are you a sane man, Poyāma?" he hollered, furious. "What make you ac so foolish? By now everyting burn to de ground!"

By force of habit, the heels of his boots made bossy contact with Wind's ribs. As before, the communication was ineffective. Feeling even more foolish, he leaned forward.

"We muss head home immediate, if you please, for make sure de fire come under control."

The rain forced LaRue to give up his chase of a white phantom thought to be a wild horse. Passing Gloria's cabin a dozen galloping strides within the tall gate of his sprawling homestead, he spotted her preparing to head into town. A conversation seemed necessary. It was a conversation he wanted to have many times before, but had always decided to just let it go. Circling back, he pulled up beside a small carriage harnessed to a fittingly small horse she had just loosed from a post.

"So, let me guess. You're going out in a driving rain because . . . actually, I can't guess. Where on earth are you going in this whether?"

"Mrs. Bailey needs her groceries for the week. This is the day I always get them for her."

"That old lady is tough as nails. She won't expire if you wait until the storm passes."

"Now is when I planned on doing it and I have other things to do later. So, if I don't get it done now . . . ." Gloria shrugged, indicating an indefinite delay.

"The ground is hard from the drought. You might run into some flash flooding."

"I'll be careful. You still planning on helping me drive cattle later?"

LaRue looked over shoulder at the western sky, rain pouring from the rim of his hat. "Of course . . . when it clears up." The clouds hung low and dark above the distant tree line, strangely dark, to his thinking.

"Something else you ought to be careful about . . . ." He looked down at her. "That Vishnu character is not normal by a long shot."

"Thank you for looking out for me, but he and I have not spoken in quite some time."

"No, and I'm glad for that." They were both raising their voices to be heard over the rain. "I just don't like the feelin' I get that you're still wait'n around for him."

"O, really? Does my life look to be on hold?"

"No, no, of course not. You're busier than just about anyone I know. I just . . . I've yet to hear an appropriate word of disgust or dismissal from you after that weasel cut off pursuin' ya without a word of explanation. I know that was a long time ago, but, every time his name comes up . . . , I could swear you brighten for every word about him."

Gloria had taken a seat in her custom made carriage behind a slight but spunky Palomino, eyelevel about three feet down from her brother's. Hat removed, she tilted her head back and let the rain fall on her face.

"Rain . . . !" She laughed. "I was beginning to think I'd never see it or feel it again. What a beautiful day." She put her hat back on and looked up at the elder LaRue. "So, I hold no malice, have no bitterness and do not judge, and you conclude something is *wrong* with me? . . . I am smitten, left waiting . . . moving toward old-maidhood?"

"You know what I mean."

Suddenly, Gloria was distant, staring into memory of the quality that lingers and spreads, ever moving nearer:

"*. . . a maturity for which my heart will yearn.*"

The words had been hers—at least, spoken by her voice—but from a place deep inside of which she was unaware before their utterance.

She looked up at her brother. "What I know . . . ," she said, still thoughtful, "is that things are not always what they seem."

Richard LaRue shifted in his seat, turned away and then back. "What You *should* know . . . , is there's a lot of men around these parts who would love to have a beautiful woman like you.

Gloria laughed again. "I see . . . , it would be nobler to be 'had' by someone because I'm pretty than to continue enjoying being me, staying the course and waiting on love. What High standards you have for your sister, dear Richard."

She reached out. After a hesitation he reluctantly leaned and took her by the hand, rolling his eyes. "I love you," she said, "And I know you care. So, thank you. As for your concerns . . . , I very much enjoy being me. When the right man comes along, he will meet me in stride with a similar contentment."

Letting go of her hand, Larue took off his hat and looked up into the pouring rain. "You're right. This rain's been a long time comin'. Gotta appreciate it while it's here."

"You know what else is like that?" Gloria asked, grabbing the opportunity.

"OK . . . , here we go . . . , how did I know it was coming?"

Indeed, Gloria was as concerned for her brother as he was for her, and marital struggles recently reported by Claudia weighed heavy on her mind."

"Just a reminder: Like your award winning wines, love is served well by patience, my brother."

"Yeah, I hear ya."

Seconds later, Richard LaRue was riding toward his house. Gloria gave the air a couple of deep sniffs, then swiveled in her seat and yelled, "The rain will be cleared up this afternoon. I'm counting on you!"

With a flip of the reigns, horse and carriage began to move, but only about twenty feet before she pulled back, halting progress. Squinting and trying to make something of a distant brightness,

Gloria leaned forward. Too far away and too distorted by rain to distinguish what it was, it appeared to her as a light topped by a bouncing dark spot. For a moment it drew nearer. Then, as the bright part widened and moved horizontally to her right, *horse and rider* came to mind, but as a question or a guess. Narrowing again, it steadily diminished until disappearing into the rainy morning distance.

Under the conditions, temptation to chase the oddness down and discover what it was did not sustain a motivating impression. "Most curious thing I've ever seen," she whispered, before giving another flip of the reigns and leaving curiosity behind.

Wind had made yet another reversal loop, at the end of which Poyāma said, "OK, heading home." He was sure of the decision, but added, "If a home still exis." Thinking the fire in the vineyards might be out, he knew even heavy rain would take quite a while to douse the kind of inferno consuming the two large buildings. Their total loss could be assumed. The question remained: how far did the fire spread?

"Can you pick up de speed?"

It did pick up, but the route felt unfamiliar. Before long the rain on the right seemed darker than to the left. Poyāma surmised there was a backdrop of mountains on that side. But, questioning whether they passed on the north, south, east or west side of the mountains revealed the extent of his disorientation. A mass of something caught his attention and amazement caused his mouth to hang open as they passed. Barely visible through the rain, some of his horses were huddled together beside a fence line that quickly disappeared into the grayness on both sides of the gathering. Xerxes was not among them.

Who fence is dat? The question was pondered well after the horses had vanished from view, as was the more bothersome concern regarding the whereabouts of Xerxes.

"We come back and fetch dem in a bit, OK?"

The ride back to the ranch felt unendingly longer than that leaving it. Finally, over the sound of rain, a distant but unmistakable cracking and crashing was heard ahead. He knew they were nearing the ranch—the barn had collapsed. The rain was so dense they almost passed under the ranch entry before it was noticed through the soupy grayness. Similar sounds to those heard earlier were much louder and closer. The stable was down. Steps were slow and rainfall dramatically lessened between the entry and the house, which was unharmed. By the time they approached the scorched scene on the other side of the house, the rain was as it was when they left.

Flames clinging to the blackened wood were low, and as expected, the vineyard fires were out. White, steamy product of smolder was thick and everywhere as they passed the two destroyed buildings. The horse continued walking up the slope, passing through destruction on both sides. Over the steady whirring of rain, rushing-watery sounds of flash flooding could be heard. Then, an eerie, unrecognized rushing noise met Poyāma's ears.

Topping the hill the horse stopped and he slid from its back, mouth hanging open. There before his eyes, the opposite hill appeared to be melting into a massive mudslide, rolling into the valley and settling around the lower stable and cellar. Water had filled all cracks in the parched earth and the hill was disintegrating. Sweeping away carriages, some were carried along as riding upon surf and some were mangled like toys. Mud was a third of the way up the row of maple doors to the cellar and rising up the walls of the stable. The long buildings looked strangely squatty.

Turning and facing the burnt mess to his left, then, turning back to the muddy mess in the valley to the right, Poyāma gawked.

"Dese are my stuff . . . why you do dis for me?"

Looking over his right shoulder, he saw the horse, turned away, unresponsive, seemingly unaware, unmoved. *I make de mistake and fall for how he amaze me.* It bent and sniffed the ground like any other animal. *Jus dis morning I meet him . . . he come to me and I so trill for lay dese eye on his glory . . . now dis . . . .*

"You do dis to a good man, you know. De rain and mud hold off long enough for how de wicked can get away wit steal tree horse and saddle dat belong for me. De mud should come and catch him for he drown by his evil way. *Dat* I could understand! But he escape and I get dis. De wicked should be destroy, not de good."

He was looking down at the cellar, mumbling, almost delirious. "De Frenchman, LaRue, come here for insult me and laugh when he see how Vishnu vineyard failing dis year." Looking back at the vineyards, then at Wind, he began hollering. "Have you bring a match for burn de Frenchman barn and vineyard? Go away! Take all you beauty and you amaze and you excite somewhere else for someone else fall for you and get ruin! You noting but disaster! Why you choose me? You noting but harm for me! You take de side of evil and wrong agains de good! Go . . . go!"

Assessing the garden vineyard, he was sickened by the damages to the Sauvignon, Steuben, Vignole and others. "How de good get treat like dis and de bad get reward of horse and saddle and laugh?"

The memory of LaRue's return visit imposed itself upon these murmurings. The terror that the horse might belong to the Frenchman was recalled along with the ideas that rushed upon his unsuspecting dazzled mind—ideas of hiding, stealing, cheating his neighbor if need be, of happily trading all his wealth and all his horses for *one* if need be.

Poyāma stood atop the hill barely breathing, turning, stunned as he surveyed the devastation. The house and a couple of outbuildings remained unharmed. At least two-thirds of his garden vineyards—all vines in the vicinity of his vantage point—were scorched. Dropping to his knees and falling forward, two fistfuls of dirt were grabbed. Rising back up, hands open, the two small dirt clumps rested there in his palms. At that moment, nothing of a lifelong romance with *terroir* remained. He cast them away, disgusted.

Holding up broken hands against a backdrop of ruin, wet black residue of ash still clung. The rain had stopped. Poyāma turned and gazed upon Wind, who was trotting away, bathed in the beautiful colors of cloud filtered sun that followed the storm. Dusk was in those colors and he realized the long ride was actually longer than it seemed, rain having distorted time awareness along with distance and direction. The other horses came to mind, last seen through the rain huddled together beside some fence out in the who-knows-where. *Now I have no way for find and fetch dem back,* he thought.

Beyond the valley of mud the delicate pastoral scene would have been a delight on any previous occasion. Horses populated the rolling hills to the northwest as before. In their world nothing had changed. This and the earlier viewing were separated only by some heavy rainfall and high winds. Down in the valley, the tops of maple doors and pieces of twisted carriage were as litter spoiling the beauty.

"De horse win," he said.

SHOWDOWN

"Gloria?"

The porch lantern was lit, showing Poyāma's breath rising. "You close up for keep warm? We get surprise wit dis hard chill in de air. Nobody see dat coming." Gazing into the dark, he worried, silent, mindful of the scanty harvest in a few vineyards discovered to have late ripening fruit for which he held out hope. Concerning his vines, he was obsessively stubborn that way.

De vine what don' get burn better hurry for ripe before de freezing come and cut off de opportunity for dis year like LaRue predic . . . like he hope bad for me.

It was five in the morning, late for an inner clock usually rousing him between four and four-thirty. Sleep had taken hold the minute two old boots completed a horizontal distribution of damp, worn out, smoke saturated clothes upon the couch at two-fifteen. A short, thoughtful recline prior to getting ready for bed had been intended by the rancher wearing them. But recline quickly became snoring. One day's sprints, firefighting, riding, overwhelmed emotions and hard labor had leaked into early morning work of another day, with barn and stable organized into piles looking like large bon fires.

He would have preferred more sleep. But a single day's weariness would not overrule such a well trained inner clock. The little white tent in the corner of the porch was occupied. There was no new web beneath it. He glanced over the land from side to side. There was no white horse upon it.

"Gloria, you too cold for hunt tonight? You missing you chance, girl. I see some big mot flying like crazy . . . ." He looked around. "Time for knock a blow." reaching into his vest, he removed the morning cigar. "OK, I don' see noting . . . no mot, no bug, no noting fly in dis chilly air. I have to quit de lying. Habit, you know . . . my whole life made of dem . . . helping me get what I value and forget what I don'. Witout de lie in de way, LaRue would have help put out de fire before it find raging and togeter we could have save de vineyard and de building. Pa always say, 'Never create a monster you can' destroy, else it gonna destroy you.' Still, sometime it feel nice, a little lie for helping."

Looking down at the blurry cigar, he tried to keep his hand from shaking. "Dat no good for lighting," he said with a chuckle. "A-a-a-h-h, yesterday I have excite for you believing my word about 'believe.' Today I say, 'Eh, what good is believe?' Maybe I was right before . . . believe is like de mood of de chameleon." The cigar went back into the vest pocket. "Cold out here, girl . . . but you don' need me for tell *you* dat." He blew on Gloria's shroud. No movement followed.

No position was more familiar to the hardened life-long vineyard keeper—knees in the soil, hands working it. The large flat stone in place and dirt spread evenly around it, he rose up and sat back on his heels.

"You deserve a stone dat big. I tink you my favorite of always."

Centered beneath the stone, Gloria Thirty-two was wrapped in a white napkin with the morning's unlit cigar—ritual. An adjacent stone, much smaller, was noticed.

"Twenty-seven . . . she de one dat catch poison from fight wit de wasp before I have time for know her more dan a few week."

Poyāma glanced over the stones within view. "Das a lot a very nice cigar in dis garden."

Reaching across several stones and patting the top of another large one, he smiled and shook his head. "Twenty-one . . . now dere a girl who have de big hunger and no fear. I remember how I worry for her when de monster mantis get caught in her web. I remind her what Pa always say: 'Don' hang you hat where you can' reach.' But she prove me wrong and have a fine meal of dat one. Den she lure in anoter one, bigger, de nex day. For sure one of my favorite right dere."

He looked up into the lengthened morning dark of late fall. Heart more than heavy, there too was a growing darkness, something previously avoided. His entire way of viewing the world had been shaken. Normally operating only on presumption about God, he woke up actually thinking about him, greatly desiring to speak a few words of complaint. Inclination to open his mouth and do so directly felt strange, given the length of time since last communication. In fact, the last communication could not be recalled. *Maybe far back as when de circuit preacher pay us a visit back home,* he thought. An idea came to mind.

"You know someting girl?" Getting to his feet, he was careful to avoid burn wounds while brushing off dirty hands against each other. "We keep going like dis for anoter fifty year, we have a nice patio." He bent over and shook moist dirt from the knees of old jeans. "But maybe after today dere be no more year for Poyāma. Because today is Sunday, if I have not lose my mind along wit everyting else. And dat mean de preacher is preaching at de little church dere in town where he will hear a harsh word today from dis rancher about God. Den we see if I keep breat for tomorrow, or if God strike me down dead for mout off at him."

Inside the house, every manner of slamming, banging and delaying type of preparation was made for the showdown. Except for weddings, funerals and one or two Christmas services, Poyāma had not been to a church service since moving to his new country. Some fine clothes were hanging in the closets . . . too fine for the day's purposes. *How do a man dress for duel,* he wondered. *I know dere muss be a gun showing for sure, in case dese church peoples have no liking for de word I bring dem and dey minister.* In the end, the usual items of dress for an appearance in town were chosen, which included his newest and most expensive boots, in *his* mind a sign of power and status.

Standing in the middle of his great-room, the house was examined for something that had not yet come to mind, but he was sure would make itself known once spotted. The blanket used on the picnic with Gloria hung on the wall above the fireplace. It caught his attention. He looked over at a small table, where the container used to hold grapes taken on the picnic held seasonal décor. The only thing he could identify that he needed was a good horse.

The nearest horse was two or three hills away. Saddles were either destroyed by fire or trapped behind doors blocked by several feet of mud. His pocket watch reported ten minutes before six. *Church start at ten*, he thought, *or do it start at eleven?* The math required a brisk walk to get there by ten. *A-a-a-h-h, right dere a problem. I stink by de time I get dere. Wait . . . dat is perfec! Dis a fight. A man should work up a good stink for a fight.*

Clutched in his right hand was a holster holding two revolvers. Suddenly, the memory of his father's voice and word's was clear. *'An angry man should not carry gun for tempt of someting stupid.'* "A-a-a-h-h-h! Who you kidding, Poyāma Vishnu?" he scolded himself. Throwing the guns on a table, he muttered, "You can' take fight to God wit gun."

Looking around to see if there was anything that ought to be brought along on such a lengthy walk, another thought came with startling clarity but no familiar voice: *I will trade you every expectation you began with for the power to make the most of this moment.*

Poyāma turned and opened the front door, attempting to close another in his mind. Stepping onto the front porch, the offer demanded a response. Annoyed, he went back into the house, snatched a piece of scrap paper the shape of a dollar bill from a drawer, grabbed a pencil from a cup and sat down to write. Unintentionally, the result had the appearance of a voucher.

I will trade you—

Every expectation you began with

For—

The power to make the most of this moment

Slapping the pencil down, Poyāma stood, stared at the paper and complained to himself, "You loosing it now, broter. What can dis mean . . . who making dis trade wit who? Where dis power coming from . . . in what form it coming . . . how do it work for dis here purpose? A-a-a-a-h-h-h!" He folded the piece of paper and shoved it into a pocket. "I will tink about dis on de way, or maybe on de returning."

It so happened that the offer was forgotten the moment he closed the door and stepped from the porch, as was the need for food and water. Soon he was passing under the entryway to the ranch, looking ahead at the sunlight shining through layered leafless branches of the wooded region to the east. The ball of light behind the dense entanglements of limbs appeared fractured, molten in patches and otherwise spread out sparkling specks.

An illusion of glowing branches catching fire caused Poyāma to stop. The picnic ten years in the past was as moments ago. Sunlight shining through tangled strands of Gloria's hair, seemingly setting them ablaze, felt present. He wanted the memory to include his voice telling Gloria how glorious she was, how thoughts of her were as the warmth of sunshine, deep like meaning, full like being and bright like the star over tomorrow. But the memory was mute. He resumed walking.

The first half of the walk into town was driven by the stressful anticipation of a public confrontation and its agitated rehearsal. Though vigorous and vocal, the practicing was imaginary. Fiery words were directed at a man behind a pulpit on a battlefield the length and width of an isle between pews loaded with goading spectators. The idea of stopping to slug it out directly never occurred to the enraged decrier.

The second half was a battle of the will centering on a question of whether arrival or expiration would happen first. By nine-thirty the cold beginning to the morning had been forgotten. The day had seen a turn, and a *return* to recent pattern—temperature rising quickly under a bright full sun. It had been many years since the owner of Percheron, Piebald, Palomino and a host of other equestrian options covering most of the rest of the English alphabet had traveled half this far without horse or carriage. New boots was an especially bad choice.

Nearly despairing for fear a delirium had taken advantage of agony and dehydration, seized his mind and sent him off course, the town finally showed itself as a speck on the horizon. The remaining distance was covered barefoot, boots in hand. Arriving on wobbly legs, he dismissed the idea of paying the church a visit and headed straight for the mercantile, which he knew would be open, but not "open." It was Sunday, and nobody would be working there—transactions were by "honor system" only. But the mercantile—which actually had a name that no one ever used: Vernon's—was to this town what a pub or saloon or lodge might be elsewhere in the world.

First stop was at the community well pump beside it, which Poyāma had ordered and paid for at the same time his own wells were put in. after filling both boots, he drank from one while pouring the contents of the other over his head, leaving him soaked and dripping like a rag doll. In this condition he stepped inside the local stamping ground, unconscious of power and status.

Dropping the boots on the floor and his posterior onto a chair, Poyāma collapsed upon the table beside it, which doubled as a checkerboard. Head buried in his arms, he called out to no one in particular, "What time is it?", realizing it had been quite a while since he last checked.

"Twelve ten," came the answer. A moment later it was followed with some humor. "You get baptized across the way and come in here to dry out?"

Poyāma recognized the voice as that of the preacher's elder teenage son. He sat up, bent brows leading the comedian to think his humor was not appreciated.

"Mr. Vishnu! I . . . I didn't recognize you when you came in . . . I, I had my back turned and . . . ." the youthful voice went silent for a moment, lacking a supply of words. It was replaced by the sound of a chair scooting on the floor, turning to face the weary traveler.

"Are you OK?"

Poyāma's frown was actually from contemplation of the time report, which brought two silent responses. The first was amazement that he was capable of walking for six hours and the second was relief that the showdown would have to wait for another Sunday.

"Yes, fine tank you . . . great . . . ." The words were barely out of his mouth when Poyāma waved them off with an emphatic hand gesture. "No . . . not fine . . . for sure not great. I am a liar and a bad one . . . always ac like de man who perfec, de man who have everyting right . . . everyting fine."

"Well Mr. Vishnu, after all, you do have . . . ."

"I have noting! I loss it all . . . but only save back my house. Everyting else loss . . . vineyard, barn, two stable . . . even my friend, Gloria, jus dis morning. But I tell her at de las, jus before she get burry in de ground, dat I stop de lying. So I feel obligate, for Gloria sake, for tell it to you straight."

The rattled young man looked as though he had received a concussion. Pretty sure he knew everyone in the area, as far as he could recall, there was only one Gloria. Squinting thoughtfully, he silently reassured himself he had seen her earlier that morning at the church.

The weary, soggy traveler said, "I take a long walk and get drink and dunk at you pump outside for look like dis jus for you. But I take de walk because I lose my garden vineyard and barn and stable to fire and my many wagon and cellar and oter stable to mud slide after de storm . . . all jus yesterday. Excep for Gloria . . . dat what happen dis morning, like I tell you. So, all in all, ting not so fine jus now."

"Mr. Vishnu, if all you're saying happened like you're tellin' me, maybe you should not be doin' as well as you are . . . , which leads me to believe you're doing much worse than either of us think."

"You pretty on de money dere. You know what time de church service end? I come to town for a showdown wit you pa, de preacher."

"One o'clock."

"One o'clock! Who can play church for dat long?"

The comment drew a hearty laugh. "Not me, I can take about five minutes of sittin' still for anything. But Dad lets me come over here when I get antsy, long as I promise to read the good book or study the words of a few a these ol' hymns." He held up a Bible and a hymnal as evidence. "Actually, they don't get started over there until eleven-thirty."

"Eleven-tirty? See, dat right dere is sacrelig. Nobody start church on de half hour when I was young, I tell you dat. De Good Lord make time on de hour, not de half hour. And nobody ever start church dat late back den eiter, no way. People afraid to get out deir bed too early dese day."

The amused and concerned youngster matched elbows to knees, leaned forward and said, "Actually, I think it's for the people comin' from far out 'n the countryside."

"Well, nobody do dat too. People far away go to dey own church back den or wait for de missionary for swing by." Poyāma stared for a moment, thoughtful. "Too bad dat missionary die so young. I tink I never see him pass de time I was ten or so." A deep sigh preceded a yawn. "I remember everyone look forward to him only coming once in awhile." Feeling tired and fuzzy, he put his head back down on folded arms.

While he rested, the young man took the opportunity to walk across the street to the little church. During the congregational singing he slipped a note to his father. It described briefly "Mr. Vishnu's losses and frame of mind." He was greatly relieved to see Gloria LaRue occupying her usual seat in the third row left of the pulpit, appearing healthy as always and singing her heart out.

"You doin' OK here Mr. Vishnu, or can I get you something?" he asked, back in his neighboring chair in the mercantile, having read aloud and pondered all six verses of one hymn and both of another.

A few seconds were needed to process the question. "Yes, de answer pretty much de same as before, tank you. What time you say it is?"

"Twelve fifty."

"What! Das not what you tell me!"

"No, I told you twelve ten the last time you asked. That was before we talked for a bit 'n you fell asleep and slept for more than a half-hour. Now it's twelve fifty."

Poyāma was out the door, boots in hand. Entering the church, he tucked himself into an open seat at the end of the back row. After setting his boots beside the pew, he spotted Gloria up near the front. Self-consciously putting his hands through wet, matted hair, he was glad she could not see him looking so disheveled, though the concern did not keep his heart rate from elevating. Forcing himself to stop staring, the man behind the pulpit quickly became the focus of redirected attention.

"And lastly, the third response, which you may also find unusual . . . Let's take a look at verse seventeen . . . ." The preacher looked down at his Bible. "'Nor do men put new wine into old wineskins; otherwise the wineskins burst, and the wine is poured out, and the wineskins are ruined; but they put new wine into fresh wineskins, and both are preserved.'" Looking up, he gazed out upon the congregation and spotted Poyāma in the back row.

"So, we have a wine answer to a technical religious question. These fellas wanted to know why Jesus' disciples weren't carryin' on as real men of God . . . why aren't they gettin' down to the disciplines of the program like the disciples of John and those of the Pharisees? And Jesus' answer is actually very straight forward: 'It's a new program and they're not ready. That's what I'm doing. I'm getting them ready.' He was answering them, in essence, 'These guys you see me walkin' around with every day are just like you—clueless to the fact that I am introducing an entirely *new* program. They are saturated in, conditioned by, and predisposed to the old program. If they're not reconditioned . . . prepared first before getting all busy carryin' on like they know what's what and how it's done, the new wine of the Holy Spirit I want to pour into them will be wasted on their old attitudes. Their fresh faith will be spoiled and they themselves will be ruined.'"

He looked over his friends slowly, seemingly thoughtful of everyone present. "Now, let's take a minute and examine ourselves. Is there any out-with-the-old kind of preparation for the *new* taking place? Is there any evidence of such tender, even if severe, mercy? If so, brothers and sisters, be encouraged, be patient and be surrendered to the Master's masterful work in you. He has his eye on you and new wine is coming."

Certain he had heard precisely the part of the message meant for his hearing, the opportunity was taken to sneak back out the door before the service ended and Gloria caught sight of him looking so unqualified. Just as he had missed the first thirty minutes of the sermon and everything that went before it, Poyāma missed the closing remarks and invitational song. Standing barefoot in the street holding his boots, the showdown was off for the time being.

I got a lot for tink about and noting ever prepare me for tink dat way. He chuckled to himself for the thought. *Dat was de very ting what de sermon was about, so you listen dere, Poyāma.*

There was an intrigue down the street. Wandering down to where it was, he watched from the middle of the street as a man was kicking one of the wheels of his wagon. On the wagon were his wife, their two children and boxes of their belongings. The wheel was obviously broken. Whether by his kicking or by another means, it was not easy to tell.

"We've spent over a week in this town and most of the money we had left between fixing this wagon . . . this one wheel twice . . . gettin' Ben's arm set, and reboxin' and repackin' everything because of that crazy storm that tried to blow us the rest of the way to Tennessee."

"You don't have to tell me, Honey, I've been right here livin' it with you. And breakin' your foot on that wheel isn't gonna help things."

The man put his hands on the tall wheel and leaned into it, head down between his arms, right foot kicking at the dirt. "We were already behind. We'll be travelin' in two feet of snow long before we get that far."

"This is a lot of things to go wrong Daddy," the boy said.

"Yes it is son."

"In one place I mean."

"Yes I know, Son."

The woman got down from the wagon and stood beside her husband. "Maybe we should . . ."

"That's not the plan! We didn't spend two years plannin' 'n workin' for this move—this 'adventure' as you call it—to cut our plans in half and wind up somewhere we didn't intend, in some little town with no job waitin' for us, no family . . . no community like there is waitin' for us in Tennessee."

"We don't know what might be here."

"That's just the point. We *know* what's there."

"I just want you to know I wouldn't consider it a failure to change our plans, especially if this was *the* plan all along . . . just not ours."

"Well I would!" the man answered, pushing away from the wagon, whirling around and walking to the middle of the street, where he stood with hands on hips. He spotted Poyāma standing nearby cradling boots in one hand and holding his vest in the other, still wet, shirt hanging loose.

"Can I help you?" the man asked, certain he was looking at a man of dim wit and even less means.

"Now, dat is a nice question you ask me from de condition you in," Poyāma answered. He walked toward the man. "Dat tell me a lot about you."

"Look, Mr., if you need a ride, we could make room, but this wagon isn't goin' anywhere for at least another day, maybe two. And we're about to spend the rest of our money fixin' that wheel for the third time. So, if you need money . . . maybe a hot meal, that's about all I can offer at the moment."

"No, I have no need of anyting. But I make a proposal for you."

Poyāma pulled from his pocket the piece of paper he had written on before leaving his house and held it out. The man took it, opened and stared at it.

I will trade you—
Every expectation you began with
For—
The power to make the most of this moment

He walked back to the wheel and resumed his former position. Every question Poyāma had asked after the thought came to him was running through the man's mind.

"I write dis down before I leave my house dis morning, no idea where it come from. Maybe it come to me for you."

They met back in the middle of the road, Poyāma receiving an aggressive hug from a complete stranger for something he would rather have had an explanation. But he never felt more wealthy than at that moment.

The man handed the piece of paper to his wife, scooped up both of his children and began walking toward the mercantile. "You guys pick out two pieces of candy each while I see if I can find something for fixin' the wheel. We need this wagon for gettin' around to see what kind of place this is that's presentin' us with all these challenges 'n tryin' to keep us here."

Poyāma walked over to the woman sitting in the wagon. "What size you husband boot?" he asked.

"Eleven," she answered.

"Well, dese one size too small, so I give dem to you instead." He set them on the back corner of the wagon. "Ostrich . . . put dem in consignmen in de mercantile and dey good for buy you all a new wheel."

"Thank you, and thank you for this," the woman said, holding up the hand written voucher.

Turning and beginning the walk back home, Poyāma got as far as the church before stopping. Disheveled appearance or not, he thought it would be nice to have a word with Gloria once the service let out. A nostalgic thought came to his mind. *I wonder if dey serve de snack in dere. I never see dat snack again since when I was a boy back home.* Opening the door enough to poke his head inside, he saw that a baptism had just taken place. Quickly, the same back row seat was snagged.

"'In the beginning was the Word . . . And the Word became flesh and dwelt among us,'" the pastor recited, coming down from the pulpit. Stopping, he stood before a small table, upon which were a plate containing a loaf of bread, two cups and a small book.

Picking up the book, he said, "Our communion reading for today is from The Gospel According to St. John, chapter 6, verses 47-57. Then he read:

"Verily, verily, I say unto you, He that believeth on me hath everlasting life. I am that bread of life. Your fathers did eat manna in the wilderness, and are dead. This is the bread which cometh down from heaven, that a man may eat thereof, and not die. I am the living bread which came down from heaven: if any man eat of this bread, he shall live for ever: and the bread that I will give is my flesh, which I will give for the life of the world." The Jews therefore strove among themselves, saying, "How can this man give us his flesh to eat?" Then Jesus said unto them, "Verily, verily, I say unto you, except ye eat the flesh of the Son of man, and drink his blood, ye have no life in you. Whoso eateth my flesh, and drinketh my blood, hath eternal life; and I will raise him up at the last day. For my flesh is meat indeed, and my blood is drink indeed. He that eateth my flesh, and drinketh my blood, dwelleth in me and I in him. As the living Father hath sent me, and I live by the Father, so he that eateth me, even he shall live by me."

Poyāma sat stunned. *How dis memory for 'eat de sun' come to me jus yesterday morning and I come here to de place I never come and listen for what dis man read from de book so specific?*

After setting the book down, the pastor picked up the loaf in one hand and a cup in the other.

"Now friends, these poor folks our Lord Jesus was talking to did not have the benefit of the understanding you and I share. So, it is not difficult to appreciate why most of his followers stopped following after hearing these words. But the word we must pay close attention to still today is this word 'believe.' It is a bigger word than *agree . . . you* know—with the Methodists, the Catholics, the Lutherans and so on. It is a word bigger than religion and broader than theology. For it is a directive concerning reality and necessity—the reality of sin separating us from a holy God and the necessity of a Savior. This little word believe has meaning as big as life itself, and *that* unto all eternity. So I ask you: do you believe the flesh and blood of the Son of God was given for the forgiveness of your sins, and have you received this free gift of salvation from God our heavenly Father? If so, then I invite you even as Jesus did his disciples sometime later: 'Take this and share it among yourselves.'" He broke the bread and set its halves on two plates, one on each side of the table beside one of the cups. "Partake," he said, "according to the Lord's command to 'Do this in remembrance of Me.'"

As those in attendance rose and filed out of the pews and formed lines approaching the table from two sides, Poyāma remained seated. His mind was busy while the line moved steadily forward. He pondered the events of the previous day, thoughts he had awakened to, numerous unexplainable influences which had come to bear upon the moment. *So dis is de encourage, 'eat de Son,' what Ma try for slip in behind de word of Pa. Howcome nobody ever tell me de snack is such a serious remember . . . de blood and de flesh of God for forgive?*

While recalling the memories of his parents, their ways and influence, the way he had treated LaRue came to mind—threatening to kill him—followed by the real reasons he could not keep good help employed. Pride that prevented requesting timely help and racing around on Wind hoping desperately for any help at all were fresh recollections. When the communion message of need for a Savior forced all other thoughts to subside, he whispered, "I need de Savior, not jus help and not jus religion of Ma and big idea like Pa." Leaving his seat, he walked to the front.

Arriving at the table, he stopped and stared down at the objects it held. He looked up at the pastor, who asked, "Do you believe in Jesus as Savior and confess him as Lord?" It was the first time in Poyāma's life anyone had directed this question at him. He was thankful it was asked on the first day in his life on which he was certain of an answer. He did not know where the answer came from or how he knew. But he knew more deeply and was surer of his answer than anything else in his entire life. "Yes," he said. The pastor picked up what remained of the loaf and held it out. After breaking off a piece and consuming it, Poyāma received the cup also.

When the service ended, he sat thoughtful, forgetful even of Gloria, while others exited. Then, on the way out, the pastor was waiting at the door.

"Sir, I listen hard for dat word you preach . . . it hit me on de mark."

"Well, Mr. Vishnu, you are an easy man to please. Maybe I should keep all my sermons to the last three or four minutes."

They laughed.

"Yes, well, I leave home around six and get dere dat late, if you can believe it."

"Is there anything I can do to help?"

"Not for me, tank you." Poyāma turned and nodded toward the lady in the wagon. "Her husband and children go for shop in de mercantile. Dose people might choose for stay here. I hear dem talking about some hope for a little community. Maybe you can see if dere is some around here for dem. I don' know what kind of skill de man have, but if he don' find work too soon, you can send him my way. I have plenty of work for a man wit a shovel for do at my place dat keep him busy a bit."

"We'll see what we can do," was the response, as both men looked down the street in the direction of the broken wagon. Turning back to Poyāma, the preacher was thoughtful before speaking again. "By the way, instead of 'Sir,' please call me Eugene."

"If *you* replace Poyāma for 'Mr. Vishnu' we got a deal."

"Deal," Eugene said, smiling as they shook hands. "I must confess a little jealousy. I like your name . . . not only for its uniqueness, but for the sound of special in it. It's not a run-a-the-mill name like Eugene. Is it Chilean or Indian? I'm sure it has a wonderful meaning."

Poyāma frowned. "Well, what a shame dat I muss correc you on all of dose nice idea. Not Chilean . . . or even Sout American, not Indian, and no meaning at all what anybody ever can tell me. Only de 'sound of special' is what come hard upon my Ma for give me dat name."

Eugene looked surprised. "In that case, if you don't mind my voicing what comes to mind when I hear it . . . ."

Poyāma was slow in answering, giving himself due time to consider whether or not he might actually *mind* before saying, "You have my full attention."

"It reminds me of a word I learned in seminary back in New York . . . a Greek word: Poēima. It was a word deep with creative meaning. If I recall correctly, our English word Poem grew out of it. It was used in the original writing of the Bible in just one place to describe you and me as . . . hmm, the *God-crafted* . . . made by God for his specific purpose in Christ Jesus."

Poyāma stared. Having difficulty making sense of the creative context stated, he focused his attention on the part that most interested him. "What kind of specific?" he asked.

Folding his arms and appearing to chew on an upper lip tucked under his protruding lower lip, the pastor processed the question thoroughly. "Goodness," he finally answered, lowering his arms, hands finding one another behind his back. "God's purpose in personally crafting us is fulfilled by our living out the good works he wills to do through us. That would be my interpretation of the passage in which the word is found."

As if the man had reached into the heavens, pulled down a star and handed it to him, Poyāma stood dazzled, feeling awkward in his handling of awe.

"Well, Sir . . , Pastor Eugene . . . I, I tink my Ma have no way for know anyting like dat when she fall in love wit de name she place on me. But I tink she will have no reason for find offense wit de meaning you explain if I borrow it."

The pastor placed his hand on his new friend's shoulder, smiled and headed down the street toward the broken wagon. Poyāma watched him walk away, certain the showdown had taken place after all and he was both loser and winner as a result. He looked around studiously. Gloria was nowhere in view, so he set out for home. Before long he met LaRue coming into town, the Morgan beneath him appearing near collapse.

"Good morning LaRue. You horse look abuse, like you drive her too hard."

"Afternoon Vishnu. Why on earth are you in bare feet?"

"Indian ting. Time for new profession . . . guru."

"You have time for a beer?"

"No tank you. You miss a good sermon today. Dat man really preach it broter. Jus now I tell you what happen dere . . . he talking right to me. It never too late to learn."

"Better than your preachin' to the vines?"

"Well, I can' really say much on dat. I like mine too." Poyāma gave his neighbor's horse a pat on the neck and began walking. "I see you soon," he said, impatient and irritated by background thoughts about how fast things can change.

"Hey, you get through that storm in good shape?" LaRue asked, turning on his horse.

Poyāma stopped and looked back, thoughtful before answering. *Here's de real tes for me keeping my word to Gloria . . . no more lie.* "Dat was a big one wit some hard result. But I make it trough."

"You need a hand with anything? Wait a second . . . you're not walking because your horses got out are ya?"

"You ask a lot a question, LaRue. I bet even you wife find annoying at you, you ask so many question."

LaRue laughed. "She would probably say that's true, Vish. Anyway, I'll be glad to help you out any way I can."

Staring with eyes of suspicion up at the man who was seeming less like a nemesis all the time, Poyāma thought their relationship was becoming almost bearable.

So, now I come to need of he help. Not so fas. And where all dose beautiful horse go anyway . . . jus disappear? How come he is sounding like de only one oter dan me who know dey get out.

"No tanks," he said, "I jus have need of some exercise today. Everyting going OK."

"Well, that's a long walk, but at least you picked a good day for it."

"Yep, time to get on wit it. See you sometime."

LaRue turned and rode away.

As Poyāma began walking, he could not have been further removed from the interaction with the young family, the proposition on the voucher he had written, the few minutes of sermon he had appreciated, the promise to Gloria Thirty-two, or his own proclamations of rejoicing from a hilltop just a day before.

"Why do I treat him dat way," he asked. "OK, so he sneak and be clever in his way. I do de same in my own way. But he try for look beyond de bad and reach out. He come to my place once in a while. In all de year I live here, have I ever visit his place but two time to see his sister?"

He thought about a life of being mostly pleased with himself. *I was a good man for all dose year. I was a good man. I do ting right, I treat oter people mostly friendly, many time maybe generous. I do for dem how I like dem do me. How dat change? How I come to find dis way for keep back alone?*

"Dat horse!" he said angrily, feeling betrayed and humiliated. "Everyting was wonderful til dat horse show up. I hate dat horse. He ever come near my land, I shoot him full of hole so he never do dis to no one again. O yes, de great Poyāma . . . 'I am Poyāma!' Poyāma who too clever for de slick French American, LaRue, but excite like a child, like a silly mama boy over a fine white horse . . . a stray horse . . . someone else problem wander onto my land . . . someone else nightmare come my way, and I say, 'Sure, sure, make youself at home . . . no, better den dat, make dis you own home for destroy however you like. A-a-a-h-h-h!'"

He was limping due to the soreness of bruises and broken blisters on his feet and the achy weariness in a number of leg muscles.

"Why you so proud Poyāma? De preacher ask you how he can help. LaRue ask you how he can help. You too good for find help? You too perfec for need help? Even de young man wit de broke wheel and no money offer he help. I could be riding home nice and comfortable in someone carriage, on someone horse. Instead, I suffer and ac like I have it togeter fine . . . nice day for a walk. Yeah, right! I suffer because I march into town like some marshal to have it out wit God, like God de one at fault for all dis. Jus more pride right dere. Pa say 'You can never fight de Devil in he hell.' But dat what I try for do by always use my pride."

After many more limping steps, contrite in evaluation of prideful errors, Poyāma's thoughts returned to the horse.

"Dat horse de oter part. Dat horse ruin me. All my life I live by de moral code dat always do me right. Dat horse show up and how long it take? Blink of an eye, dat all, and dere I am making secret way for keep horse even if it belong to my neighbor. I ac jus like I judge him treat me but ac like I am good in how I do it and he bad.

"So, wait . . . ." He stopped. "Did de horse bring dat to me or was dat dere already? It muss have be dere already for it go to affec so quick. But why I lose my good style and ac so low, so foolish? 'Da evil a man do follow him.' Now I know what Papa mean when he always say dat word. He mean it follow because of exis inside, and de man can' get away from it. Where him go, dere he be."

Resuming the walk, mental images of his father were surprisingly clear. "I remember anoter word he say to me. 'You can' suck cane and blow whistle at de same time.' But I don' listen to him on dat word. I use lie to make de bad me hide from de good so I can walk wit de two but tink I am only always de one . . . de good Poyāma who always in de right. I should listen to my own word too . . . dat word I preach up on de hill . . . 'rejoice.' I forget divine and lose rejoice. Dat de problem right dere. Poyāma too much impress wit Poyāma good, like I don' need even God help . . . like I have special right for be good . . . like de French tink dey de only one who get de wine always right jus because dey French."

Stopping again he said, "So, dat where de sermon, Rejoice, come from . . . leak right out my own soul all over de vineyard, and I tink it about keeping vine. I know someting strange from de beginning yesterday, like someting coming I desire and someting coming I hate for see."

Walking on, the dirt road was hard like rock, having absorbed the majority of the rain from the storm into its dry depths and given up the rest to the heat of the sun. Once in awhile a rock poking up from the surface bruised the hiker's already sore feet, adding a hobble for many steps.

Hearing hooves on the road behind him, Poyāma turned and watched LaRue riding up on a fresh horse, another in tow. Soon they were face to face again.

"LaRue, you a good man . . . *dat* is a taught dis brain never come up wit before."

Laughing, LaRue held out the reins. "And you are a wealth of surprises to mine also, Vish."

Poyāma took the reins, took hold of the saddle, put his foot in the stirrup and stopped . . . staring. His eyes pinched shut as the memory of the day he lost his brother commandeered control of his mind. A wealthy French neighbor, one of the partners of The House, had lent them two horses for a day of fun and adventure. Halfway through the day they decided to trade horses. His kid brother was just a few feet away, mounting the horse when it took off, leaving him sprawled upon the large rock at Poyāma's feet, lifeless. Locking thumbs behind his neck and wrapping arms around his head, shock became a fit of panic.

Forehead pressed against the saddle, mind playing and replaying the entire scene, he tried to will the vivid memory away. The foot came out of the stirrup and he stepped toward LaRue holding up the reins.

"I can'," he said, animated in the shaking of his head back and forth.

"Vishnu . . ."

"Why you call me Vishnu and ignore my name for proper calling?" Poyāma asked, agitated as he handed back the reins and once again set out on foot for his house.

"Com'on, Vish . . . look, I stopped in at the mercantile after I ran into you earlier, and I overheard a few folks talking . . . about what happened to your place."

Poyāma stopped. "How nice! Now de pity of de whole town get fix on 'Poor Mr. Vishnu and he problem.'"

"Not the whole town, Vish, just . . . just the preach *you* enjoyed listenin' to so much . . . and a few others who care about you."

"Why you call me 'Vish', what not any of my name?" Poyāma was walking with some renewed strength, disguising his hobble the best he could.

"Then I met a young family that was in a predicament because of a broken wagon wheel. They had a pair of fine boots . . . could be had for the right price, I learned. As I was lendin' a hand with the wagon, Judge Barnhardt walked up and bought them for a pretty penny. That was a nice thing you did there, Vi . . . broter."

Poyāma once again stopped and turned toward LaRue, by this time seventy-five feet away or more. "Why you make fun of my talking?"

"Is it OK for a 'broter' to help you out?" LaRue called. "I know your feet have to be sore, and you still have half the distance left to get to your place."

Still half remain! He have to be kidding, Poyāma silently complained, looking over his shoulder and sighing deeply. He shook his head. "I can'."

"Why not?"

"I have stric forbid . . . stric forbid for ride anoter man horse. Dis I never do . . . ever!"

LaRue chuckled and shook his head as he rode up to where his neighbor now stood. When he got there, he hopped down from his horse.

"Hey, I understand the importance of pride to a man."

"Dis not about pride, trus me. Dis stric forbid. I never, never do dis ting, believe me on dat word."

"I get the forbid thing, already. But if it's not about pride, what is it about?"

"Dere a word call karma . . . you know it? I believe dat word. And horse have de own karma. De horse know to who it belong, you can believe dat. Dat why a man break horse, pay money for horse, brush horse, feed horse wit he own hand, saddle horse wit one saddle if he know what he doing, and provide cover for horse. De horse paying attention to all dese ting and have a pride of he own he ready to guard. Did you train dis horse for Poyāma to ride?"

"Well, no, but . . . ."

"Dat horse know it, believe me. Unless you raise him from foal for everybody service and he agree wit it . . , trus me, dis no kind ting you do for invite me to hop up on his back for maybe he do me wrong."

They stared at one another.

"I have a question for you," LaRue said.

"What it is?"

"Why do you call me LaRue?"

The staring continued, Poyāma not thinking of an answer, LaRue not waiting for one, but extending his hand.

"Richard, but you can call me Rich, because that is what I was and what I am going to be again some day."

"Poyāma," was the response as they shook hands.

Simultaneously nodding, the walker turned and resumed walking and the rider got on his horse.

"Tank you rich man, Rich, for de nice ting you try for do, but I can no way oblige for stric forbid."

"I understand, Poyāma," said a less proud French American.

A less proud Indian-Chilean-American stopped once more and turned. "Dat sound too much like wrong coming from you. Go back to Vish. I like de way you exis someting new dere for jus between we."

LaRue turned on his horse laughing, gave it a spirited kick and smiled for the first mile of the ride back toward his ranch, periodically shaking his head. Then an ugly thought turned his mood. *Now what? Now he's like a friend or something. I'm betraying a friend, that's what! You see what you've done Richard. Trying to cover your conscience over with a little bit of Mr. nice guy, you went and made the guy a friend.*

"Why did I do that? Boy, am I stupid!" he scolded aloud. "Now what am I gonna do. It's too late to turn back. Miller was so excited he said he was leaving immediately. That means he and his men are on their way and will be here in the morning. In the morning!" he yelled into the wilderness.

He pulled back aggressively on the reins, dismounted before his horse was able to stop and immediately began pacing. "What am I gonna do? Even if he hasn't left and I could get a message to him calling it off . . . which I can't in this amount of time . . . still it would be embarrassing . . . humiliating! He will never do business with me again. And *he's* also middleman to over half my wine customers." He kicked the dirt. "Wine customers? What do I care about wine customers? I don't have enough wine product to call it a business anymore. Horses are my shot at turning things around, and Miller is the only man I know that's a bigger horse fanatic than Vishnu and has the money to buy these animals."

Spotting a loose rock, he ran a few strides and kicked it as far as he could, spun around nearly a full revolution on the follow through and sat down in the dirt.

"I should call it off anyway. When he gets here I will just have to tell him I don't have any of the fancy horses anymore . . . they broke out and got away."

He stood and walked to his horse. Halfway into his mount, he stopped and got back down. Leaning against the horse, forehead pressed against the saddle, he mumbled, "I can't. I can't do it."

Grabbing the hat off his head, he stood fists on hips and closed his eyes in thought. *This is all the money I have headin' in . . . , a couple years to keep us on our land with food in our bellies. If I send Miller on his way with no horses he's gonna charge me for him and his boys stopping everything and comin' here. That's more money goin' out and none comin' in.*

This thought demanded more pacing.

"I'll figure out a way to get the money back to Vish. I'll work for him . . . right, how will I explain that without telling him I sold his horses? Plus, he doesn't want money, and he can buy any labor he needs. He wants his horses. Those are his treasures." Spinning around and raising his hat in the air, he yelled, "Richard . . . You idiot!"

By the intention of slamming it to the ground, the hat came down with some force. But LaRue did not realize how close he was to his horse following the spin. When the hat collided with the horse's back end, both horses lit out for home. For a moment, LaRue stood and watched as if they would turn around, head back to him, laughing upon their return and say, "Just kiddn' boss."

Looking up at the sky, he said, "Stop laughing." Then he started walking.

Continuing the ruminations begun on the first half of the journey, Poyāma had progressed quite a distance opposite of LaRue, a comic dual-limp enabling him to ignore his sore feet. "A-a-a-a-h-h, see dere, now you should feel ashame. Dat man try for do a nice ting, riding home to fetch a horse and bring it back while you imagine he collec up you horse for he self. And you still walking, even after a man bring you a horse for ride. How dat happen?"

This last rebuke deserved some thought. Keeping the memory of his little brother out of his mind the best he could, he thought about the basis for "stric forbid." *Superstition! Superstition de only explanation for dat. I choose superstition over face a ting and call it what it be.* Poyāma took a moment to detour a few paces and sit down. Arms wrapped around his knees, head tucked between them, he stared at the ground. Tears fell making dark spots in the dirt. *Sad feeling and pain is what it call,* he silently concluded. *Fear dat I fail to be in control at all time and worse fear dat when I am, bad ting happen . . . like what happen to Vishwaas. So I hide from de pain by make de serious rule about believe in horse karma.*

Right there in the road, Poyāma laid back and recalled a number of sad things he had been powerless to do anything about. Sitting up again, he looked out at the horizon. "If I tink about dis sooner, maybe I never get rich," he quietly pondered aloud. "Maybe I never own fine horse eiter . . . maybe I never leave my country and my family for dis lonely way for make grape and horse my everyting." Suddenly back on his feet, the walk was resumed and the thinking out loud much more lively. "Dat too big a ting for tink about jus now. Dat too big for anyone to decide. Who know, maybe I make more rich. Dat de wrong ting to look at. De ting I learn today is dat i's never too late for learn. Lie and superstition only get in de way. No more . . . no more for dem. Now to find dat horse, Wind, and apologize. He de start for all dis." Limp and all, the pace was brisk.

"Everyting about de day he show up was differen from de start. Before he come I never do noting unusual. I never do noting outside exac plan for make busy. I never do noting like preach sermon for inspire de vineyard for rejoice. I never tink about rejoice. Before de day of Wind come I never do noting like take time for talk wit LaRue. I never do noting like stop and write ting on paper dat I don' know what it mean. I never do noting like walk six hour into town, drink from boot, go to church far late, listen to de message, care for meet stranger and he family. Before Wind, I never believe to hand anoter man de piece of paper what mean noting to me and expec it have meaning for him. What meaningful to me . . . dat all dat matter before Wind come here for complete disrup. A-a-ah-ah-h! What if I miss one of dose . . . jus one? What if I don' stop for pay attention to de proposal . . . enough for stop and write it down? I muss find dat horse and apologize and tank him for all he do for me." He walked the rest of the way on sore but eager feet.

XERXES

Bursting through the front door of his house, Poyāma
tossed his vest onto a chair and began throwing a few
things together. He located a thick pair of socks and his
favorite pair of boots and put them on. Something he thought was
completely random came to mind. Going to the desk, he grabbed a
small stack of the scrap papers and a pencil. On each piece of paper
he wrote the contact information for one of his international wine
distributors. After stuffing the papers into the pocket of his jeans, he
gathered several pieces of fruit, wrapped up some jerky and cut up a
loaf of bread. Before long, a small wrap was packed with provision
enough for a several hour hike, if it should take that long to find the
horse and deliver the apology.

Wanting to take care of his thirst before doing anything else,
he went to a hook on the back of a cabinet beside the kitchen and
stood arrested. *Where is my canteen,* he thought. Two just like it were
kept at the lower stable. He considered perhaps it had found its way
down there with them.

"Jus like everyting else about dese very strange couple of day,"
he mumbled, bothered.

Taking hold of a wine sack, he went out the back door headed
for the lower well. Deciding it was too long of a walk, he turned and

went back inside, picked out a bottle of wine, opened it, took a drink and poured the remaining contents into the sack. Another bottle was opened and added without any attention paid to compatibility. He walked back outside. Stopping him in his tracks, there on the top of the hill was Wind, whiter than white against the darkening dusk. It was seven o'clock.

"Hey . . . you return back!" Poyāma yelled, dropping all he had in his hands and walking toward the animal. "Tank you for come back. You muss know I don' mean noting of dose terrible ting I say."

It was not quite the apology he was eager to make while approaching the ranch; more needed to be said. Turning the corner around the Steuben and heading up the hill, he slipped and stumbled, but regained balance before hitting the ground. "No, no . . . too fass on my feet for *dat*," he said with a laugh, feeling he had cheated gravity of some ornery fun. But, raising his eyes to the top of the hill again, he saw no horse. In a breath the cheating had turned on him. His steps were quick to the hilltop, from which he saw Wind charging through the valley below and up the next hill.

"See dere . . . jus like dat you make me angry again. Why you do dat?" Turning and heading back down the hill, trying to ignore the burned blackened sights to his left and right, he was emphatic: "Nope, not dis time, not a chance. You on your own dis time. No more falling for noting. I got a lot of work to do. I give de apologize . . . we square."

Compulsion to turn again and go after the horse required clenched jaw and teeth-grinding resistance. *Why dat horse have power like dat for upset?* A foul mood shoved aside the former apologetic one. Pushing through efforts to ignore blackened evidence of horrific loss, it crushed resistance. He stopped and looked around.

"Time for strap on my gun and hunt you down for kill! I make myself dat promise, else you come back for bring more harm!"

He heard visitors arriving in a wagon out beyond the house. Reaching the bottom of the hill, he walked past the house and out toward the entry of the ranch to meet them. Before long he could see it was the young family he had encountered in town. They met a good distance from the front of the house.

"Welcome to de Vishnu Ranch and Vineyard . . . witout de vineyard and much of de ranch jus now. We never actually meet. Poyāma Vishnu," he said, extending his hand.

"Sam Willis . . . this is my wife Anne, our son Ben and daughter Emily."

"You fix de wheel fas, what look like it have no way for fix."

"Actually," Sam said, "we bought a new one with the money we made selling the boots you left, and we had plenty of help getting all of our luggage offloaded, the old wheel off and the new one on. Thank you."

"O, dat was a small ting. Everybody else help you more dan me."

"We didn't use all the money and wanted to bring you what's left," Anne interjected.

"And we heard you might have some work that needs to be done," Sam added, holding out the money.

Poyāma laughed, discretely waving off the money. "Hard work!" he said. "Lots of shoveling is all I have right now." He took a seat on the back of the wagon and rode to the house.

Once stopped, everyone offloaded and stepped onto the front porch.

"Come in, we talk for a minute," Poyāma invited. "But I am in a hurry for go out for a while. I muss watch after some business dat take who know how long. Make you self at home. Check you heart for stay as long as it like, in case you muss wait more long of my returning."

After picking up his vest and slipping it on, the holster on the table was buckled into place. He opened the back door and walked out onto the porch, pointing northwestward.

"Over dat hill you see a valley, and in de valley you see de shoveling I talk about." The wine sack and wrap of provisions were picked up. "Some mud slide shut in my stable and wine cellar."

The two children were passing curious looks back and forth. Nor did either of their parents have any idea what to make of the situation, the sparse details or the freshly burnt surroundings, barely visible in the darkening landscape but strongly smelt.

"De horse covering de hill beyond dis one belong to we. Help youself for whatever you need of dem. But no saddle, harness, bridle, yoke, noting can be reach until shoveling free de door to de stable. I hope for see you soon. O, leave a note telling which of de room you sleeping in, for if I get back in de middle of de night I don' step in on anyone. Dere is plenty of room for everyone to have dey own. De kid might enjoy which ever one along de hall back from de lof."

Poyāma turned and began walking up the hill, noticeably limping. The small family was left speechless on the back porch of his fine home. Stopping at half the ascent, he turned and looked back. "Sam," he called. "If you miss seeing me back tomorrow or de day nex, fix a fair salary for youself and talk to de banker for pay Friday." Shortly, he crested the hill and passed from view.

The kids ran inside to explore the loft.

Sam looked at Anne. "I guess we won't be staying at the inn again."

"I guess not," Anne answered. "It looks like we have a place to stay . . . at least for the night . . . and a job for the time being."

"Nice place."

"Very."

"Looks like the amazing barn and stable we heard about were there and there," Sam said, pointing to the right at two enormous, smoldering piles of black lumber.

A flash of white in an opening between far off trees to his right, and Poyāma was setting out on a northeasterly pursuit. A mile of walking, climbing and stumbling forward rewarded him with such weary legs he was unable to lift his feet for proper steps, a constant reminder that the walking actually began fourteen hours ago. Darkness, a significant drop in temperature and no recent sighting of a white horse were causing thoughts of turning back and questions of where *back* was. But this was no ordinary determination driving a common pursuit. This was a man leaving all other pursuits behind, driven, unconscious of reason, smitten by desire he had yet to identify. A mile further, keeping east and moving into taller hills, he stopped.

"Dis strange, why dere a horse path up in dese hill I never know about. It run right between all de tree like somebody make it."

Feeling encouraged by easier footing, he followed the winding, up and down path until finding himself in the middle of thick woods wondering how long it had been since he left the path.

"A helpful path is suddenly not helpful. How dat happen?" He looked up at a canopy of darkness. "Too dark in here for see noting. If I get out of here I see by light of de star and moon again." He decided to head downward to his right, believing that to be south.

Free of the woods, Poyāma pulled out his pocket watch and flipped it open: twelve-thirty. Sprawling hills and intermittent rock formations seemed infinite in the dimness of starlight. A large rock outcropping was no more than ten feet below where he stood. *Dat look like a good place for a man to res wit jerky between he teet,* he thought, examining the area. *Maybe knock a blow after dat.* The vest was checked for a cigar. Glad to discover a faithful habit of preparation had not failed him, he sighed, pleased.

Sitting on the rock, the wrap of provisions was opened. A piece of bread, two large pieces of thick jerky and an apple were enjoyed, leaving a bit of bread and jerky for later. Hungry enough to consume three or four times that much food, or at least all he packed, melancholy overruled appetite. He wondered about a few scattered apple trees showing no effects of the drought, escaping the death toll in previously thriving groves. An attempt to follow dinner with some tasty, satisfying wine was rebutted by a weighty disappointment. When the opening was put to dry lips they puckered and he pulled back, staring at the mouth of the container. Instinctively, he made a circular motion with his hand before sniffing. Smell and taste were in agreement. The contents were moribund and flabby. Poyāma stared, surprised by revulsion.

He took another sip and pulled back. "De wine sack is not good for *dis* wine." Disregarding the fact that contents of different bottles of wine were thoughtlessly poured into the sack, he stared at the opening, one eyebrow raised and one dipped. "Dis like a wine what don' say noting strong. All de wrong kind of sweet dat stuck inside itself. It forget how wine are make for burst out and state all de where and what dat contribute for make dem."

He thought for a moment it might be the strong aftertaste of recent events that contributed to such disdain. By contrast, any wine might be flat. He took another sip. No, the wine lacked personality by any standard. And it was a peculiar disheartening kind of flat. Assessments of a number of tastes were being made on the lingering reports of his tongue. Before attempting another drink, he raised the round rim to his nose. A puzzlement of ingredients rose from the opening in a wrong complexity of aromas. He tried another sip anyway. A slosh of disappointment was promptly spat out of his mouth into the darkness.

"A-a-a-a-h-h-h! Noting! . . . Weak and hollow, noting for balance, noting like take risk for sharp tase or take chance . . . like it have no secure and protec all de sweet for make only happy tase. If I learn anyting at De House and from Pa, I learn happy tase alone keep no memory in de mind of de one who drink." Perturbed, he licked the top of the container and frowned. "And dis wine have de wrong kind of bitter, de kind dat don' come forward straight and help for balance, but only work from behind to make annoy and leave memory dat spoil enjoy. Many flavor, but hollow and weak . . . no power of good wine."

Poyāma took the critique personally, as if the one thing he knew he was good at, the craft he had spent his life perfecting came to nothing of value. With disgust, he dumped the worthless contents of the sack onto the bolder beneath him.

A kill sent a pack of coyotes into a night-splitting party of celebratory song no more than twenty-five yards up the hill.

"I jus come from dere," he said with a bitter chuckle, turning and looking up the hill. "A-a-a-h-h, de sound of de *bloodtirsty* . . . a man got to love dat word."

The cigar was next. A brief knocking of the end against an open palm satisfied compulsion and concluded with the announcement, "Time for knock a blow." It was mounted between his teeth. His eyes closed. *A man could grow to love dis kinda life.*

After two days of blurred activity and consequence, the tangible strangeness of missing thoughts hung in his head like an empty clothes line after a storm.

Eyes again open, he stared, wanting details useful for summation. They stayed away. For the moment, his consciousness was one dimensional. Even the dark layers of landscape and starry sky seemed flat.

He looked over his shoulder. Within scooting distance, a large sloped rock invited reclining. There was only one match, so the pressure was on for a successful first light of the cigar. A few minutes later he was settled. Legs crossed, hands clasped behind his head, smoke rising, stars shining, from the corner of his eye he noticed the burned out match that was thoughtlessly tossed onto the rock. A thin stream of smoke was rising from it, barely visible.

"How I entertain Gloria Tirty-two and all she ancestor wit dat silly game for so long I have no idea. And I never win even one champion. Time for new game."

After a period of continued blankness, contemplations gradually came into play, like the difference between a rock in a boot and a rock in a stream. The contemplator mulled over the apparent randomness of his muses. Odds were greatly against catching the white horse on foot in the hills at night—a recurring subconscious annoyance; and jagged emotions about earlier events had smoothed in the fluid blankness of many minutes rushing by between each new set of smoke rings.

"So, we should examine dis picture," he finally said, as if the horse were near by. "Right now, de mountain show me some cold, and de temperature still dropping. I have no idea where you have lure me and it look like dis rock might be my bed tonight. Jus *one* day remove me back and I was a man of healty mind . . . I find respec in all my way and dealing . . . proper in whatever ting I do." Pauses to tap or grind his teeth were frequent. "Den, I fall head long like drunk man for *you* . . . a *horse* . . . who quickly help for spread fire dat destroy my hard work, my vineyard, my barn, my stable, and chase all my special horse to de four wind."

Processing was stopped for a smoke. Soon, the largest, most perfect smoke ring he had blown or seen blown hung above him, spinning, suspended like a halo. Closing an eye, fifty stars were counted inside the ring before it broke apart and dissipated into the night air.

"Dat ring show me cause for de new game."

Smoke from another deep drag on the cigar was sent six feet overhead, straight up like a geyser. *But no game tonight,* he thought, looking at the cigar before indulging its warm taste again.

"On de oter hand, I have a couple new friend," he said, getting back to the breakdown of the last forty-eight hours. "I quit from de way of superstition. Dat happen on returning from de town where I make friend wit de preacher. I never expec for see dat. And I make Gloria Tirty-two de promise for stop de lying before she pass. All togeter, maybe not so bad."

Poyāma stared at the cigar. Lips tight, teeth pressed together, his jaw muscles flexed, pulsating. He had been working it and it was short. *I never smoke one of dese down dis small so fass,* he thought, dimly aware he was not actually as relaxed as he was attempting to be. The coal was large and hot—consuming the stubble that remained—too hot and too near the end to allow room for fingers *and* the one more smoke he desired.

"What I can' understand is how it happen. How can I be weak and not know it. How can such a ting sneak up on me? How a horse can teach a sane man for chase after noting . . . walk all day, hike into de night and not fall from exhaus? It all have someting to do wit dat horse for choose me and not me for choose him."

Less pinchable stubble than hot coal, the cigar fragment was ground into the rock. A black smoldering smear of ash on the cold, hard, dark gray surface, it seemed to have a mocking voice: *See, de rock have no complain for burn!*

"But de rock have no living in it," was the whispered response. That quickly, Poyāma's mood was blackened, like the smoking smudge on the lifeless rock. Staring at it, he recalled the words of the preacher's son: *"Mr. Vishnu, if all you're reporting happened as you've told me, you really should not be handling it as well as you are . . . , which leads me to believe you're doing much worse than either of us think."*

Tears glazed his eyes. He was like a volcano—tremors, groans, emotions swelling like magma, pushing to the surface, the pressure moving him to his feet, eyes burning, heart pounding, mind racing with angry protests. With fists clenched and every muscle tense and flexed, head back and face to the heavens, he drew in a deep breath, preparing to let loose some fiery eruption. A scream shattered the molten moment. It was not his.

"Xerxes!" he exclaimed with a dry, throaty, cough-like expulsion. Wide eyes darting, he tried to catch a glimpse of the horse's shiny black coat on the dark landscape. The shocking sound had come with such surprise he had no clue of a direction in which to look. Chills of excitement coursed his back and shoulders, contradicting the sickening disappointment felt in his gullet and gut, left by the suppression of rage.

Again the angry voice of Xerxes sounded forth. This time his owner immediately sped left and leaped recklessly from the rock to a ledge below. Traversing the here-and-gone moon-lit ledge to its end like a cat, a lower ledge was spotted and met bluntly after a short flight. Knees and chest collided on the landing, knocking the air from his lungs and imposing a momentary rest. In the silence of breathless agony, the distant rumbling of countless hooves suggested the scattering movements of many horses.

When able to rise and refocus, a tiny black movement in the distance held his attention. Back and forth in a straight line, less then one hundred feet below the ledge on which he stood and fifty yards out from it was Xerxes, pacing furiously along a fence line.

A fence out here? Poyāma wondered.

Many other distant and disorderly movements were part of a confusing scene, activities obscured by the dead of night. He heard the sounds of wood planks cracking and falling to the ground. He heard a voice. It was the voice of LaRue. He seemed to want the horses to leave the corral. Spotting LaRue, he saw the open section of fence just broken out. One by one, Poyāma identified moving specks as horses in the huge enclosure. Squinting, he followed the fence line on the far side of the corral and saw the open gate.

As he climbed down from the ledge, Xerxes was running the fence line to its end. He had identified the open section of fence and was fired up at LaRue for the harassment of the other horses. Poyāma raced down the steep and rocky slope before him as the angry stallion reached the end of the western fence line and bolted east, heading toward the broken section in the southern boundary. Poyāma hopped the fence and ran toward LaRue, who was unaware of either intruder. His attention was focused on the uncooperative horses he had chased off to the east end of the corral. By the time he heard the thunderous hooves of Xerxes, he turned to see the great black stallion baring down on him like a freight train. Reflex put right hand to revolver, but his long coat caused a rare fumble and the gun was on the ground.

"Xerxes!" Poyāma yelled at the top of his voice, bending the animal's flight to the north, away from the paralyzed rancher and in a big loop to his master. Soon, all of the horses were gathered in one place near the western fence line and the ordeal was dissolved.

"Close de gate!" Poyāma hollered.

LaRue did so after locating the dropped gun and returning it to his holster. He then walked to the broken out section of fence and propped up the damaged pieces to create at least a visual barrier. Crossing the corral, he came to where the displaced animals were gathered, reunited with their rightful owner.

Without a word between them, both men hopped the fence as Poyāma lead the way to the place on the large rock he had left his meager belongings. LaRue, kept a suspicious eye on the man he had attempted to dispossess of a corral of prized horses. That Poyāma was wearing revolvers on both hips was itself a loud warning. Being pounced on and manhandled in the stable the previous morning was a close memory. His hands were prepared for action in case of a bad turn in the dark.

Feeling obligated by former habit, Poyāma was trying to devise the bad turn, but lacked something essential. It seemed only right that he should be viciously angry. Yet, knowing he had more than enough justifiable reason for vengeful wrath, its absence was a frustration and curiosity. Aware of a profound alteration in his nature, he wished he could return to his prior self for this one confrontation. Nevertheless, with all the thoughts running through his mind, not a single idea for malicious action was among them.

After reaching the destination, they stood in long silence looking out upon a landscape cast in shadow. When Poyāma finally sat down, he requested that LaRue do the same. But LaRue was mindful of the best positioning for a quick draw, and he was not about to let anything cause him to fumble his gun a second time. The request was ignored.

LaRue glanced over shoulder, a frown on his face. "I smell wine."

"Yes . . . me too," Poyāma countered. Explanation about the emptied wine sack was not given, and the subject was dismissed.

With his back to his neighbor, ears attentive to sounds of movement, and sweaty right hand hanging by the thumb from his belt directly above his gun, LaRue stated rather matter-of-factly the details of a deal with a man named Miller. He told how he took a chance and made an overnight dash to Rockford in northern Surry County, hoping to meet with Miller, knowing he could likely find him prospecting at Unanimity Lodge Thirty-four. The trip was a success and a deal was made. He was returning home on his weary horse when he met the barefoot Poyāma along the road.

He explained the subsequent decision to release the horses in the night, how unexpected friendly developments between he and

Poyāma had led to the decision, how knocking out the fence and claiming the horses had broken out and escaped seemed the only way of getting out of the mess he created.

After a time of tense silence, Poyāma spoke. "Dat was some fass work on you part, a very impressive ting you pull togeter in a day."

He turned and stared up into the wooded hill behind them. *Somehow dat horse lead me here for discover all dis,* he thought. *How his timing always so perfec?*

LaRue was humbled by the evident opportunity to work things out in a reasonable way—no guns, no shouting, no threats, no legal action and no insults. Though a man of many acquaintances, he treated friendship as synonymous with inconvenience. Its welcome—offered to Poyāma earlier that day—had been regarded as a mishap. But there on the rock, under the night sky and the strangest of circumstances, it had returned.

"You know, Vish, my sister was quite taken with you before I took to planting some foul seeds and turned her away. On my second visit to your house yesterday morning I promised you I won't be doing any more of that. Actually, I'll be workin' on . . . on 'fixin' it back', as you would say."

LaRue had no idea why that particular thought came to mind under the circumstances, or why he did not brush it aside as he typically would have. What left his mouth after a long moment of quiet was a greater surprise.

"I'm sorry Vish."

It was not at all like the tactical apology of the previous morning, but thoughtful and sincere. He swiveled to look over shoulder at Poyāma.

"She's an amazing lady and worth another try if you think you're still interested."

"I forgive you . . . and tank you," Poyāma said.

Pause was punctuated with nods of acknowledgement.

Leaning back, Poyāma slipped cold hands into the pockets of his jeans. The fingertips of his left hand discovered pieces of paper. They contained the names and contact information of his most treasured professional relationships, hand-written before leaving his house.

A suggestion entered his mind: *Give them to Richard LaRue.* In an instant his hands went from cold to sweating.

The idea of writing the information down had come to him in the same mysterious way he had been compelled to create the voucher before the hike into town. Likewise, this suggestion was identical to the one causing him to give the voucher to a stranger in the middle of the street—a little awkward, but easy. This was different. These papers were as keys to doors opening to industry advantage. And the man suggested as their recipient was a competitor, a rival, a man who had just attempted to rob him.

Inside the pockets, hands balled into fists. *Dis man try for sneak away wit all de horse what I treasure,* he thought, immediately realizing he had said, "I forgive you," but had not done so.

Finally, standing up and handing the papers to LaRue, he said, "You know what my job call for at de vineyard in de early year back home? Shipping! Den I move to customer service, still when I was young, like teenage year. Dese customer distribute all we wine for market all over de worl. I make so many friend, so many great contac in dose day, broter, you can' believe. I work de vineyard too and learn what make good wine from Pa. But when I come here and get start, dose contac make everyting happen like lightning.

"On dese paper I write for you each of my main distributor. When we get pass de drought dey do you some good like you can' believe. Even now dey make sure you move inventory what you have. Use my name, it for sure give you a big advantage. Forgive how I keep back such ting from you and you family before now."

LaRue did not know what to say. This was something he would never do for anyone, friend or family. He stuffed the papers in the pocket of his coat and stared out into the night.

"What kinds of horses have we got here?" he asked after a lengthy silence.

Poyāma thought about the horses that had gathered around him down in LaRue's corral, he recalled releasing the twenty-eight horses from Xerxe's side of the barn first. That not all of those and several from the other side of the barn were among this group puzzled him.

"You make dat deal witout knowing what horse you have here?" he finally responded. "Broter, you a trader deluxe!"

"Well, I made educated guesses on most of them. Ya got those Red-man war horses for starters. Some people take offense to those, but my goodness . . . yours are the most striking Pintos I've seen. And, let me think . . . I don't know anything about Japanese horses, and Miller doesn't either. So I wasn't able to factor that in as a for sure . . . ."

"Yes, he is down dere," Poyāma interrupted. "Hocaido. Dat one fass like you never believe," he said, picturing vividly the swift strides of the sleek import from Japan. "If he born wit long leg like de Toroughbred, he for sure win all de derby."

LaRue squinted as if doing so were the same as turning a lamp on each animal as he called them to mind. "The Percheron and Camargue, of course, are French. There's a Lusitano, a couple of especially stately Morgan . . . ."

"Dose two are cousin," Poyāma interrupted, "bot straight from de state of Vermon, only four generation remove from 'Justin Morgan.'"

"Several Arabian," LaRue continued, trying to act unimpressed . . . "a Lipizzaner, and . . . What's the little guy?" he asked.

"You kidding!" Poyāma exclaimed. "Criollo? Da's de horse of de Sout American cowboy. Dose horse rule de place I come from."

Not impressed, LaRue moved on. "I described the ones I don't know and Miller seemed to know what they are, except on a few of them, he was just throwin' out guesses."

"De biggess one, de one wit de dark head and de white feet, is Shire horse," Poyāma answered, adopting the squinting technique. "Fjording . . . de Sumba from Indonesia, Akhal-Teke—anoter very fass horse . . . Comtois, Appaloosa, Canadian . . . a-a-a-and let me see . . . Pura Raza." The collector closed his eyes. After a few seconds they opened with a flinch.

"O, how I forget de King? Xerxes! Fresian . . . de war horse for de knight in armor. But *he* make a change from normal Friesian. Someting rile him up to his own way for rule." He went over the inventory one more time in his weary mind. "I tink da's about it."

"Miller asked specifically if there was an Egyptian Arabian in the group. He said he would pay more for one of those than any other. Based on the description, I told him no."

Poyāma gave a shrug and stared, thoughtful. He actually had twin Egyptian Arabian mares among the horses on the side of the stable freed last before the fire. He remembered them being among those circling him in the corral in and out of the smoke. Wanting to recall if they were with the ones he saw returning to the stable later, the memory was not clear enough to quiet his concern.

Why would anyone place value on Egyptian Arabian higher dan all de oter horse? He wondered.

"It's a bit late for herding," LaRue pointed out. "I can round 'em all up with a few of the boys and bring them back in the morning."

Wet eyes gazing in the direction of the horses, Poyāma weighed a decision as if staring into the bright, fiery eyes of Xerxes.

"Na-a-a-h-h. Keep wit de deal you got wit you friend Miller. He find dem each a good home. I have no stable for keep dem now. What he pay, you keep back a quarter for you trouble, give a quarter to de young family dat stay at my place for dey get a good start, and give de ress to de preacher for care back at people who suffering hard in dis drought."

It was quiet again. The horses were lined along the fence staring in the direction of the conversation on the distant rock as if listening for the news of their fate, or hoping for another round of attention from Poyāma. LaRue stood up and put fists to hips. Shrunken numbers resulting from the imposed accounting were hurting his head.

"Ya know what I'm thinkin', Vish?"

"No."

'I don't want to tell you"

"OK."

"It's embarrassing to admit."

"More embarrassing den stealing horse, what belong to a broter?"

"Maybe . . . maybe it is. I'm thinkin' I'm angry about what you just said . . . about the way this thing is goin' down. Twenty-five percent to some kid for just showin' up and havin' a family and a broken wheel! The same as me, your friend, who did all the work roundin' up your lost horses and puttin' the deal together and stressin' over the whole thing 'cause a takin' all the risks . . . how does that work? How does a perfect stranger rate the same as me on this one?"

The truth of the matter was quite different. After the hard rain, LaRue had discovered the horses huddled together outside the corral near the fence, the fear of Wind in them. He simply opened the gate and all but Xerxes went in. *The darnedest thing*, he had thought at the time.

At the sound of a rumble from above, Poyāma turned and looked high into the woods, certain he caught a glimpse of movement through the trees.

LaRue looked up at the stars. "I heard that!" he yelled. "Very funny! I'm gonna go break all the wheels on every one of my wagons and see what kind of fortune you send me!" Snatching the hat from his head, he spun on one heal, hands raised as if being ordered by a sheriff.

"I know . . . I know, Vish, they're not my horses, they're your horses and you are being very, very gracious here. Still, fifty percent to . . . to who? How do we know money just dished around like that is gonna get in the hands of hard workin' folks who have actually been fightin' the drought and hurt by the drought? How do we know anyone's really gonna be helped that way?"

"Dat what none of my business is looking like."

"I know, it's none of my business either, Vish! But . . ."

"You know, Richard, dat preacher and he son have good heart, and between dem keep up on everyone."

The frustrated horse trader slapped his hat across a thigh. "I know I helped myself to your horses and got us into this mess by sellin' what wasn't mine to sell. I'm sorry for that, but they were wanderin' free and . . . and I found 'em. Someone else mighta found 'em, then what! But I'm the one that took 'em in and took care of them beasts. Don't lose track of that little detail."

"O, I keep track for detail. How else I come to give you twenty-five percent on sale of *my* horse?"

"Your horses! Yeah, well . . . it's not like *you* were out roundin' 'em up. Remember the unwritten law of the land: if it's not branded . . . ."

Poyāma stared, recalling the thrilling ride in the rain, the actual "roundin' 'em up" by Wind, then leaving them gathered beside an unknown fence to attend greater concerns.

"No, I was working for keep back de fire," he answered.

"I know . . . I know, I heard about that, Vish. That was a shame, it was . . . and a big distraction, I'm sure. But you can't expect free rangin' horses not to fall into that up-for-grabs category just because you're preoccupied."

"Maybe da's de cause for me getting noting from dey sale. You lose track of dat little detail."

LaRue stared as if stuck. He spun and flung his hat from the rock, into the night. "Still, twenty-five percent!" he protested, unstuck. "And seventy-five percent to strangers who did nothin'!"

"OK, look for see it dis way: I get one hundred percent, or I take dem home back."

They stared at one another.

"Of de one hundred percent I get, I give away twenty-five percent to you, my friend Richard, de criminal in de whole ting, and seventy-five percent de way we talk already."

LaRue hung his head, shaking it back and forth. Several minutes passed.

"See why I didn't want to say anything about what I was thinking?"

"Yes."

"Like I told you, it's embarrassing. I like to think of myself as a pretty good guy, Vish. I bet most of the people I know think of me that way. But look at me. Why am I like this?"

"I am de same." A shudder attested to the difficulty of the admission.

"No you're not."

Hesitant, another shudder preceded Poyāma's response. "You know de white horse you come ask about? I lie to you about dat. He come to me. I fall in love wit dat horse immediate. Right when I lay dese eye on him I feel de scare for maybe he was *your* horse or belong for somebody else. So I hide him in de house . . . in de house! He was in de house when you come sit on you horse and ask about him. Lucky ting he a horse wit manner, or I find some trouble wit get de smell out de house."

"That makes me mad, Vish. I found him first. By rights he should be mine and you should hand him over."

"Dat horse belong for nobody and cause noting but trouble. I promise you dat!"

"Yeah, well, that's not the point, is it? You hid from me the horse that I found and was trackin'."

"Yes, and dat *is* de point. We de same, like I tell you. Here is someting else: you know dese paper I give you . . . I have dis information all along. I keep it back from you all to myself until now. All de time I like for tink everybody know Poyāma Vishnu better for make de wine dan de Frenchman, Richard LaRue."

"Wow . . . wow . . . stop tellin' me this stuff, Vish! I was beginning to like you." LaRue shifted his jaw and shook his head. "And how do we know that I wouldn't be right there with you, getting all the glory a Frenchman deserves for winemaking, if you weren't so stingy and I had the advantage of these same contacts all along?"

"We don'. But we each start wit his own advantage, me de international connection from my history and you de *French* from you ancestor. We choose for share we self or each keep back his own and hope for suffer less dan de oter guy."

"You must be freezing," LaRue said, thinking of taking off his coat and offering it to his shivering friend. Picturing himself shivering, he decided to keep it on.

Poyāma blew warm breath into cupped hands. "It muss be down close by forty degree. Good ting dere no wind." *It gonna push close to freezing up dere tonight,* he thought, picturing Wind making his way higher and higher into the mountains.

LaRue was statue-like, grinding his teeth. The mention of the white horse brought back to mind Miller's questions concerning an Egyptian Arabian horse, *"White and unmistakably special . . . worth more than all the others combined . . . quick to reach full speed, like lightning, very intelligent . . . the things sometimes point like bird dogs . . . unusual proportions, you'd know it if you saw one." No wonder the shrewd Vishnu is willing to walk away from the rest of these,* he concluded.

Peering at his friend out of the corners of his eyes, suspicion was grating. Each hand went into a coat pocket. His right hand discovered the papers stuffed away earlier and quickly pulled them out. They were elevated in an attempt to coax a slight illumination to find the surface of the top page. Giving up, he lowered the papers and stared.

"Does this say Garrison on it?" he asked.

Poyāma nodded. "Dey help me get start before I set foot on dis soil. Very good people and good friend."

"Distributors," scoffed the Frenchman, becoming consumed by resentment. "Vish, my problem is drought, harvest, product, not distribution."

"Hungry mout for distribute is like demand dat knock at de door. It make you exis someting new, find way dat create harvess and keep produc flowing to de barrel in de cellar."

"O, I see . . . you think I'm loafin' and using the drought as an excuse."

"No."

The papers took brief turns on top for examination. But Garrison remained the only discerned notation.

"Distribution contacts . . ."

Poyāma nodded before adding, "International."

"Garrison . . . If I'm not mistaken, they're known for common mercantile items . . . groceries, hardware, textiles . . . cheap . . . not fine wine. Are these all like that?"

LaRue's analysis converted the generous paper offerings to implications about the quality of products created at his neighbor's vineyard. The ungenerous critique was understood. Poyāma held out his hand. The contact information for key players in international product distribution—two of them elite French wine distributors to a growing European restaurant industry—was returned. The papers were jammed back into his own pants pocket.

"Richard, you like de idea of 'fine French wine' more dan de work for make de fine wine. De man who make good wine make for he self and he own high standard. He know what he make good and feel happy for all who enjoy what he create. Someone else high opinion have noting for add to he love for make de wine."

LaRue walked to the end of the large rock and hopped down to the ledge below.

"How am I gonna get across my field with that Xerxes in there?"

"Go around de fence."

"I'm not lettin' that horse scare me from my own property! Around the fence is an additional quarter-mile walk."

Again traversing the ridgeline and descending toward the corral, Poyāma followed after his neighbor, concerned. "I can stand at de fence and see dat he behave."

"I would appreciate that!"

Upon reaching the fence, LaRue spotted Xerxes far away near the opposite end of the corral. He hopped over the fence as Poyāma stepped onto a fence rail beside him.

"If he charge you, jus stand you ground. He like for show off, but he always stop or go to de side at de las."

Hearing his owner's voice, Xerxes turned and began trotting in their direction while LaRue moved across the long corral with long, agitated strides. As in parade formation, the other horses were on the flanks of the marshal. Without warning they sprung into full gallop, charging on the playful whim of their leader. The impression was war-like to LaRue, who stood frozen as the stampede covered the field quickly. Poyāma jumped the fence. Arms swinging overhead, he moved away from LaRue in an attempt to divert the direction of the pretend marauders, but Xerxes was having too much fun. Lowering his arms, he watched in horror as LaRue lost his nerve and began scrambling backward, certain he was a single stride from being trampled by a hateful beast. As Xerxes planted his back legs to stop, his front rose upward and he looked larger and more threatening than ever in the eyes of the terrified cowboy. The revolver was drawn and three shots fired. As the other horses flared off to the sides and scattered, the great animal crumbled and tumbled to a stop between the two stunned men.

Stepping toward the shiny black heap, Poyāma stared down in disbelief and fell to his knees. LaRue walked around the wounded stallion, studying it to determine if it was dead, stopping where the long black main was spread upon the ground. There was no movement.

Until that moment, Poyāma had little real appreciation of a proud, deep connection to his prized "King Xerxes." But with the helpless animal's head inches away, weak, failing eyes spoke of an imminent departure and the measure of invincibility. He knew right then the reason for the choice to allow the crooked deal with Miller to go through. Exile would have preserved a mythic youth and vitality of the mighty Xerxes and spared his owner a moment like this, the moment when legend ends. He reached out and stroked the horse's face.

He felt Larue near, standing to his left, hovering. Something was missing. It made itself known in a wish to reach back and grab a handful of hate, some wrath-worthy judgment, anything useful for just this one moment, something through which to interpret the whole situation and produce a blame-worth rage of punishment. Sitting there overwhelmed with grief, he tangibly missed it—a faithful companion for all those years, but not there for him when he most needed it. All he actually felt was profound sadness. Turning, he looked up at LaRue.

"What!" The defensive response was instantaneous. "What could I do, stand there and let him run me over . . . trample me to death? It was him or me!"

Poyāma looked back down at Xerxes. Large brown eyes blinked and looked up at him.

Seeing this, LaRue set the revolver on the ground and began walking away, as if inviting guilt-ending fatal punishment, daring Poyāma to choose who to use it on. But the mourner just wept. LaRue was at the other end of the corral when the gun was lifted from the ground. It was not until reaching his barn half a mile away that he heard the distant shot.

Making it back to where the lifeless horse lay, LaRue was carrying two shovels and a pickax. He leaned a shovel against the fence beside his neighbor, who was staring high up into the hills anticipating another glimpse of the white stallion—three times during LaRue's absence Poyāma had seen white movement along a straight horizontal line, visible through clearings in the trees.

For an hour and a half an audience of horses stood by in the dark, watching two men work side by side. The only sounds heard were those of pickax and shovel moving earth and the occasional breaking of rock. By the time the massive carcass was rolled into the enormous hole, all four hands of the laborers were bleeding from broken blisters. When the hole was filled and excess dirt spread, Poyāma handed his shovel to LaRue, who, in turn, handed him his coat.

"I saw you starin' up at that hill like a man who dreams. It'll get chilly up there tonight. Bring it back whenever."

The rancher slung his tools over a shoulder, turned and headed home. The dreamer climbed the fence and returned to the rock where he had left a small pack of provisions and an empty wine sack. Far beyond exhaustion, but incapable of sleeping, he headed straight up the hill and into the woods.

III

New Wine

EXILE

L aRue was right. The climb up the mountain had steadily gotten colder. After five-hundred feet of arduous ascent, Poyāma stopped . . . bothered.

"So, a man always have his own righteous . . . no matter what. Steal a man horse and call it 'find', but no way make wine for de common we, no way use distributor who distribute to de ordinary mercantile. Kill a beautiful animal what God create and call it, 'him or me', but no way accep noting *new* as way of de French vineyard. No, de ol French way alone make pure and exac."

Fifty or sixty determined steps and his head was buzzing, demanding a halt to progress. "Poyāma de same," he said with a miserable kind of self-mocking chuckle. "Always find new idea for make de wine for serve all over de worl and make million of stranger happy. But only one idea for my neighbor—keep back from him. He is de special kind of wrong, not my kind. I only work for keep bitter, for strike back and make him feel small de way he do for me." He shook his head. "We all have we religion of we self."

Twenty more forced steps and he took another break. Groggy-minded, attempts were made at an inventory of factors contributing to the loss of Xerxes. Too expansive and too few factors on the list directly attributable to LaRue, he quit the project. Even after abandoning the inventory, one too many factors suggesting his own responsibility became cause for renewed effort applied to ascent of the mountain. Weak and woozy, but otherwise beyond any of the usual characteristics of hunger, the thought came to him that a bit of fuel would be helpful. The food hastily wrapped at his house was felt for inside a deep pocket of the barrowed coat. Puniness of the remaining fragments in relation to need for fuel was offensive. "Wortless," he muttered, disgusted for even having acknowledge the scraps. He had already begun disciplining his mind away from a constant annoyance of an inner noise of thirst, knowing he only carried an empty wine sack. But the noise was only growing, even by the necessity of the discipline.

Just ten more steps required total concentration. It was not his imagination; the climb was becoming steeper. Too little strength or oxygen for fueling upward movement on legs alone, he employed hands and arms to help, grabbing hold of nearby trees and pulling, then pushing off from the upper side. Finally, there was nothing resistant to the temptation of a bed of leaves at the base of an aged oak. A tug on a chain and flip of his thumb showed a watch face reporting three-forty.

Arms crossed, elbows on his knees, he sat staring down between his boots. Something had recently changed in him that he did not want changed. Every thoughtful movement toward bitter judgment was paired with an echo of reason. The resulting uncertainty concerning LaRue's fault left a hollow, unsatisfying feeling. Wanting to direct his mind elsewhere, a target was readily identified: he was exceedingly thirsty.

Leaning back against the tree, the insides of his eyelids were as screens displaying images of the fancy barn and stable before both were reduced to ash. A moment later the lids sprung open and he looked around, so strong was the smell of premium cigar. Memory of discovering a glob of ash when placing his hand on the porch rail ignited visions of the beginning patches of fire in the vineyard. Pride was tangible as a statue erected there in front of him. Because of it, spitefulness and the greedy concealment of the white horse kept him from asking LaRue for help putting out the fires when they were small. Tongue beyond the clinging pastiness of common thirst, his mouth was dry as the ashen memories.

As if under indictment by a conspiracy of the senses, a recent boast from his own voice entered the mind of the accused: *"Some farm wake to rooster, dis one wake to voice of a king . . . King Xerxes."*

The mutual attitude of superiority was not unique to the two neighbors. But, being that they were the most prominent vineyard overseers in the region, a tension regarding status, supremacy of practice and orthodoxy of views encumbered their interactions from first meeting.

Memory of prideful enjoyment in Xerxes' intimidating impression upon LaRue was symbolic of contributions to a managed contempt. Shifting repetitiously, his face bent into a frown. Eyes half closed, reclining against the tree, and cold, discomfort proved unfixable. Suspended between awake and asleep, thoughts were slipping around freely in Poyāma's head. Questions about making a difficult climb up the steep grade in the chilly dark instead of being at home sleeping in his comfortable bed were a constant annoyance, like a backdrop to all else.

A horse . . . no . . . horses . . .

Recognition of horse sounds was fuzzy. Groggy sensations of vulnerability accumulated into a jolt. He sat straight, then leaned forward, twisted to the left and glanced up the hill, feeling certain of the presence of Wind. "OK, keep back if you like! But don' tink I care for you listen," he whispered, convinced all of his sleepy muttering had been heard. "Listen all you want for what I say!"

For the moment, he had forgotten the entire reason for being out in the cold dark climbing the mountain was to chase down the troublesome white stallion. Turning back and resuming the former repose, drooping eyelids bounced half-open irregularly, as if poked by thoughts or the jitters of overtiredness. Again, sounds of horses were heard. "I know you up dere," he mumbled, barely audible. "Listen all you like." His brain was too drained to produce a care for the difference between sounds of one horse and several. A snicker induced rocking of his head against the bark-covered support. "We all have de *me* religion . . . de shrine to we-self. How am I any . . . ?"

Heavy eyelids could no longer resist gravity. If the question was completed or answered, it was done so in his sleep. A constant rain of leaves fell and many found the slumbering climber. Gentle, like fingers, they touched his hair and caressed his face, which was transformed by a smile. They *were* fingers—Gloria's fingers! She was smiling back, drawing close. He, too, moved toward her. Fingers in his hair . . . falling, grazing his cheek, his neck . . . He could feel her breath on his lips, big beautiful eyes staring into his, blinking, once, twice . . . A tension of near touch was all that separated the tips of their noses.

She stepped on his feet . . . again . . . then kicked and scuffed against them. How odd. Why was she doing that? He wanted to look down, thinking it disruptive, unromantic.

When his eyes opened they were squinting, adjusting to the dark while attempting to see what it was that batted his feet around so furiously. *A beast?* He thought, trying to focus in on whatever was responsible for sounds of foraging. The dark of the early morning hour appeared to have grown blacker than that which he had stared into before falling asleep. Horizon line seeming to move, he blinked hard several times. Movement did not stop and he knew it was not the blurry effect of heavy grog.

I remember de tree right in front of me before I sleep, he thought. *How de horizon come before and dey behind?*

Feeling something shove his boot again, all was instantly in focus. A black bear was digging in the leaves at the end of Poyāma's outstretched legs, trying to make something of the napping, yet unrecognized human. Its body covered nearly all of Poyāma's field of vision. A twitch of terror caused a responsive lurch and rotation of the startled animal. They were face to face, a few feet apart. The bear made a sound Poyāma found difficult to determine with certainty as a growl or groan. Against all effort to keep silent, the sound that escaped the leaf-covered subject of the bear's curiosity was a gasp.

The animal was still for a moment, seeming equally paralyzed. Then it cocked its head as if, being a wild speaking bear, it was puzzled by the more domestic utterance of the visitor in its forest. Evidently interpreting the noise as an invitation to dinner, acceptance in its wild language was a maniacal transformation beginning in the eyes, lifting the muzzle to expose teeth and gums, the spewing of vicious sounds and foul smelling fluids and squaring to pounce.

Thunder rumbled down from high in the hill and the bear's attention was redirected. It turned and ran. Poyāma leaned to his left and peered around the tree. A glimpse of whiteness disappeared like a wisp over the peak of the hill. There was no sign of the bear when he turned back.

"Yeah, right!" he called out. "You come back for dis I teach you someting for take home and warn you cub."

Looking down through the dark sepia tinted grays of interior forest, struggling to make out details or perceive distance, it was clear that he could not have slept for long. *Morning was not much furter off dan dis when I stop and sit,* he thought. *It still de same dark.*

For the moment, the near memory of the flashing whiteness topping the hill tempted a desire to get up and follow, which was firmly rebuked. *A phantom! How can I trus what I see only a piece wit two sleepy eye? No way! Dat might jus be someting crazy in my head.* Turning and looking up the hill once more, everything was exactly as he remembered it being when first coming to this place and sitting down. Disgust and annoyance followed. *A-a-ah-h-h! Dat white could be noting at all dat come quick to less . . . someting I imagine and it slip from my mind, not over de hill.*

He turned back. The pocket watch was right where last seen, in his left hand, open: twenty after four. It was time to wake up by the normal setting of his internal clock. The watch was returned to the pocket.

Reaching up to feel something on his head, several leaves were discovered. Scanning his body, he saw that many leaves had collected upon arms, shoulders, torso and legs during the brief nap. His legs were completely covered, but for where the bear had removed those on his ankles and boots. "De night still cling like dese leaf," he muttered, annoyed by the realization he was too awake to hope for any more sleep. For the time being, thirty minutes of slumber was all he would get. Some calculations were made from memories of the past few days. "I sleep maybe couple hour in two full day," he said, disgusted.

Reaction to feelings of profound hunger echoed the response to sleep deprivation. Unable to recall a time he had ever felt so purely grumpy, he wondered if the bear had actually been part of the dream, a subconscious invention animating demeanor.

Another leaf fell from its balance on his head and slid down his face and neck on its way to a resting place among others. The dream of Gloria, her fingers on his face, seemed as real as the bear that had interrupted it. He was agitated, angered. *How come Gloria only come to me in de dream and all my memory and tinking? How come she never come for real, make it easy . . . say someting like, 'Hey, how 'bout we get going wit you and me.' Not everyting have to wait for me.*

Joining forces in spite of his rebuke, memory of the picnic long in the past was fresh as the dream of only moments ago. They mingled in his mind: presence, longing, tension of nearness, her breath on his lips, light touching hers, rounding her chin and falling on her neck . . . ease of conversation, her smile, laughter, silence in her presence lighting fires in his heart and soul, the scent of her hair.

As to a siege big enough to topple a kingdom, he responded promptly, shutting down his mind leaning right and pushing off the ground to get vertical for resuming the hunt of Wind. But the hunt would have to wait. Instead of getting to his feet, dizziness cast him face down on the leaf covered slope of the mountain. Gravity aided a roll over onto his back, but not an attempt to sit up. Hunger and fatigue had gone from upsetting to haunting as dizziness prevailed. Heart palpitations sent out a flurry of fluttering sensations before overwhelming disappointment darkened into despair.

What Have I done? was a mortal concern floating through the haziness of the moment like a leaf on the chilled air of the forest. And like a pile of leaves, the question, *How have I spin so out of control so fass?*, was the result of accumulated errors. Poyāma, who prided himself on doing well, being well and, above all, appearing well, was sickened, feeling anything but well.

Having released themselves from disabled denial, the questions were not attached to any anticipation of answer. The early hours in the forest remained gray, as did fuzziness of mind, brokenness of spirit, weakness of body and absence of resistance. In that stillness, gray became the color of clarity.

I love her, he silently admitted to himself and to the universe.

The moment was a first. Many times he had enjoyed pondering the thought he *might* love her. It was safe. It was manageable, like a stall in a fancy stable containing a beautiful, sleek, shapely horse, its flattering name carved into the door. *Might* was a reservation. *Might love* was an escort service for the kind of love that was self indulgent, inspired by self-consciousness, subject to convenience, based on calculated interests, born of a highly fashioned sense of personal preference and connected to prescribed social conditions and expectations.

But *I love her* was not about him at all. It was entirely about her. It was about her loveliness, how lovable she was, who she was as a person that he recognized as desirable, enjoyable, compelling and irresistible. There was something about her that defied selfish nature and practice and called him to lay aside preference and take up service and sacrifice. He sensed a dangerous affront to self-preservation, willingness to risk his very life for her care if need be. No other interest or compulsion had ever led him there. Only one explanation stood out as feasible. It was Gloria he loved—the essence of who she was. *She* was the reason.

The admission grew. *I love her, I desire her . . . I need her. She de one who make me hungry . . . weary for keep on too long witout her, weak for disappoint dat I never do right by her, never tell her how I believe de word Wonder, and Excite, and Treasure, and Special and de whole English language get create jus for speak of her.*

Enveloped in the early morning gray, he thought it was less dark but more fuzzy. So much new, though nothing that had yet entered his mind was a total surprise. All had been there, just previously unacknowledged, resisted.

"Tank you," he said, not sure to whom or exactly for what.

His pondering was not quite like the rigors of real pondering. It was more like dwelling, or lingering. He felt as though a door had been opened into another dimension and he had stepped through, wandered around and lost track of the door. A bothersome awareness of intent to relocate the door contributed to the increased fuzziness. Puzzlement about himself was another contributor, as if familiar things were suddenly curiosities.

How come I never take my heart out from where I keep it always hide, always careful . . . never show her me.

The word *me* held the most unexpected revelation of all. The one person he thought he had an understanding of was the man to whom his life had been devoted, the man he thought to have built decision by decision—the man he called "Me." But he had never before thought of or referenced himself in the context of greater emphasis on someone else's worth. Reason suggested he should feel diminished by elevation of Gloria's value to that of preeminence inspiring his sacrificial love. But the opposite was true. It was his former self—the one left behind on the other side of the door—who appeared pitiably small and flat, like a graphite stickman rendered on a piece of paper.

By comparison, he felt dimensionally exploded, infinitely expanded.

Ten year! he thought, astonished. *It take ten year to admit I love her?* The contemplation was painful. He recalled a shift fallowing the picnic to the rule of a possessive assumption: *Gloria will be mine someday soon.* Treasuring a person became focus on acquisition. He went to work on it. Beautiful, easy, unmerited celebration of relationship had morphed into substantiating a claim. The real Gloria was replaced by ideas concerning her. But she was never forgotten. Quite to the contrary, every corner of Poyāma's world was populated with evidences of misplaced longing for her: honorific monuments, tributes, Gloria relics and Gloria fixations galore.

Staring into the past, thoughts of the fallout from the second wine tasting event at Richard LaRue's commanded a deep sigh. *When dat happen, what to do nex I have no idea. Back home, it all work out easy. Pa take over. He get together wit her Pa . . . done deal! But Pa stay way back far away. And Gloria have no living Pa, so her broter take over. De problem wit her broter make everyting worse. No deal!* Pursuit of Gloria, he recalled, had been deferred in favor of a naïve confidence: "Someting will happen to correc everyting. Someting always do."

The gray was darker than he remembered it being the last time he had made note of it. Thirst was greater, severe, angering. The pocket watch came out and its lid was flipped open: 4:10. Frowning, he stared at the hands as if forgetting how to tell time. Perusing the mottled gray forest, clues were not detected.

"Time run backward? Someting very out of de ordinary happen jus now," he muttered. "No, de clock muss have break. Eiter de clock break or . . . ." Shaking his head, the watch was returned to the pocket. Dizziness gone and weariness greatly reduced, he was able to sit up, clear away what he thought was a remarkable accumulation of leaves, and scoot back to the tree he had left and rolled away from.

The pocket watch came out again. He stared at it, putting together that thoughts of Gloria and realizations of love, seemingly only brief moments in length, had actually been spread out over many hours. *I jus now wake at de usual time*, he thought, and then muttered, "So . . . I lose a whole day . . . but catch up all my sleep and den some."

Picking leaves from each arm, one in particular demanded attention. It was by far the largest. Something else begged his attention. Eyes rotating upward as his head did the same, a long, thoughtful stare up the tall trunk at the canopy overhead was intercepted by observation of a falling leaf. When it hit the ground he looked again at the large leaf in hand. "Fross!" He looked around. "All de leaf grow fross! You hang on long up dere for eat de sun, but de fross bring you down." He licked the leaf for the moisture of frost on its surface. Unsatisfying, frost was cursed for being a tease.

The leaf was discarded and Poyāma closed his eyes and rested his head back against the tree. A burdened image of the vineyards at home was surprisingly clear. *De grape wait long and hang on long to de vine for harves. Maybe too long and freeze ruin dem all.* He consoled himself with a reminder that temperatures upon the mountain were considerably lower than those down in the valley at vineyard level.

"I hang on long too . . . all dry and shrivel like dese leaf."

The feeling ran deep. Yet, it was contradicted by a feeling from a place deeper still. As if producing the result of an evaluation of the two conflicting feelings, a third announced, *Time for get up! Time for go!* There was a hesitation, a silent debate and a conscious decision to suspend response until later. Thirst and fear-motivation were indistinguishable and one or the other kicked slothful decision in the shins.

Time for get up and go now!

His eyes opened widely. The announcement was not to be confused with a suggestion. And the feeling behind it was not one of those of common describable proportions. It was more like that in a rooster at dawn of a new day. It was this feeling that drove him and did not rest while he slept. It was not obliged to wait for the sun's slow rise. It was a feeling bigger than the sun. It was a feeling louder and greater than the combined capacity of all natural, comprehensible feelings, being ruler and purpose of all.

"*I am Poyāma,*" he recalled from the sermon, "Rejoice!" His eyes blinked demonstratively, awakened. A slap to each thigh and he was on his feet. Staring down into the steep descent, he was eager to reverse the efforts that brought him high up the mountain, go straight to find Gloria and set things right. Hearing a noise, he turned to see Wind proudly topping the nearest ridge above. Poyāma stared. Turning, he looked back down the mountain weighing a decision. When he looked back up he saw nothing but trees.

"O-o-o-o-o, you got to be kidding me," he grumbled, looking up into the steep darkness of the hill. Its appearance was actually much less daunting in the modeled dullness of that hour than it would be if in detail illuminated by daylight. One step began the long climb and instantly it was as if the distance shrunk by ninety percent, so confident was he after taking that step. But had he known the difficulty of the ten percent, more seated leaf collecting would have been the outcome.

After two-hundred feet of elevation, feeling decrepit, he stopped. "Why everyting so hard, so confuse. Why not jus an easy way dat Wind belong wit me, comfortable wit everyting else? He connec me wit my right tinking for lead me and set right . . . *and* destroy!"

The recollection of standing on the rock hours earlier was clear and close. He remembered the emotions, pressure building toward eruption like internal magma, head back and fiery wrath ready to blow. But its re-creation was far from reach. Wishing he, instead of Xerxes, had been the one to let loose with an angry protest, disappointment was the only response he could muster. *One match, one cigar, stars, smoke ring, plenty of relax, smashing hot coal and stubble into de rock . . .* He tried to retrace everything leading up to the combustion of feelings cut off by Xerxes' voice piercing the night and robbing him of the explosive moment.

"I really feel de heat for dat coming," he said, shaking his head and resuming the climb. "I really want for let loose wit dat one big!" He stopped again and stared down the hill. "Xerxes steal it right from me." Twenty steps or so brought him to another stopping point. "I take too much pride in de tunder of dat horse . . . in de wild and de fire of his power . . . his voice . . . his spirit . . ." The early call of a gliding hawk was far off, but compelled a glance just in time for its shadowy flight to be seen through a break in the trees. ". . . and not enough in my own," he whispered.

Realizing the sky beyond dark cover of leaves was waking, the next hundred and fifty feet went briskly. Terrain was an even mixture of rock, soil and fauna. Greenness could not be altogether suppressed by the carpet of brown leaves or the lack of light. Moss covered rocks pushed through both to make an almost musical impression—a high note or two upon the generally melancholy tone of things. The trees were tall, one hundred feet or more and lacked limb and leaf until reaching the roof of the forest. Stopping and looking around, the scene was enjoyed as a giant-size version of lying in a sugarcane field as a boy when visiting relatives in British Guiana. Pleasure accompanied the visual image. But the following steps were especially sluggish. Coming to a ridge, a trodden path could be seen until disappearing into the woods west and east.

A horse pat up here? No wild horse live in dese hill. Dis muss be what de native people create.

"'Exile,'" he whispered, gazing down the path westward. "Dat word what Pa tell me—'Born for anoter man possess, move by anoter man choice, work for anoter man wealt, sing for anoter man we song of home for ac like we happy anyway.'" He stared, heavy, as if swept away on the spirits of Native Americans. "'Indian' . . . ," he said with a chuckle. "Right dere what begin de exile . . . de name dey get for captain of he ship get loss on de way for India." Lament set his head wagging back and forth. "Wes dese Indian take for exile, like Pa get send sout and I take nort on my own. We all learn de way for exile." Exile converted to agitated consciousness of thirst-misery. As if weighted, his eyebrows sunk, then converged, nearly touching.

Three gun shots and the sickening sight and sound of Xerxes hitting the ground came to mind. He recalled leaning against the fence, looking up into the wooded hill and several times seeing Wind's whiteness passing through breaks in the trees. Spinning around, an opening in the trees welcomed his viewing like a large open window. He ran down the path to his right and found another significant opening about twenty-five yards away. Further on there was another. Climbing on to a rock just off the path, heart pounding, he tried to identify features of the landscape far below in the pre-dawn light.

"Dis it!" he exclaimed, hopping down from the rock and crouching. "He was here on dis trail when I was way down dere looking up. I catch sight of him when he pass dis opening. He lead me here, I know it." There were fresh hoof prints on the path. Some very large, fresh prints were studied and touched. Looking over shoulder up the hill he whispered, "Jus some small evidence . . . see how dat is all it take?" He laughed. "How I set out for kill dis horse and find inspire wit every sight of him?"

Standing, he yelled, "Here me Wind! I know you up dere and I track for kill you. What Poyāma track, no way noting keep me back for find!"

Hearing a faint echo, the inspired hunter looked around. Nothing in view offered explanation of such an echo. He looked down again and located the large hoof print amid others, all much smaller—normal size. Walking the path he saw that the smaller prints were many. Some were more recent than the large ones, often upon them, and others appearing beneath them. There were boot prints and other signs that someone else had also knelt to examine the larger prints made by Wind. Suddenly, he felt uncomfortable for having yelled out. Further investigation revealed some of Wind's prints to be over the boot prints.

"Some oter horse and dey rider come trough here recent . . . while I sleep. And Wind come here before and after dey pass. He keep watch."

Recalling the curiosity of the echo, he looked around, then gazed up the hill. Twenty feet up from the path trees appeared to be rising from the ground at mid-trunk. He climbed quickly. Coming to a ridge and peering down into near blackness, it looked as though a descent would reverse the last two hundred feet of climb before more upward progress could be made. At the sight of it, the momentary inspiration was also reversed.

Studying the situation, it was readily apparent that quite a walk would be required to scout out possibilities of circumventing the problem, with no guarantee of success in discovering anything better. The thought of extra steps in any direction for any length only to confirm this to be the most direct route was at once an encouragement and a dare to proceed forward and downward.

"It is black like de bear down dere."

Hearing the echo again, he mumbled while beginning with cautious steps. "Fourteen year and I never climb dese hill for know someting about dem . . . always too busy . . . too busy for make success in dis land and never take time for explore."

Familiar or not, the descent would pose serious cause for concern and second thought under bright sun on a normal day. But three days of serious strain on his legs and very little food resulted in a depleted and sore condition that magnified the value and ease of downward movement and impaired evaluation. He no longer had any idea what he hoped for as an outcome of following Wind. Yet, not following was not a consideration. The great white stallion had last been seen atop the ridge above the horse path. Wherever he went, Poyāma was taking the only way he knew to get there.

Drop in temperature was directly correspondent to descent and increased density of darkness. But the environment was actually pleasing to him. Tree trunks rose from spaces between rock and their vertical grayness shared a statement with the horizontal grayness of the rock formations. The illusion was that of wetness, like long drops running down a window on a rainy day, washing together as they neared the bottom. Surrounded by the tall trees, it was like being in a large room of such windows. The dark sepia world was left behind and the darker world of cool grays was entered.

Half way down the steep rocky slope Poyāma came to a seat-size rock and sat down. Arms wrapped around his knees, he stared down at the moss covered surface between two old boots. Aching legs and pains in his blistered and bruised feet were contributors to the decision to stop and sit. But a fuzzy sense of danger was mainly responsible for a prolonged break. Long, empty silence gradually gave way to thoughts, then words.

"You know someting? I tell you a secret if you believe." Arms unfolded and legs lowered and hung off the rock. "When I show my face at de harvess party dis year . . . dat showing was all dat matter . . . all I care about. In all de game we play, my turn was de only turn for I pay attention. All oter turn only make me wait for get mine back."

The words were spoken to Wind as if he were standing right beside the rock. Getting to his feet, Poyāma gingerly brushed his hands together before brushing the seat of his pants.

"Da's it. Da's all I have for say."

WOUNDS

The next step was a physical calamity and an emotional catastrophe. It was a step implied by shadows, but in fact, not there. Realizing the fallacy too late, Poyāma whirled around in an attempt to reach back and catch hold of some help. This was partly and painfully successful. Rather than falling the entire twenty feet to the last tier before the final descent to the bottom, he bounced and scraped his way down. Though many aches, bruises and stinging superficial lacerations resulted, the borrowed coat prevented a more severe outcome. The first bounce turned out to be the worst. An outcropping rock passed through the center of flailing arms and met his chin, causing a nasty bite to his tongue. He lay still, stunned, occasionally spitting blood onto leaves and mossy turf. Amid the storm of pain, an unfamiliar feeling resulted in an attempt to wipe the left side of his lower lip. Discovering the tip of his tongue hanging by a sliver of flesh, it was given a yank and tossed away.

There were too many focal points of burning, angry, bruised flesh and bone to assess the signals coming from any location in particular. But their amassed excruciation did come to a focused intent. Extermination of the horse by which constant harm had been introduced was a renewed fixation. Spite was as a brush dipped into the warm blood pooling in his mouth and painting the horse's image upon the white-hot canvass of his mind. Pushing aside the coat, a revolver was drawn out. He was stalking still, waiting for one of those glimpses of white moving in the woods.

While waiting, India came to mind. India—a fantasy land of idyllic scenes, relationships and encounters made of equal parts Pa's oft-spoken memories, lore and Poyāma's own imagination. *Who are de English for rob a man of Indian heritage?* Haze supplied a slight numbing relief to a body experiencing shock. *Sugarcane and grapevine . . . who de English and de French tink dey are for lord over we?* South America followed—a perfect boyhood if not for that one horrible moment. *Dat what spoil everyting!* The U.S.—*I get it almos perfec, right until de horse show up.*

It took more than half an hour for most of the sizzling nerve endings to quiet down enough for him to notice his splitting headache. That was about the time he lost consciousness, an inflated tongue holding his mouth open.

He came to in deepened darkness, welcomed by unrelenting and ever-worsening thirst, soreness and bone-rattling chill. Staring straight up, some of the tall trees became discernable, separating ever so slightly from the star-lit night sky. Darker than before the fall, it took a few minutes to process the disorienting visual and realize another entire day had passed. A feeling of *really scared* was suddenly like hands around his neck, constricting and impeding breath. But its grip was quickly loosed by the council of recent occurrences, all the kind any sane person would most fear, and all survived. The revolver remained finger-wrapped, stiffly, as if rigormortis clung, cheated by his revival. With trembling effort and great concentration, it was returned to the holster. Reaching for the pocket watch, a broken chain was discovered. The watch was gone, snagged and plucked away during the fall.

Rolling to the left to aid rising, an injured shoulder said, "No, not this way." Rolling to the right, top and bottom of the hip and all three points of the elbow on that side dared him in unison. Attempting to pull up by summoning the accordant strength of abdominal muscles not punctured, torn or cut, the roll call returned laughter.

The laughter was painful, but the strange, helpless predicament rendered a silly interpretation. The more laughter, the more every wound made itself known. Complaining the loudest and finally bringing the absurd humor to an end was his tongue. Swollenness was greatly reduced. The same was not true of soreness.

Poyāma stared, miserable, thoughtful, as if back at the top rethinking the decision to climb down. *If I know dis pain coming for take dat way down, I would chose for run and jump.* He lay shivering, thinking about the cold and the damage, both reduced by half because of the coat. *If I don' have dis coat dose rock shred my body for sure.* LaRue, the man who provided the coat, was presently his best friend ever.

Choosing shoulder pain, he rolled to the left and tried to create enough momentum to get onto all fours and crawl to the edge of the platform on which he had landed. But the protest of injured hands and knees forced a collapse upon the injured shoulder and a subsequent time of breathless anguish. A different approach was needed. Getting back onto the only padded, unharmed meat and tissue remaining useful for bearing weight, he scooted on his backside and led with the heels of his boots to manage a slide down the short grade leading to the bottom of the original two hundred foot decline. Mission complete, having plunged forward in the dark of the previous morning and then conquering the treacherous slope in just under twenty-three hours, he was motionless but for the blinking of watery eyes.

A hollow, dungeon-dwelling growl was heard and demanded double attention when repeated low and faint by way of echo. *I never hear a stomach so loud for make echo. How long since I las take food?* he wondered. *OK, I toss a bite down quick as I can move for fetch someting.* Pulling a wrap from a pocket on the right side of the coat, a piece of the spicy jerky was located. But the instant it was inserted between dry lips, the wounded tongue retracted so violently it threatened to stuff itself down his throat. The jerky was thrown and the wrap it came from flung to the ground, its few contents spilling out. All stomach complaints were ignored from then on.

The confession made before the step resulting in the tongue chomping blow to the chin and countless other injuries was recalled. Release felt good when the confession left his mouth. But he was not used to the effects of confession. Like tossing away a small bit of debris that turned out to be essential to regulation and containment of a critical tension, a sense of lightness had followed. Poyāma wondered how it might have influenced the misguided step, if he had felt too pleased . . . had his guard down.

The admission made to LaRue, "I am de same," came to mind. He wondered if it too had interrupted shrewdness, playing a part in the loss of Xerxes. Studying the previous few days as if reviewing an accounting leger, something critical to his usual navigational dexterity appeared to have been discarded among burdens attached to confessions. Its loss, he surmised, was what threw off a normally precise balance of caution and ambition, balance dependent upon constant calculation.

The contemplations melted into annoyance.

However it happen, it happen! De step happen and it belong for mine . . . I mess up big dere for sure. There it was again. Silent or vocal, acknowledgment of personal error was followed by a lightsome sense of being. And again, it felt good, though a very different kind of good from its forerunner. It felt outrageous. It felt conspicuous. It felt tangibly connected to more. It felt like an invitation to show his mind. The magma was back and rising.

"Perfec . . . perfec . . . no more perfec!" he declared with frustrated, tense restriction due to minimal movement of his tongue. Confident of listening ears, he continued. "I tell you someting if you don' keep it secret. Perfec only cause hide. Perfec what demand compare wit LaRue. And he sister . . . I never decide for pursue my love because perfec plug my ear and blind my eye wit pride. LaRue have no power for keep me back excep what I give him by how I take offense. Gloria never tell me he de boss of she. I keep myself back for embarrass by what she might tink after what he say. But I never make chance for fix what he say."

He was on a roll and feeling more than merely good about it. He was alive. "I keep back from de town and all de people for protec what I hear dey tink about de great Mr. Vishnu, de master for horse and wine . . . de dark-skin foreigner who have mystery way wit success, who always keep to himself, who always keep quiet, but when he speak he speak wise and walk de secret road of his home country."

Momentum and catharsis came to a blunt stop. As if the tail of the last thought had whipped around and slapped him in the face, the reminder of "home country" in present context inflicted a pain that caused Poyāma to forget all others. Gritting his teeth and squeezing eyelids together tightly, back arched, torso raised, throat producing an uncivilized sound, a downward thrust of hips and forward throw of shoulders popped him to his feet. Tears that had been pressed out to the sides of his face now flowed downward. Eyes opened wide, spotting the white horse halfway up the opposite hill, staring back.

"I tell you someting else for you big ear like to listen." Glaring, ignoring the pain in his tongue, voice shaky and mostly air, he was doubtless the animal could understand every word. "I leave my family and all what I love back home for wonder what dey tinking of me about my little broter loss. Everyone say it not my fault but treat me differen. Pa never blame me. But he call me "Perfec Son" always before and never after dat happen. I know one ting what true for sure: perfec make for exile. Since de day of my birt I watch out for my time to be like Pa, for make way of my own. But I decide in my heart for exile de day of my broter loss. Now you come here and find me. You destroy my place and ruin dis exile I spend all dese year for make perfec."

The pistol had been thoughtlessly drawn as he spoke. Right arm raising, gun loosely held in a sore, stinging hand, he made an effort to aim that was negated by the shaky struggle to pull the trigger. A shot was fired and hit a tree. The gun landed on the ground, ejected from weak, pained fingers. Echoes lingered on the chilly air. The horse did not move.

Ok, good, Poyāma silently fumed, *you stay dere and wait for I pick up de gun I bring for keep my wish for kill you.*

The horse lowered its head, shook its mane and turned away, walking slowly through the trees and up the hill. Keeping his eyes on the horse, Poyāma bent over until stopped by ache and stiffness. Glancing down, darkness was all he saw. The gun would have to be felt for with shuffling boots and a method for bending down and reaching it figured out once it was found. Another gun remained mounted at his left hip, but he was no gunslinger, and the fact never entered his mind. When he looked up the horse was gone. Long tall shapes were barely discernable on the dark hillside, all clearly defined illuminated trees seconds earlier. But well after losing touch with that amazement, conflicted longings kept his attention fixed on the wooded slope.

Now I know for sure dat horse know my heart. Somehow he know when I lie and what my heart speak true. He somehow know I have no wish for kill, but only hunt for keep near him. And he come near only when I show true.

A falling leaf hit wet hair and dragged along his ear on the way to a shoulder landing. Turning away from the hill, arms and head hung weighted by uncertainty about practical matters, like where he was, why he was there and how he would get home. It was not the horse but his own obsession for the horse he wanted to kill for the sake of recovering some normalcy.

Consumed in thought, Poyāma slowly found a way to a seated position on the cold hard ground, mostly oblivious to his lightless surroundings. An attempt to identify details relating to the brief history of the obsession was quickly diverted by the cry of Xerxes in the background of memories reviewing the initial phase of adoration. This was replaced by other memories of standing on the same porch, fawning eyes delighting in the young Xerxes and each of the premium steeds in turn. *De obsession for all horse,* he thought, feeling informed. *Dere begin de weakness.*

The enraptured moments following Wind's early morning arrival tempted grasp. Trying to recall the most irresistible of the first impressions, a near sensory remembrance of groping fingers traveling the contours of glowing white muscularity transformed into images of lusciously bulbous clusters of grapes, ripe on the vine, held in hand. He stared knowingly—*de firs cluster of harvess.* Bigger than birthdays and more desirable than candy, every activity of every year throughout his life was measured by this greatest of anticipations. Round, sweet, juicy and satisfying, back home it was called "Heaven's 'Yes.'"

First clusters and the beginning of harvest represented more than tasty beauty and bounty. '*Work, waiting and worry,*' he recalled, were inventions of winegrowing, according to the lyrics of a favorite song. Of course, '*festivals, family and friends,*' along with every activity of merriment and all forms of blessing were also bound to the '*life of the vine.*' The experiences of his youth formed into essence of all he recalled as happiness and Gloria's smile came to mind. The scent of her hair was like a perfume poured into his memories. There she was, among them all, as if they each had born anticipations of her.

Someting about her I always know deep inside.

After turning and feeling for obstructions, the level area behind him was deemed clear enough to lie down. He did so slowly, gingerly.

So, obsess have start wit de fruit?

He had almost forgotten the examination of obsessions responsible for the disaster of the past three days and currently loathsome circumstances. More songs came to mind. The sounds of flutes, drums, guitars and many voices singing brought an internal smile. Songs, too, in those early years seemed to burst forth from the taught skin of plump grapes. He once loved listening to his little brother play tunes upon the flute. Like those tender sounds long silent, it was long before Poyāma's mind produced any other thoughts or memories. He stared, numb, as if afraid to remember.

The House imposed on the blankness. If buildings were capable of pride, that one presumed to broadcast self-importance. *De House would find welcome between de barn and de stable before dey burn,* he decided. Never before had he consciously acknowledged the replicating of architectural character in buildings he had designed for his own vineyard and horse ranch. Realizing the obvious fact, he chuckled at the irony that pride had prevented admitting it sooner. He liked "nice ting," as he categorized all things fine and exclusive. But more than nice things, he relished association with impressive things. And above all, he took pleasure in what could be recognized and envied for belonging to him.

OK, now I see I have obsess for many ting. But obsess begin wit me, he concluded.

Setting out from his house convinced of a hateful determination to hunt and kill the horse, he had come to see the expedition as disguised obsession, bringing more harm to himself and none to the tormenting animal. Poyāma closed his eyes. Reliving the introduction that began as a flame in the distance quickly lighting visions of fortune in its capture and service, he squirmed. Moments later, in radiant dignity the white stallion had stood before the simple one who, from a wooden porch on a field of dirt, would presume upon it such crude indignities as ownership and control. More squirming and his eye lids squeezed more tightly together beneath a deepening frown.

"How I come to ac like dat?" He whispered. "How I become a man who tink so wrong like dat?"

Beauty like none ever seen, power like none ever imagined, thunderous authority like none to which he had ever been exposed, yet he had sensed a gift of personal devotion in its arrival. There was no mistaking the clear fact of its chosen destination. Amazed at the vulgarity of the reflex to make use of such selection for an impression of importance, he wished for a place to hide from the memories or a way to erase them. But, imprisoned for the time being at the bottom of the cold, dark fissure high on a mountain, he was possessor of nothing but memory and thought, without even the luxury of a distraction with which to busy himself.

It always become more hard for keep fill wit wonder. De grape enough for provide wonder when I was young. Song and friend and celebrate and many nice ting do it after dat. Change to new country take over from dere . . . Gloria . . . den I replace her wit de excite of success . . . den collec all de fine horse . . . now what?

When Poyāma opened his eyes, long trunks of the surrounding trees converged into the black canopy overhead, drawing attention immediately to a single star high above. Its light shined through an open spot in foliage suddenly feeling very near. Its brightness and singular clarity was like the other side of a silent conversation. His heart and mind were united, equally clear and bright in whispered answer: *Dat star immigrate to dat spot like I immigrate to dis one for we have dis meeting in de universe God create.*

The idea was so foreign to any previous inclination of his mind it was recognized with certainty as a revelation. Another followed: *I have no exis apart from all what God create. He make all togeter one unite for he self. He alone keep always able for supply de wonder dat keep me fill.*

Due to its nightly migration across the sky, the position of the star in the small space between leaves changed steadily. Its sparkling light had a place among former thoughts of desirable things, wonders. It went black. Assuming it had disappeared behind the leaves, he moved his head to the right. Many similar adjustments were made. It was not found. He waited, thinking it might have been covered by clouds. The loss felt significant, like something for which he wanted an explanation or an answer. While waiting, wishing clouds away, he realized there had been no anticipation of the star, no feeling about it prior to its appearance; yet, feelings of anxiousness, distress, loss and longing were introduced by its outage. It did not reappear. But the revelation about God's perpetual novelty did.

As if gazing up into heaven through the small space between leaves, Poyāma muttered, "You make all of dis. You make all fit togeter like glory." He was blank for a moment, suspended, feeling something. When the feeling made itself clear, he spoke in full voice, as to a person. "I never tank you for dat. I never tank you for make me part of dat. I never tank you for make a way dat come to be Indian, English, French, Sout American, United State. I never tank you for Gloria . . . for Richard LaRue . . ." There was a long, blurry, sniffly pause. "I never tank you for my family . . . for my broter, Vishwaas . . . for de way you give me his name when I come to dis country for carry him close always . . . for all de oter bright ting dat make for find my way in dis worl. Maybe dis one small voice down here in de dark have no way for reach out long like de light of dat star, but . . . tank you."

Left in the void of abrupt disconnect from the star was a sense of urgency to find Wind. Thankfulness was much more than a revelation. It was evidence of transformation. Thrilled by it, Poyāma's pendulum of evaluations had swung back to favor the white stallion. *Dat horse do me so much good I have no loyal dat remain in my heart for anyting but follow where he show de way.*

Straining with neck and shoulder muscles, his head lifted until in position for surveying the situation. Slightly diminishing blackness gave loose definition to the actual length of the earlier coma-like slumber. Resulting from a jolt to his head from the impact of the rough landing at the end of his fall, he had gone unconscious and stayed so from one early morning to the next. Soft rays would soon precede the sun over the eastern horizon, climb the mountains and begin seeping down into the shadowy woods. He was seeing the minimal effects of the decrease in darkness, feeling hopeful and trying not to think about the staggering loss of two full days to *sleep*. Had he a better understanding of how much his body needed the depth and amount of rest, more thankfulness would have been enjoyed.

Recalling periodic glances at the facing ascent while drawing closer to it on the rocky climb downward, memory of large cave-like spaces warned of equally difficult vertical conditions on that side. At the moment, shadowy saturation remained too thick to allow for distinguishable features fitting the recollection. In fact, even the tall, limbless trunks of the timbers lost their vertical statement as if submerged in pitch near the fissure floor.

After getting back to his feet, Poyāma employed cautious shuffling to cross the narrow breadth of level ground between the two steep grades. He came to the rocks at the base of the opposite slope. Reaching out and feeling through the visual murk with both hands, he stopped at a rock outcropping just before finding it with his forehead. Reversing the last several steps, an assessment was made while everything substantial lightened in grayness and all hollow places stayed black. Glancing up and over shoulder, half expecting to see the horse, the deep gray-blue sky above showed itself against the dark underside of leafy canopy. A horizon somewhere beyond the succession of tall hills could no longer keep the first rays of dawn from tinting the heavens.

Eager to make progress and able to see its most promising possibilities, rock shelves terracing between infrequent but large trees were scanned. All led upward until meeting a hillside much like the one that dumped him onto this ground level of the great crack in the hill. Narrow soil chutes between rock were few, steep and crumbly, even if their softness was tempting. Several were tried before being rejected in favor of better footing on rock steps. The decision brought quick progress, a misfortune resulting in a precarious situation fifteen feet up the incline. Standing on a narrow ledge, the target platform leading directly to hike-worthy terrain was frustratingly near and awkwardly beyond reach.

Blistered and bruised feet protested the delay, which required heels-raised weight bearing and balancing. Dirt and rock fragments had found every split and groove of wounded hands complaining of the responsibility for holding the position. Just a few feet up and to the right was the platform. But no handholds adequate for stability were between the current ones and there. If he could lift his left foot about two feet, there was a solid ledge from which to push up and over. Two feet was an ugly mile with an uglier dead-end according to a squinting visualization, which made both knees begin shaking.

"What you do now?" he yelled. Looking at the situation downward over each shoulder with the aid of increasing illumination discharged the unhelpful declaration, "Stupid!" Feeling empowered by the chastisement, suggestive of an inner judge capable of better sense, he added, "You should stay wit grape, what you know how for do. Maybe you should have stay in Sout America!"

The left foot maneuver emerged as preferable to backing down and reversing all progress. The leg lifted slowly and the ledge was felt for by boot tip. Its counterpart's shaking became swaying, then shifting. When the right foot slipped, panic sent the left hand on a flailing search for a grab that did not exist. The twisting movement spun him around, facing outward. In a blink he was back where he started from, progress reversed and no unharmed meat and tissue remaining. Every bony protrusion and all fleshy padding back and rear that could clip a rocky edge on the way down seemed to have done so. Collision with the ground sucked all oxygen from both lungs. For nearly two minutes pain prevented their function for its return. Mouth open with no sound coming forth, Poyāma just writhed in the dirt.

When heart rate, blood flow, and oxygenation reestablished brain signals, a voice trembling with rage rasped, "I hate dat horse."

Rocking to create momentum, gritting to keep back tears, groaning just to vocalize fomentation of an overdue blast, he generated enough oomph to roll over and creep along, stomach to the ground like a molten mass. Drained and deflated, a limit was reached more than a destination. Intention to get onto all-fours, and from there stand, ended in collapse, knees wedged between body and ground, derriere propped up on the backs of heels. Thus he stayed, as if stuck, face to the ground, forehead resting on crossed hands. Throbbing in wounded knees supporting this position added nothing noticeable to the general misery.

"I hate you," he murmured, before breaking down and weeping uncontrollably. Loud tearful lamentations served no anesthetic deliverance. And when they stopped, only words could satisfy as replacement. Pushing off of the ground with all remaining might, his broken upper body rose until upright as a tree on folded lower limbs.

"You here me!" he yelled, "I tell you someting what is true. I only lie before now because I tink you come for bring me even better fortune. I stay too long wit believe dat for expec you turn all dis trouble and harm around to someting good when you see how hard I work, and how hard I try and how I only keep up for deserve you. But you bring only seduce for all dis harsh betray. You tink you really special and mighty? I only say all dose praise and flatter for make you owe someting back. You tink I really love you, you crazy! I love de hope for maybe you be a special prize like you look! But you only take away all what I already earn for make me happy. I love de tought of you help me look proud for everyone who see us. But you turn everyting around so I look like a fool who watch his good mind and character run away far . . . so far it maybe never come back.

"I see how you bring me up here by you deceive for dis final destroy. And now I see you win always. I have no strong anyting lef for chase or kill or follow. So before I lay down and die like a dog, I tell you my true heart for make sure you know . . . for make sure you have no satisfy for tink I fall hard for love you. No way! I only fall hard by dis desire for own you and use you for serve me! I am a fool for dat!"

Having set things straight, the unsmitten, unimpressed, defeated pursuer fell forward onto his hands and then onto the ground. A shudder made several laps up and down his bruised spine. Within seconds he was dosing, body overcome by shock, emotions overwhelmed by numerous forms of pain. Within minutes the sound of sniffing and gentle nudges of a large soft nose made a rousing impression. Staring into large eyes and slowly getting to his feet, breathless and trembling, the hunter knew this was more than a spell.

"I forgot," he said, resmitten.

Poyāma followed Wind over to where he stopped parallel to a knee-height ledge, waiting. Stepping up onto the ledge, he leaned forward and slumped onto the horse's wide welcoming back. There was no inclination of a movement-prompting kick to the ribs, no thought of command or suggestion, only rest, face buried in silvery fragrant mane.

HEALING

"Gloria...."

Poyāma walked around the tasting table taking in the ambiance, closely observing every face awaiting the appraisal, including his—the kind of thing you can do in a dream. But this was no mere dream.

"Paradoxical... plump and plain, yet exotic and luxuriant...." Pausing, Gloria drew the grapes up to her nose and it was soon pressed against them. "Basic and magnificent... one and many, meager and plentiful, simple and complex... round..." Her fingers traveled the surface of the fruit. "Abundantly classic... deep and enduring."

It was more of a revisit or replication, somewhere between exact memory and out of body recurrence. He stopped and watched Gloria.

Staring into the cluster of grapes in her hands, she took a few short sniffs and a deep breath. They were returned to the table's centerpiece. "Quite difficult to describe in a few words or phrases really."

"The wine, Gloria dear... we are all familiar with the grapes."

"Gloria...."

Her eyes closed and the sip was drawn in. The rim was lowered. Behind wet lips the wine was rolled on her tongue as it was also swirled in the glass, releasing the scented riches. Gloria smiled.

"Bouquet rises from this glass like luster from a fine diamond . . ." She frowned. "Intricate and multifaceted, yet elegant, a concentrated nose, muscat-like, black currant, wild cherry . . . lively tannin, young and firm . . ." She opened her eyes and pulled back from the glass, watching the wine roll around its interior, again frowning. Rim again beneath her nose, she added thoughtfully, almost dreamily, "Yet, old-fashioned, even ancient qualities . . . woody, blackened smoky-burnt-woody with a slight hint of tobacco . . . windy, as if the winds of an Indian summer swept long and strong. Late harvest . . . browning leaves, snowy whiteness . . . enjoyable . . . it will age nicely toward a maturity to be relished." Staring into the glass, she whispered, "A maturity for which my heart will yearn."

The tall oaks prevailed. Surrounding, dense like the fused planks inside a giant barrel of wine, they enveloped the woozy, bouncing traveler as the word *destiny* bounced around in a mind wanting to stay with the fond revisit of the past. It was a momentous event, the wine tasting at the LaRue's table and Gloria's inspiring description. Creative confidence and soulful flourishing expression were its offspring, bottled and distributed with wild success. Her voice and presence felt near.

Never had Poyāma felt so glad for rest, so able *to* rest. Not even curiosity could force his eyelids open. The wounds were healing, tangibly, toxins sprinkling away like salt from a shaking, jostled, cracked and chipped container.

Still, the ride was fairly smooth. The enjoyment of it seemed long to a weary mind in a dreamy state, maybe days. He had stayed on with no effort, no applied cling. However long they had traveled, it was a matter of days since a drink last went down his throat. He craved water like no craving he had ever experienced. The craving made him feel angry. As it continued, seemingly for additional days, he wanted to yell at someone for not taking better care of him. *A simple drink of water! How hard dis little ting for come by?"*

Remembering the empty wine sack, he longed for it anyway, for perhaps a remaining drop or two. Focused effort was needed to pull up his right arm and feel around for the wine sack. Drawing it from the large side pocket of the coat, it was discovered to be full. The cork lid was thumb-pried and lost. Wet refreshment flowed into and mostly back out of his mouth, some flying away on the swiftly passing wind and some mixing with sweat as it ran down Wind's shoulder.

Thirst was immediately quenched. More important to healing, taste and scent supplied the very satisfaction hoped for before disappointment led to the wine's rejection and the emptying of the wine sack onto a rock. Unconcerned with how it had become refilled, Poyāma drank and drank, long past fulfillment of need or want.

Strong tannins with sapid character, ginger, tree moss, lichen, fennel, mushroom, ginger again, but stronger . . . It was Gloria's voice, but now describing wine characteristics corresponding with the wooded environment through which they were passing. *Basil, dill, licorice, thyme, angelica . . . acacia, resin, ivy, grasses, leaves . . . jasmine, heather, chamomile, walnut, wild berries . . . .* The descriptions came in patches. He hazily sensed the space between them in terms of dimensions, as opposed to seconds or minutes. *Herbaceous, fruity and floral meadow smells at forest edge mixing and rising like ingredients from a baker's oven . . . sumptuous and sweet, very ripe, a vast array of perceptible scents . . . a rich, almost chewy, waxy profusion of flavors . . .* the taste of wine on his palate and the surroundings were changing harmoniously.

Leaving the woods, the meadow pleasures in the winemaker's nose were seductive, luring current awareness into a delicious merger with the former memory of long-treasured assessment of product from his own vineyard. In a sleepy mental image, the hold on the wine-filled sack in the pocket became Gloria's delicate grasp of a wine glass' stem. The horse's movements were as its swirling.

Refined, fullness of personality like that which I have only found previously in the longings of my imagination. This wine one could deem heavenly if not for such earthy flavor. It is the wine of kings and queens, the wine of . . . sunshine!"

Stepping from the shadow of the forest, a startling full bolt of sun was like a slap arousing retreat reflexes. Poyāma's head was sucked in, mostly covered beneath the coat collar. Squirming, recovery was slow, due to the grip of marginal consciousness and confused interpretation of the shock. When his blinking, squinting head emerged like a turtle from its shell, the smoky smell of charred wood was near. Rising up and looking around, nothing was recognizable. However, two forceful thoughts—*home feel to de lef,* and, *home smell to the lef*—suggested the direction from which the burnt scent snaked over the hills and reached their position. Wind turned right.

Should I say someting?

The thought was couched in ambivalence. His desire was to go where Wind chose.

But dere are some ting I ought to look in on. Maybe dis all new for we bot and he jus waiting on me for speak up.

An irregular hop at the front end served as warning and Poyāma had only time to reach out and take hold of flying mane. Any hesitation would have left him pondering directional and communication issues in the dirt on his sore rump. Thankful for the grip created by a lifetime of hard work, he held on, waving like a flag in high winds, pelvis bouncing off the top of Wind's tail now and then, keeping a centered flight. They charged down a hill, across a valley and half across a river before the pace slowed enough for him to drag himself up the broad back to a seated position.

Again there was an urge to contribute a suggestion, something about the importance of communication, particularly prior to dramatic maneuvers. He was glancing back and forth frantically over both shoulders at the water rushing by, alarmed by its speed. Quickly, Wind's body was completely submerged and rushing waters threatened to separate horse and rider. The white head of the great stallion looked strangely small in the water, partly covered, drawing back and thrusting forward. It was impossible for Poyāma to perceive any progress toward the far bank comparable to the sensation of being swept briskly down the river. But the two movements were about equal.

Thinking he was drowning Wind, whose head disappeared under water momentarily, a lean to the right was ill-timed to the horse's sudden footing in shallower waters. As Wind rose triumphantly, Poyāma tumbled off to the starboard side and discovered the true speed of the waters. Submerged, tumbling and racing away on the current, the breathless deafness of under-water cut off all connection to the world outside the river. With legs churning wildly, attempting to find the bottom, all sense of up and down was lost in topsy-turvy. There had been no chance to inhale before the plunge. Lacking air, the frantic motions slowed, and then Poyāma's body became limp.

A boot popped out of the water and bounced like a buoy. It was snagged by Wind, who had been speedily traversing the river's edge, following the action closely. He dragged his sputtering displaced rider to the shore and dropped him off. Overrunning the spot and circling back, muscles flexing nose to tail, mane flying, a ferocious declaration made it known he was exhilarated by the save.

Curled up and holding the boot encasing a foot feeling crushed by the jaws of his rescuer, the soggy, blue-lipped survivor grimaced between gasps for breath and water expelling coughs. The fight for restored air to water ratio in his lungs was short and volatile.

"That was unbelievable!"

Though the words were spoken loudly, Poyāma barely heard them over the stuffiness in his ears and the roaring waters. Craning to survey the area, a man on horseback was partially visible, dismounting on the other side of Wind.

"I mean it! I aint never seen nor hear 'bout nothin' like that. I seen people git baptized in the river, but not this one, not here anyway. That was special. And we had the privlige a watchin' the whole dern thing."

Not liking the sound of "we," Poyāma struggled to his feet and limped toward the man. He did not get far before disbelief slowed his steps. Behind the first man were two other men on horseback with a long row of familiar horses between them—Poyāma's horses! They were the very horses scattered in the fire, which Wind rounded up and LaRue put in his corral to await the arrival of Miller and his men. But this man was no businessman, the way LaRue described Miller. The fact meant only one thing: dangerous. Soppy but revived, Poyāma guessed that somehow these fellows had strong-armed the collection of fine animals from either LaRue or Miller.

Coming around the back of Wind and sizing up the man, he appeared to be a minimum of six and a half feet tall. Lean, ugly-bearded, six-shooters on his hips and a grin on his face, he turned and held out a hand.

"Name's Pitman . . . Parker . . . Parker Pitman."

Certain the man was lying, Poyāma obliged. "Hulsecam . . . Winslow . . . Winslow Hulsecam." Where the name came from he had no idea.

Laughing as they shook hands, the tall aggressor said, "This here is a mighty fine steed ya got. A man might give up a number a fine animals for a horse that'll rescue 'im from a river. As ya can see, we're in the business. How much ya want fur 'im?"

"No way he for sell by me."

The next thing he knew, Poyāma was dazed and seated on the ground. He yelled out in pain while popping his dislocated jaw into place. The long fingers of Pitman's right hand flexed open and shut several times. An abrupt shake evidently expelled any pain resulting from the collision. Both hands moved toward their respective revolvers before hanging from the belt by their thumbs, message-like. "Everthin's fur sale, now aint it . . . Mr. Winslow? I don't care much fer liars. I knowed a few Hulsecamps and none of 'em would take kindly to a fella like you callin' 'em kin."

"OK, I lie about de name, but tell you de trut about de horse. You do better for ask him what price he take for he rider dan de oter way around. Dat horse belong for nobody. He set he own price . . . Try him, you see."

The man turned and stared. "So ya ride this guy bareback, do ya?" Looking over his shoulder, he added, "How does a little fella like you git on this beast?"

Poyāma stood, walked over to the man, bent over and hung clasped hands for a makeshift stirrup, receiving a suspicious look. "*You* got de gun," he responded. A few seconds later Wind had a new rider. A few more and the new rider was hurled into the river, just after the words, "OK, big boy, let's see what ya got."

Following Wind's example, the two horses carrying the other two rustlers charged straight into the water, stopped and ducked, ridding themselves of their brutal burdens. Poyāma watched until losing sight of the three bobbing figures, rushed away on the turbulent waters.

"For sure I learn some important ting jus now," he announced. "Firs, I really muss get out from de ranch now and den. I have no idea dis place exis. I never know a river like dis pass anywhere near my home. Where dis river come from? You put dis here?" he asked Wind, rubbing his sore jaw with one hand and stroking the horse's long white mane with the other. "And second, I get what I deserve by forget de promise I make my friend, Gloria Tirty-two, before she pass de oter day. No more lie. Anoter man lie have no command over me for lie."

He limped over to a large rock and put his bitten foot up against it and felt for broken bones.

"Tird, I learn never tink dat I run out of way for get damage when you and me keep togeter. Dere always someting new for get harm."

Wind came to the rock and Poyāma stepped up and got onto his back.

"And lass, I see for sure dat de one who try for take posses of Wind come quick upon some very hard lesson."

Wind walked up to the first in the line of returned equestrian exotics and nuzzled as Poyāma leaned over and untied the rope keeping them all together. The same was done at the other end of the line. It had run through makeshift rope yokes on each horse. These were also removed. Wind's silent intentions had been understood and together they had accomplished the freeing of the horses. The realization was meaningful . . . a beginning. No consideration was given to where the horses might go and how they would get there. These were possessive concerns from which *he* had been freed. But the opinions of the horses were different, if such simple, instinctual responses could be expressed word-wise. They had been redeemed from captivity and returned to their beloved master.

A lengthy bit of sitting and no movement finally alerted the rider that communication was needed.

"Wherever you want for take me . . , take me."

THE ROAD

ind set out westward tilted slightly north, strong in stride, fluid and deliberate. The speed at which they traveled was more of a normal horse at gallop than that at which they had charged across fields and hills toward the river. A glance over shoulder revealed an astonishing sight, and the reason for the accommodating pace. A string of horses followed at a distance. Long study for the purpose of count and individual identification nearly cost their owner his head as a turn was made into a grove of low-limbed maples. It was Wind who discerned the moment and leaned to the left enough to dodge the blow to his oblivious rider. It was not the first time, nor the last.

Slowing, all horses were once again together, moving at an easy and organized four-beat gallop. Serpentine turns through the trees impacted breezy tones in their branches as the gait of all pounding hooves simultaneously became a three-beat cantor. Other distinct tonal fluctuations were in the air, caused by synchronized changes to the length of time in which no hoof was pounding the turf. The coordinated percussional qualities were unmistakable, and the lone rider was transfixed by the sounds. Leaving the enchantment of the grove to memory, a bouncy two-beat trot took over that made for brisk passage of a two mile slope, before giving way to a four-beat gait with a lateral movement crossing a wide but shallow stream. This left the experienced horseman laughing and applauding on a two-beat march into thick wild grasses.

"Ah-ah-ah-ha-ha-a-a-! Whoever know such ting happen in de worl?" he yelled, gleeful. "De only ting what make it more perfec would be if Gloria can be here for share wit me!"

He leaned and patted Wind's neck, knowing it was no small thing to get Thoroughbred and Morgan on the same beat, that lateral movement was unnatural to all but a few and Wind's lead was the only explanation for such inspired coordination. "You have some power no man or horse ever expec," he said, moved.

A random memory interjected itself. He pondered having dumped the contents of his wine sack onto a large bolder near a corral on LaRue property. Reaching into the pocket holding the wine sack, he realized immediately it was empty. The cork was discovered to be tightly in place. He frowned, recalling the nearer memory of drinking wine from the sack, using his thumb as a stopper, the cork having been lost. Looking around, the sight of grazing horses in a sea of tall grass conveyed a sudden and surreal transition to utter tranquility.

Gloria's voice . . . those earlier descriptions—harmonious with travels through the forest and the meadows before the big river . . . loss of the cork . . . wine spilt on Wind's shoulder . . . these were swirling like wine in a glass. He looked down at Wind, white as white could be where the stain ought to be. *It was a dream,* Poyāma thought, looking at the cask and cork in hand. Reaching forward, he patted Wind's sweaty neck. "I have a dream about we. De voice of Gloria describe de joy of we travel togeter like wine, a wine fine like wonder. But more dan a dream . . . ." Absence of thirst was knowable, meaningful, calling to mind the former long agony of thirst, though only as a momentary discomfort in the distant past. Raising a leg, he leaned, swiveled and slipped off Wind's tall back. He walked out into the field holding the container, looking off into the layered grasses thoughtful of the good wine of being with Wind.

"You know how you remind me?" he said loudly, turning to walk back to the mighty stallion and bumping into him nose to nose. "How you so quiet for so big?" He laughed. The wine sack was returned to storage in the pocket of the coat.

As if peering out from behind a waterfall, the deep blue eyes of the mighty horse stared beneath flowing strands of hair gleaming in the sun. Poyāma reached up and brushed back many of the hanging strands for a better look at the eyes. He rubbed the tall, proud ears and stroked the broad forehead admiringly. His arms would not reach around the great muscular neck, but they wrapped as far as possible and held on.

"You have power and a way dat remind me of de wine press. I tink of dat back when we fly like crazy over de hill and into de meadow. De press break open de grape and let out all de ingredien inside, what flow for make wine."

The memory of Gloria LaRue's appraisal at the wine tasting came back to mind. Every detail was savored. Every nuance held ruminations of the recent events . . . of Wind.

"I know a fine lady who describe you once, like she speak ahead of you coming."

He combed strands of blurry-bright mane between scarred fingers, noticing the absence of tangles. Reviews of their journey were playing in his head and they were seen as if moving upon the luminescent white contours. Walking slowly around Wind, left hand light and lithe in its traveling caress, head slow-dancing, meandering nimbly to the lead of eyes enraptured, ears attentive to song, passing dips and rises, billowing bulges and smooth plateaus, the myriad scents of harvest filling his nostrils with every breath, the sweet, round fullness of personal pleasure rolling over a delighted palate . . . he drank in the moment and it satisfied all thirst.

"Really, you remind me of noting," he whispered, coming around again to an intimate eye to eye gaze. "Because I never see noting like you before. You fresh like breeze and crazy like wind. You wild like water, and beauty like sun dat sparkle on it." He smiled and drew in a deep breath. "OK . . . maybe you remind me of de perfec wine for what I always imagine and strive but never tase."

Wind reached out and gave Poyāma a shove backward with his nose. This was followed by an upswing of his head that was so evidently communicative it translated the shove as directional rather than playful. The message was: "Go Taste!"

He whipped around wildly and ran off in the opposite direction. The other horses scattered, startled. One by one they each began to take off after the flash of white that left them behind. But across the stream and halfway up the long hill, Wind stopped and turned to face them. As he rose up on hind legs, they also stopped. He whirled and bolted up the hill.

For an instant, just as Wind was topping the hill, Poyāma experienced some confusion as to whether he might have watched something winged take flight and pass beyond view. He stared long, finally attributing the phenomenon to blur of movement and great distance. The other horses turned and headed back, gathering around their stunned owner.

"I will make a new wine, what help make everyone rejoice," he told them, emotional. "Wind Wine!" Poyāma announced, as the breese moved tall grass in waves, brushed the horses' manes and made him aware of tears on his cheeks.

There were a lot of interruptions in grazing to stand looking eastward, watching for Wind's return. Each horse was examined, patted and lectured about learning a lesson from leaving the ranch and running wild because of a few flames. The saddled horses were looked at last. Coming to the first of the three, Poyāma immediately recognized the Thoroughbred and saddle as his own. After a complete assessment of horse and tack, the other two were also looked over. Dried blood on both saddles indicated wounds belonging to their former occupants. Provisions were plentiful and each of the three horses carried a rifle and a canteen. After lengthy hesitation, weighing the risk, one of the canteens supplied a drink.

It had been days on very little of anything. How many days, he did not know. The last attempt to eat was recalled—the spices shocking his tongue and the rejected jerky. Famished, but warned by experience not to dump a lot of food into a long-idle stomach, he tore off a piece of bread and ate it slowly while contemplating worrisome thoughts connected to three horses and their saddles and supplies. All were seen disappearing over a hill at the time of the fire, led by a diminutive thief. Somehow they came to be in the possession of the rustlers. He wondered if LaRue had something to do with it. With no reason to believe such a thing, he rejected the idea and denounced that type of thinking as something of the past. It was replaced by concerns about the wellbeing of the LaRues and everyone else back home.

A bit disoriented, Poyāma turned and looked in the direction to which Wind had nudged, pretty sure home was in the opposite direction, the direction in which he had charged off—southeast. A feeling of urgency to take some kind of action was met with the dilemma of what action should be taken. He stood contemplating options.

Do I choose for ignore de direction Wind give wit his nose and follow de direction where he run? He stared over his right shoulder. *Do I wait here for see if he return back?* He turned and looked out over rippling yellows of winter-ready grasses, across the shallow stream and up the long hill. *Or do I trus de direction what he point wit his nose? De same problem show up in every direction.*

In each case he would be in some way following Wind. If he eliminated the horse from the problem it was an easy decision to go back home immediately; or maybe not—doubts about present location were naturally linked to doubts about the location of home. In the end, a decision was not necessary. He had made one already— one of transforming magnitude—a decision to follow Wind. This was his new path and he would not depart from it, whatever the consequences. And there was no mistaking the intent in the push with his nose. Anything going on back home would have to be handled by someone else for the time being.

Mounting a Thoroughbred, he rode no more than fifty feet before the horse's rough, jolting walk and the hard leather seat forced a dismount. "A-a-a-ah-h!" he complained, beginning to walk.

Soon, Limping badly, it was again necessary to stop. The horses were sprinkled across a square quarter mile or so. Only one, the Lipizzaner, had not left the original field. Deciding bareback was the only way to make progress, he looked over the scattered horses. The Shire Horse was chosen. It was not as comfortable as riding Wind, but wide-backed and tolerable. The further they traveled, the more overwhelmed he felt by the vastness of the land and his smallness within it, and the more uncertain he became about the chosen direction. What kept him moving on was equal uncertainty about traveling in any other direction.

Night fell and travel was concluded for the day without any concern for the whereabouts of several horses. The three Thoroughbreds were relieved of their saddles. Blankets were unrolled and used to create a buffer against the rough, hard ground. A meal of cheese, venison sausage and bread was washed down with water. Though extremely tired and sore, sleep was delayed by thoughts interspersed between frequent repositioning.

Tree horse and saddle get steal from de far stable, what nobody guard when California hire my help away. But how de food supply from my house come to de tief?

Every position found areas of wounded flesh averse to weight bearing. Memories of a clunking sound in the kitchen while out by the porch with Wind, the empty basket of fruit, a missing canteen and LaRue's early visits carved furrows in his forehead.

LaRue is far from perfec man, exac de ting what make him a less perfec friend. Maybe dat de very way God make him de perfec friend for me.

Every position had its length of pain tolerance.

I remember de word Pa speak: 'Forgive is let go of expec fix for wrong.' Maybe friend need each oter for practice forgive. In dat case, LaRue a very good friend for me and me for him.

No position was tolerated for more than a few minutes. A turn to the left was aided by groans.

A dusty golden glow of dawn revealed a gathering around the bed of blankets. All horses were present. In such a short time, the long training of his body clock appeared to have been displaced. It was no earlier than six-thirty, he surmised, staring at the horizon from which the sun was rising. Poyāma looked around, puzzled. His bedding was laid out in the exact orientation to the surroundings he recalled from the night before. Yet the sun rose in a place on the horizon very near to where he thought it had set. He stared, squinted, shook his head and moved on.

It was chilly, somewhere in the upper forties, overcast, and the clouds were low as breakfast was enjoyed. The menu was identical to dinner the previous night. Afterward, the three Thoroughbreds were re-saddled, more for transport of the saddles and provisions than any other reason. Then, another broad-backed ride was chosen—the Percheron—and the entire group was led out into a new morning.

By mid-day the selected direction of progress felt progressively questionable. Thoughts of home were weighty, involving people he cared for more deeply than previously realized. Continuing required perseverance fueled by nothing more than commitment to a choice to do so, which thus far appeared unrewarded.

"I never see so much big about noting nowhere," he informed his horse. "Dese field big like de ocean and empty like my wine sack."

Pulling up to a saddled horse with its nose to the ground, Poyāma reached over and loosened a leather strap holding a canteen in place. Each of the Thoroughbreds came with a nearly full canteen of water, which he was glad to have, once past the difficult thought of the grungy rustlers having drunk from them. The first of the three had been consumed by the end of breakfast. It hung empty from the saddle of a nearby mare he was keeping a close eye on. It was noon and, other than the two provisioned animals at either side, only eight horses remained in view, two of those like specks before the rear horizon. The third saddled horse, and thus the other canteen and provisions, had not been seen for hours.

In the unfamiliar prairie, careful rationing seemed wise, so drinks were now modest and infrequent. Replacing the canteen lid, the sound of a far off wagon was heard and a trailing dust cloud was looked for and identified in the distance. *A Road!* he thought, and leaned down to put the canteen back in its place. Turning and craning to scan a mostly vacant landscape, the whereabouts of out-of-view horses was deemed beyond concern or control.

"Hey, all you horse!" he yelled to those in view. "I leave it up to you for keep up or go you own way!"

Looking to the left and then right, the two saddled speedsters held their heads high, staring and waiting.

"You two stick wit me? OK, time we have some fun. Ha-h-a-a-a-a-a!"

Neck to neck, they raced across the open land chasing down the dust cloud. As they drew near, it left its straight course on the road and began behaving erratically, first looping to the right and then going serpentine. Overtaking the wagon thirty feet to the left of it, Poyāma's eyes widened.

"Dese fellow have dark skin . . . darker dan mine!"

The wagon stopped, and one of the two men on it could be seen holding a gun. It was pointed at the three-horse horseman, who was looping around as if on trained circus animals in formation. Pulling to a stop, the three winded sprinters faced their two fatigued, wagon pulling counterparts. Sleek, dark brown horses with empty saddles flanked a dappled gray, wide-bodied Percheron and its bareback rider. The whole thing made an impression that was reflected on the faces of the two wagoneers.

"Put dat gun down!" Poyāma hollered. "You know who live in de heaven above you head? He de King wit might like no oter. He de one who call me 'son.' You lucky I don' shout out for he send his white horse for quick stomp. Den you find youself in bi-i-i-ig trouble!"

These words had their greatest impact in his own ears. Believing every one of them, a shudder shook him like a funny punctuation. The gun was lowered and the horse-master sprung athletically from the back of the center steed. Masking a painful landing with just a slight limp, he strode toward the man with the gun, stopping a few feet from the wagon in excellent gunslinger style, feet planted, coat back behind hands on hips. With one pistol on the floor of a dark chasm in a tall hill and the other at the bottom of a raging river, the empty holsters at his sides made a mysteriously bold statement.

"I come wit a fine gif for bot of you," he said, perceiving a providentially prepared situation and nodding back toward the two animals bearing empty saddles. The two men on the wagon looked at one another and exchanged shrugs. The gun was handed over. Opened chambers revealed the reason for the easy arrest. "You kidding me!" Poyāma exclaimed in a chastising tone. "You point at a man wit empty gun? Dere exis no faster way for get bot of you kill!"

Reaching behind his back and retrieving bullets from their belt-mounts, he refilled the gun. The prisoners looked terrified until he turned the gun around and handed it back to the man who surrendered it.

"Why you give up you bluff so easy? How can I know you have no bullet?"

"The white horse, that's why," the gunless man answered.

Poyāma looked around. "You see de white horse?"

"No sir. Ya said 'e was yurs. So I gave ya the gun," the gunner responded.

"I never say noting like dat for get in bi-i-i-g trouble. Right now we get one ting straight. I belong for he more dan de oter way around. Come down and we talk."

Both men did as they were told and stood on opposite sides of the wagon.

"Where you two going so fas."

"We don't know, Sir."

"You travel like train dat blow smoke for go nowhere on a road I never know exis and you don' know where to?"

The two men looked at one another extendedly before looking back at their questioner, puzzled.

"How you don' know where you going?" he tried again.

"We're runaway slaves, Sir."

"A-a-a-ah-h-h! I was hoping for you can tell me where dis place we meet is locate."

"No Sir," answered the ex-slave with the gun, slipping it barrel-first into a back pocket of his pants while steeling glances across the horizon. Such anxious glances were continuous.

Poyāma was thoughtful for a moment, studying the two men. He thought they could not look odder together. The one to the left who drove the wagon was shorter, disheveled and thick as an old oak. His tone was rough. The gunman was tall and gangly, gentle and proper in voice and appearance. The shorter man was white haired and the taller appeared to be much younger.

"Start from where you begin. How you come to be here? You get chase here jus now?"

"There was a fire, Sir, and we saw a chance to run. The white horse come outa the fire in front of us. We followed 'im like 'e was a sign 'n 'e kep appearin' like he was one."

Head wagging, Poyāma stared in disbelief.

"It's the truth, Sir. If we told you the trouble that horse's brung us . . . and brung us *through,* too, you'd never believe us. But we keep followin' 'n come to here. 'Til you stopped us we was ridin' 'n talkin' 'bout if we was right for keepin' on followin' him."

Poyāma walked to the front of the horses hitched to the wagon and began unhitching them.

"Whataya doin'?" demanded the white haired man.

"You drive dese horse to dey grave quick. How long you keep on de way like when I see you?"

"All mornin'. We been pushin'em pretty good for days, but really got on it earlier this mornin' when we spotted two travelers a ways back who seem to be followin' us.

"A-a-a-ah-h-h! You don' serve dem good like dat and dey don' serve you long."

After giving the two horses a slap on the rear, the disgusted horseman pushed the wagon to the side and stood amazed. Horses scattered far and wide were coming their way. He counted. All accounted for, he turned back to the two runaways.

"I like de sound of Sir, but we make friend. All my friend call me Vishnu . . . Vish if you like."

The two men looked at one another wide-eyed.

"What happen dere?" Poyāma questioned.

The younger man looked too scared to breathe, so the elder spoke.

"Some days back, three outlaws put us 'n 'at wagon, covered like cargo 'n tell us we aint gonna make no sound if we's wantin' to keep breathin'. One sit 'n back wit us 'n the two sit up front like you seen we was doin'. They's talkin' up a plan fur getin' help from a fourth steelin' a famous collection a horses they heared about b'longin' t'a man name Vishnu. The fourth fella was some old pal who was the one 'at told 'em 'bout the horses . . . 'parently the Vishnu horses was near where the fourth man was stayin'. The three that caught us was headin' fur his place fur meetin' up later on after we run into 'em. They was braggin' 'bout them horses bringin' 'em big money. We was all worked in cordin' t'the plan."

The younger man elbowed in. "We wasn't gonna do none of it, Mr. Vishnu, Sir. We was listnin' 'n figurin' our own way out until the lawmen come lookin' 'em boys up. See them holes where the wagon get all tore up? That was happnin' all 'round us 'til the fightin' 'n chasin' went up into the mountains. The Good Lord musta had 'is angels pertectin' us. 'Cause not a single one a them bullets even graze either of us."

"'At's how we come by 'at ol' wagon 'n 'em ol' horses . . . you jus took apart," added the man who started the story.

"Poyāma looked at the horses with pity in his eyes, shaking his head. "Dose horse only get you caught when you try and use dem for get away. Where de mountain you talk about?"

Both men turned and pointed. "Straight back where we came from, Sir."

Poyāma stared in that direction. "Time for eat," he said, having difficulty imagining the road leading to mountains. "How long since you take food?"

As the two men looked at one another blankly, their captor went to a saddlebag and pulled out some food. Sitting down right where they were, a meal was shared and a detailed lecture on proper horse care delivered. It turned out that both men were named Jim. As Poyāma's collection of horses reassembled, one by one the Jims were introduced to each. Both men were far beyond hungry, but both had to be continually encouraged to helpings of food. It was a fine spread of apples, sausage, cheese and bread. A canteen was shared.

"Like I tell you, de two horse I meet you wit I give as a gif for you safe deliver." Poyāma had finished packing the food away after lunch. "Dis one, and . . ." He walked over and grabbed the reins of another saddled horse. ". . . dis one." Reins and ownership were handed to each man. Retrieving the only remaining full canteen from the saddled Thoroughbred not part of the gifting, he swapped it for one of the empty ones. He did this fully aware his homeward journey was yet a long one, but confident water would be provided somewhere along the way. Both of his new friends had tears in their eyes as they mounted the horses, speechless. More instructions were given as they came to mind while Poyāma made adjustments to each set of stirrups—the furthest possible adjustment up for one man and down for the other.

"Nobody catch you on Toroughbred horse from de Vishnu ranch. Believe me, dey very fass! Dey short on stamina and rough for walk, but very fass! Only run brief and back down slow. Make time for take break regular. I trus dem to you for you good care like I teach you. Whatever else you do, if you see him, make sure you always follow de white horse no matter de trouble you tink he cause. He bring us togeter as friend for I hand over dese horse and you direc me to de road what lead to de mountain. He will bring you home safe . . . wherever dat may be. Dese rifle are of de fine hand-make.

Dey very good for help you drop game for keep you belly full. When you finish you journey to a new home . . . ."

Poyāma pointed to a signature on the stock of one rifle and to a name branded into the leather of a saddle. "Dese horse and gun and saddle fetch you fine pay for help you get start. And las," he said, pointing with his left hand in the direction he had been traveling, "I sugges you keep nort."

The final adjustment made, he looked up at his two friends, both wearing strange expressions.

"What happen dere?" he asked.

After some hesitation, the long legged Jim spoke up. "That direction where you pointed, Mr. Vishnu . . . ."

"Yes?"

"That aint north, Sir."

Poyāma's mouth gradually began to hang open as the confident look on the other men's faces proved convincing.

"Ya can trust us fur knowin' north 'n south," declared the white haired Jim, adding a big smile. All three broke into laughter.

A distant cloud rising from the road in the east got the attention of the direction challenged adventurer. Seeing the dramatic change in his eyes, the other two men turned and saw the tiny black dots causing the dust cloud. As the two horses began moving forward, both men leaned down and took hold of one of their benefactor's hands and expressed a hurried but hearty thanks.

"Hey, what name have you give de white horse?" Poyāma called out before they took off in earnest.

"He comes 'n goes like the wind."

"So we call 'im Wind."

Poyāma smiled broadly. "Dat have a knowing sound to my ear," he yelled, waving. "You keep dat name on you tongue my broter," he said quietly after the runaways had moved beyond hearing. They soon had the thrill of their lives discovering the true definition of "very fass."

One saddled Thoroughbred remained. It was walked back to the road and mounted. Healing was progressing, so the saddle was bearable though uncomfortable. The other horses followed slowly, much better along the road than they had in the fields. Poyāma continuously surveyed the land, taken aback. *How I get everyting flip?* he wonderd, realizing trust in Wind's parting nudge insured he was headed in the direction of home all along. Upon meeting the oncoming riders, a man and woman, he nodded in response to the tip of their hats while pulling up side by side.

The man sported a long handlebar mustache, its curly ends thin, but impressively round and symmetrical. "Where's your help?" he asked.

"On vacation in California," Poyāma answered.

"Looks like slow goin', drivin' 'em alone."

"Not too bad. Dey well behave."

With a closer look as the animals each drew nearer, the man and woman were evidently familiar with the breeds and stunned by the collection of fine horses trailing behind their owner.

"Jus out for a ride?" Poyāma inquired.

"Actually, we're bounty hunters trackin' down a couple a runaway slaves in a wagon. They been eludin' us in the darndest fashion for a few days now. We brought a little cash along for any valuable tips we might git along the way."

"Well, I see a wagon what break down wit no horse attach jus back a bit."

"Just what we were hopin' they wouldn't figure out," the man answered. "I don't reckon they're riders, let alone accustomed to ridin' bareback, but anything is faster than them poor horses pullin' a wagon day and night."

The woman had a different interest on her mind. "You're not lookin' to sell any of those horses are you?" she asked.

"How much cash you bring?"

"O, not enough for . . . ."

"Which ones you considerin' partin' with?" the man asked, cutting in.

"All or none, excep de one I ride."

Having a general idea of the value of the collection, the hunting team broke into laughter at the suggestion, then went into conference.

"Try me wit de bes offer you come up wit," they were encouraged, and the two stared at one another with that expression suggestive of early retirement from a job they really did not like.

A LONG HINDRANCE HOME

As some loose coins jingled in a saddlebag, the horse moved at a relaxed gallop. The deal was far inferior to the one LaRue had made with Miller. It was the deal of a lifetime, in fact, for the couple. But they were permanently diverted from their pursuit of the runaways, the part of the purchase price most important to the seller. The fineness of their own horses, their quick recognition of the rarity and value of the collection and the ga-ga in their eyes assured Poyāma the horses would be treated with premium care, another major factor. And he was now free to make fast progress toward the mountains reported by the two Jims. Money the man and woman carried served a down payment. The greater part of the sale price was a good faith arrangement that would be easily squared by the profit made on the resale of select horses. But their retirement hopes were in the breeding of Arabians, Pintos and the two impressively large draft horses. It was an excellent outcome for both sides.

Clouds that had hung low and threatened rain began breaking up and lifting, as is often the case during droughts. Within two hours the sky on the horizon was mostly clear and the distant mountains could be seen. *How did we travel so far?* Poyāma wondered, thinking about him and Wind. There was a lot of travel for which he could not account, especially in the beginning. Even later on, thrill and enjoyment obscured perception of speed and the scope of their sweeping movements. He recalled the charge in the rain following the fire—how fast they covered great distances.

"De raging river I never hear of . . . probably it flow no less dan a hundred mile from de ranch. Dis a very long journey for a young horse." He leaned over and gave the horse a congratulatory pat on the neck, then proceeded to tell him about a very long journey made from Chile when *he* was younger.

Many thoughts about both journeys made time and miles pass quickly, though, there were many breaks and changes of pace for the horse's sake. One day blended into another. Sun setting on the second day's approach of the mountains, tall hills were looming but still a lengthy ride in the distance. It would be another night under the stars and a good part of another day before they were reached.

After a meal that felt like reward for a day of many accomplishments, Poyāma laid down with a full stomach and a contented disposition. Only one blanket was between him and the ground, but he was back in the land of fallen leaves. He had kicked some together for a buffer between blanket and ground. Even for a man accustomed to the finest of domestic comforts, it was a gentle, welcoming wilderness under an infinite array of twinkling miracles in a cloudless sky. Still early, the intent was to lie quietly and contemplate the newly acquired wealth of memory. A mental image of Wind up on two legs before charging up the hill was bitter-sweet, *Like good wine*, he thought.

So much had transpired since then, it seemed disorientingly long ago. And just days ago . . . fire . . . rain . . . Xerxes . . . wounds from falls in the forest, still sore, but somehow smoothed, like stones under rushing water. Continuous shifting and turning produced no discovery of a wound-free position. But sleep came and swift was the sun's return.

Breakfast was skipped in favor of eagerness. Leaving the road, he headed toward the hilly ranges leading to the forests and mountains. Around eleven o'clock he came to the crest of a hill and perused the landscape. *Good drain . . . a good hill for vineyard*, he thought naturally. A small house was spotted through some trees at the base of the hill. A boy was outside chopping wood beside what looked to be a monumental pile.

O, now, dis feel like a dangerous situation.

A nudge of heels to its ribs and the horse started down the hill.

Dangerous how? Poyāma wondered, stopping to question his intuition. *So, a young boy is chopping wood . . . alone, no Ma, no Pa . . . no smoke coming from de chimney of he house, no animal for ride or work de land . . . .*

He squinted. Lips moving, the sound leaving them was but a wisp. "A stench roll up from down dere."

Another nudge of the heels and the horse continued down the hill. *A grave, fresh fill, between de boy and de house, de shovel sticking up from de end*, he imagined, expectant.

"Yes, dis look to have potential for a long hinder."

After tying his horse to a tree, Poyāma had a look around. The boy did not pause or look up from the work. The door of the house was partly opened. He knocked. Walking in, all below the bridge of his nose was covered by a fully buttoned coat and raised collar, ends clenched tightly together. Burning eyes released tears that mixed with perspiration. It was necessary to step over debris. Flasks and bottles were scattered throughout, some filling holes in the floor, others on shelves, tables and chairs, mostly lying over obviously empty. The dreadful stench of decaying flesh was prominent among bad smells threatening harm; rancid, sickly, foul . . . smells he could ill afford give any imaginative, far less, practical consideration. It would have been a violent experience for anyone's senses, but his were the trained senses of a wine-master and the coat was wet with emotional reaction. Some tears traveled further, breaking on the floor after his lurching forward put them to flight.

To the left and around the door the body was sprawled, blood spilt and dried, no doubt the boy's Pa. He remembered trepidations while descending the hill, the imagined grave freshly filled, a shovel sticking out of it, and knew the boy should not be spared witnessing the burial of his father. The dead man was bound in sheets and blankets and dragged to the space between the wood pile and the house. A pickax and a shovel were located. Two hours of pounding through hard ground with the ax earned the right to use the shovel. It was nightfall before the hole was refilled and the shovel left standing in the broken dirt.

He watched the boy swing the ax. The swinging had only stopped once—a pause to observe the body being lowered into the ground. The pile of wood was mountainous, far taller than its contributor and twenty or more feet in diameter. That the scrawny lad might be its sole creator was a terrible likelihood. The boy was thin in a wasted way that naturally caused intrigue as to when he had last had a meal and wonder at the oddity of his strength and energy. Observation produced guesses that put him anywhere from eight to eleven and five foot tall-ish. Hair sweat-matted, long and stringy, face sunken, taught and angry, it was decided he was an intelligent youngster intensely wrestling with difficult thoughts. The intensity was assumed fitting of the offenses generating those thoughts.

After the propping of the door and opening of windows, the house was left abandoned for the night. A more thorough search of the property turned up a tumbled blanket beside a molded area between bales of hay under crude but walled and covered storage. How long it had been since the boy slept in an actual bed in the house was added to the list of curiosities. Back out at the woodpile, there was a noticeable drop off in the child's productivity. Several attempts at a log ricocheted wildly. There was little strength left in his arms for lifting the log back into place, but when he did, somehow the ax was swung again. When the child stopped for a breather, leaning against the ax handle, Poyāma walked over and drew him near.

"Time for stop."

These simple words were expressed with a tone of compassion the little lumberjack had not heard in a very long time. Collapsing against his uninvited house guest, he began to rumble with tears. The two dropped to their knees and the small bony body was embraced in strong but quivering arms. He was soon hard asleep and covered by the blanket found in the hay bed—under pain of conscience, without dinner. A saddlebag stuffed with food was set beside him for an immediate meal upon waking. His hands were inspected. "No blister, no crack . . . tick as hide dat make boot," Poyāma whispered. The blanket from the horse was added and tucked between boy and hay.

Respectful of the personalized sleeping space, and weary of the noxious odor spilling from the house, the caregiver rode up to the top of the hill from which he had first looked down upon the modest homestead. A search for a spot on the moonlit landscape was brief. The peak of a small, knob-like hill was chosen. With his back to the ground, hands clasped behind his head, Poyāma stared, thoughtless. And unlike the night before, sleep did not come easily. He had spent his entire life around alcohol and had never once been drunk; nor had drunkenness been associated with the wine masters of The House, nor the village or home in which he was raised. A feeling of disgust for "inebriate" persisted long into the night.

In the morning, a significant meal was slowly consumed and deeply savored before the work of cleaning up the house began. Starting places and priorities were dauntingly populous. The collection and disposal of debris was a disturbing foray into another man's mess. *A man crush by de grip of inebriate*, Poyāma thought often, amazed and shaking his head. Wood removed from a disassembled outbuilding and stacked in the house began the process of rebuilding the floor. Several times over the course of the day, gagging, a dash was made for the side of the house opposite the boy's resumed chopping. Many *more* times he stood at the window and watched the felling of another dead tree—victim of draught—and subsequent wood splitting. He could not have been prouder if it were his own son.

Skin and bone, but he swing de ax and strike de wedge like a man.

At dusk two bowls of vegetable chowder were poured, a pot was left simmering on the stove and a fire was crackling in the freshly cleaned fireplace. Every move was made carefully, aware of enlarged holes where broken, rotten and blood saturated planks had been removed. It was slow work. Their replacement would have to wait another day. Until then, a bit of hopping from joist to joist was needed in certain areas. Standing in the middle of the modest domain, equally modest progress was surveyed, but enough to call it quits for the day. It was dinner time.

Out by the machine-like wood splitter, a sense of gravity accompanied the prospect of disruption to inertia of vocal avoidance. Strangely nervous, Poyāma's lips felt stuck, as made of wax. *Soup* seemed to bear a worthy force and the most efficient announcement of dinner. But when he opened his mouth to speak the word, something unexpected and entirely different came out:

"Winter have no feel for you pain."

The boy stopped himself in mid-stroke. They stared at one another. Casting down the ax, he turned and ran off. After fifteen minutes of mortified contemplation, the offender turned and went back into the house. The soup went cold, the fire died and the hilltop retreat felt like asylum.

On the third day, hearing the sounds of hatchet, chisel and hammer over several hours, the boy left his ax. Gathering a stack of reworked planks and placing them beside a section needing work, he watched every move of his chosen mentor and duplicated each precisely. When the last piece was in place, they simultaneously sat up, propped on heels and gazing intently at one another. A silent question about the words spoken the previous evening was upon the boy's face. So it was answered with a shrug first, a frown, a few seconds of head wagging and finally, words:

"It jus come to me like wind . . . from somewhere . . . I don' know."

The boy bore a look of suspicion. He nodded before returning a shrug of his own. "He always said that to get me to do the chopin'."

They cleaned up. A new batch of soup was created together. Since neither could stomach eating inside the house, dinner was enjoyed in silence out on the hill behind it. When finished, both departed to their separate sleeping spots, the boy to the hay in the dilapidated storage building and Poyāma to the hilltop.

The night was cold, so the exterior sleeping arrangements were difficult to take, knowing the fireplace was clean and functional and a mountain of wood awaited fueling its use in warming the house.

Yet, even with the doors and windows remaining open, repugnant smells lingered. The following morning saw an agitated removal from the house and cleansing by fire of anything capable of holding scent—even where the use of a hatchet was necessary for shaving off a top layer of wood. When that was finished, the mountainous wood pile was stacked and organized and hay was used to make two beds in preparation for the move inside. But the doors and windows remained open for several days.

"How long since you smile?" Poyāma asked one night, After another dinner was consumed in silence. The boy stared back, blank. "I know a lady . . . ." There was a long pause. "I promise . . . if you see her smile . . . you smile get fix immediate."

He stood and went to the open doorway. Peering out into formless dark that seemed all too familiar, he wondered if the question and following assurance had actually been for his new acquaintance, or for some lost boy inside his own blankness.

Over the next few weeks, in exactly the same fashion that the floor was worked on together, a small corral was rebuilt for the horse, three outbuildings were either replaced or repaired, a porch was added to the house, wild game was hunted and dressed, wild vegetation was gathered and meals were cooked. An aged black bear was taken down by a single shot between the eyes by the youngster who was turning out to be a very quick study. Neither enjoyed the meat, but once dried in the air and sun, both liked the look of the black rug in the middle of the new cabin floor. Through the many activities and hours spent together, only the teacher spoke, and mostly to himself.

At the end of the fourth week, while enjoying a meal of roasted rabbit with stir fried onions, greens and mushrooms, the boy said, "My name is Malcolm."

A question followed as a mere cover for surprise: "Where does de name like Malcolm come from?"

Though it seemed plain enough, the inquiry was like a magic key opening a door to treasures of information. The boy had a good bit to say about the name Malcolm. Fact or fiction Poyāma could not tell, but either way, he felt a little jealous, having no such knowledge about his own. Beyond that it was learned that Malcolm had lost his mother—who he described as "tough 'n maybe a little mean"—over three years ago. She had gone off in a rage during one of her husband's drinking binges. "It was probably to just get away for awhile. She like to sit 'n the woods 'n cool down," he explained. His father too drunk to go after her, Malcolm did so when evening fell and she had not returned. A storm set in that night. It took him two days of constant searching to find her—by then weak and sickly. "She musta gotten lost 'n confused 'caus a the storm," he reasoned, distant. He muttered while recalling how he was able to get her home, that it did not take long for the pneumonia to set in. His father sobered up enough to help with the burial.

Poyāma was curious about a grown woman just going off and getting lost in woods around her own house. *Maybe she was drunk too*, he thought, hoping Malcolm might clear it up. But the boy said nothing more about the ordeal. It was evident he could not.

Malcolm's father, who already had an excessive fondness for alcohol, gradually declined into a perpetual drunken stupor. Once a marginally dedicated and mediocre farmer, the farm animals had long ago been sold. Acquaintances had been reduced to those few moonshiners who supplied his habit, which in turn required an occupation for payment, albeit nothing as extensive and demanding as farming. He turned to occasional horse thieving, for which he employed his son as scout and lookout.

The thieving events had become the highlights of Malcolm's life, the closest thing to the "normal life" he had known when it was a family of three. Forcing his father to sober up somewhat for a few days, the challenging heists required actual communication as they planned the activities together. Otherwise, due to the man's more general comatose existence, for the past year and a half Malcolm had lived a silent life. With no adult doing any hunting or cooking and no way to travel into town or pay for food, he had done his best taking care of the two of them by use of some skilled thieving and some paltry resources supplied by an elderly friend of his deceased mother, who dropped by infrequently to check in on him. The decision to sleep out in the hay had been made five months earlier and maintained throughout the summer and fall.

It was in the drunken condition that three former friends, fugitives, found his father when they dropped in unannounced to present their plan for "gettin' on with the stealin'" of the prized horses he had told them about. More essentially, they had a need for three saddled and provisioned horses. The law had been following them closely, but was ditched in the woods after a recent escape involving gunfire and the abandonment of their transportation and two runaway slaves they had hoped to make use of. These were among accounts Malcolm heard from beneath a window. It was he, however, who then provided information pinpointing direct approach and optimal timing. The vital particulars were product of investigative expeditions, which had become a favorite way to pass long lonely days. The young snoop had come to be possessor of more knowledge than anyone on details pertaining to the daily activities of ranches, farms and homesteads throughout a region covering ten to twenty miles in every direction. One such detail was the timely departure for California of six brothers employed by Vishnu Ranch.

Poyāma was, of course, enthralled with every revelation, especially those implying the nearness of home and connection to his own recent experiences. Questions were continually fed to the informer to keep the disclosures coming. Based on his best efforts to piece things together, three Thoroughbred horses had been saddled and supplied by Malcolm the morning of the fire and it was he that was sighted from an adjacent hill leading the horses away—a hill just a few miles from the little house. The boy had offered to steal and deliver the provisioned horses himself, not liking the ruthless talk of the criminals about ambush, raiding and killing "if necessary."

Malcolm had seen the beginning of the fire from inside Poyāma's own house, where he was stealing provisions. He had also watched the collection of fine horses escape, which he was glad to report to the villains. It was this information, supported by black smoke seen rising above the southern hills, which diverted their plans from an attack on Vishnu Ranch. Hunting down the loosed horses became the replacement plan. Once possessing the three Thoroughbreds needed for the job, keeping information regarding their whereabouts from the law and snuffing out witness to their criminal activities necessitated the shooting of Malcolm's father. Marked for the same demise, the boy had slipped away and spied from a favorite wooded refuge. The wood pile had begun the minute the outlaws departed for the hills to track down the coveted collection of horses. Shock, compulsion and lack of any alternative for dealing with the horrific consequences of involvement with wicked men had fueled dedication to the endeavor.

When all details had been heard and the most logical conclusions drawn, amazement was in the form of grief, gratefulness, outrage, urgency, worry and excitement all at once. The little hill on which Poyāma had slept several nights was at the base of a succession of larger hills separating them from the beginning of his property. The land features were not recognized because Vishnu ranch was so spacious he had never visited or approached it from beyond the northwest corner.

Poyāma chuckled and shook his head, amused by the thought of Malcolm waking up with the provisioned saddlebag at his side—the one he had personally packed and stolen.

Exactly how the three men came to be in possession of the fine collection of horses, and where they were headed with them, remained somewhat of a mystery. Poyāma recalled examining hoof prints intermingling with those left by Wind on a path high above the LaRue property. Remarkable as the odds seemed, evidence suggested the villains came out of the hills and stumbled upon LaRue's remote northern corral sometime after Xerxes had been buried and before Miller and his men arrived later that morning. Concerns for the LaRue family's wellbeing were greatly increased with every recall of sounds and shadowy movements in the woods the night of Xerxes' death over a month in the past. How the thieves got to the place where Poyāma encountered them was the one thing for which there were no clues. However it all came about, there was no doubt they were the three men swept away in the torrents of an unknown river.

Looking back to angry words yelled at a small horse thief disappearing over a hill, Poyāma stared at the boy thinking, *He save my life.* Looking over his shoulder as if seeing right through the south wall of the house at the burnt barn and stable, he whispered, "Dat fire save my life."

HARVEST

While preparing for bed, it occurred to Malcolm that he had given an awful lot of information without receiving any. Mentioning the fact, their introduction—a month in the making—was completed. As a rustler, he had only seen the rancher from a distance and never dark-faced as the bearded man before him. Upon hearing the name Vishnu he almost ran from the house. This was precisely the thing his guest was also resisting, so eager was he to ride the hills between the two homesteads. It was not the lack of pillows or the annoying prickles of hay beds that kept them both from sleeping much that night. Neither had the ability to turn off their busy minds.

In the morning, it came as a shock to Malcolm when he was asked to consider a flip-flop of house-guesting arrangements. When it was further explained to the young homeowner that his parents had left him the blessing of a nice inheritance of property, he finally did run from the house and resumed his former wood chopping endeavors in order to process the unforeseen flood of change in fortunes. While he whacked wood, Poyāma cleaned the house, packed their things and prepared the horse for travel. It was a mild December day in the mid-fifties and two o'clock before the youngster leaned his ax against the woodpile and ran to the side of the tall horse to be lifted up.

Fifteen minutes later they crested a hill and stopped.

As tears streamed down Poyāma's bearded face, the lower stable, cellar and winepress complex down in the valley appeared as a beehive of activity. Loaded wagons were met and unloaded, cargo taken into the press building. Several wagons, having been crushed under force of mud, were receiving final repairs. The surrounding grounds were so clean it was difficult to imagine their recent need of shoveling. To the right were the lower hills speckled with horses. Malcolm had never seen the land before them without being at ground level and studying the positions of horses while preoccupied with remaining unseen. Relaxed and seven feet off the ground on horseback, the view was much more extensive.

"How much of this is yours Mr. Vishnu?"

"Pretty much," Poyāma answered, reaching behind him to pat a knee, which was less bony than when they had met.

"That's what Mom 'n Dad had, pretty much. Dad liked farmin' before the whisky got 'im. He didn't mean for it to."

"What he didn' mean?"

There was no answer.

"What he didn' mean, Malcolm?"

"You know . . . to get like he did. I know he didn't mean to get with those bad men either."

Home was a hill away. Previously, nothing could keep the man of supreme focus from something so desired, important and near. But even as heart rate reflected excitement, a moment stood between him and his destination. It was a moment not to be lost. After Malcolm was lowered to the ground, Poyāma dismounted and bent to one knee before him.

"You fill in for him . . . dis no good. Dis ting you try for do is no good." He reached out and placed a hand on the boy's head. "You try for fill in where he leave off and fall short of de idea of 'Pa' you have in dis head. Den you muss fill in for 'Ma.' Den you muss fill in for 'I', den for 'we.' If you try for fill what only stay empty, de filling in never stop. Let go of what you expec, what let you down and cause you hurt. You muss look straight at de man and see him always for who he be. Let de idea pass . . . like de man who die . . . let it pass."

Tears, rolled down Malcolm's cheeks.

"Filling in for disappoin for we idea about all we expec only show de way for lie. But filling in for 'Pa' is de worse. If you fill in for Pa, it teach you how you muss fill in for God by build idea dat prop him up too. Dis de ting no man can do for God who already perfec full and have no need for prop. Dis de ting dat make for always keep a man back from de true God who show himself always for who he be."

Poyāma stood and took a small shoulder in each hand. Gazing down into eyes fixed on his, he said, "You pa *yield*. Yield is step aside. Yield is invite anoter power for take charge. Yield was de choice he make. We muss be true always for see what we see in every man." He picked Malcolm up and held him, long. "Only yield to God have power dat reverse yield dat cause harm."

Remounted on the horse, they rode the seemingly effortless gait of the racing bred stallion down the hill and into the valley. A few more powerful strides and they were atop the hill directly above Poyāma's house. To the left was quickly progressing construction of a new barn. To the right were trimmed vines, cleaned up of all blackened debris. Never had so many people graced the property. Most were recognized as town-folk. Many of them stopped what they were doing and stared up at the hilltop. Beyond the burnt portion of the vineyards, baskets filled with grape bunches were ubiquitous. Anne Willis was near the porch, waving. Her husband and children were finishing up the loading of a small wagon driven by pastor Eugene. He too waved.

Reaching the midpoint of the hill, LaRue was spotted over by the barn project. After laying down some lumber, his steps were quick toward the man wearing his coat. Malcolm under one arm, Poyāma dismounted. He set the boy down and covered his half of the distance between he and his friend with equal speed. Coming together, they grabbed each other by the shoulders and shook and shoved one another around vigorously.

"How is my broter?"

"Where've you been? I've been worried sick!"

"If I tell you, you never believe it. And I have more cause dan you know for worry about you too."

Seeing tears in one another's eyes, they were still for a moment, staring.

"I have some bad news about your horses and the deal with Miller," LaRue informed, breaking the silence.

"Don' worry, I sell dem to some bounty hunter."

"You what?"

"I catch tree tief wit dem by de raging river."

"What raging river?"

"Exac what I tink! I tell you all de detail later when you have time for a long story."

Others began gathering around as they talked. Sam Willis walked up with his two kids, one at each side. They shook hands heartily as if life-long friends.

"We were beginning to wonder if we would ever see you again," Sam said soberly. "But Richard kept reminding us of how tough and resourceful you are." He looked back over shoulder at the vineyards. "And this . . . who ever heard of yield like this in December? Although, these days more resemble late September, early October."

"I gotta hand it to ya Vish, you're a genius," LaRue interjected. "I thought the burning technique was a little extreme. It obviously got a bit out of control. But it sure woke up all the vines that didn't get scorched. And your patience, which I scoffed at, may be the key to your success." He laughed. "Changing the season . . . wow! Who'da thought?"

"No way! Dis no technique of any kind. I have no idea how dis . . ." Poyāma looked around the vineyard. "Dis a miracle dat have noting for do wit me, I promise. De season back home always hold out anoter mot. But I only talk de lie about exis someting new dat push back de season here for make you frustrate."

LaRue laughed. "O, sure, like I'm gonna believe that one. All I know is, you called it and it happened. You're the master. I'm finally ready to admit it." Poyama opened his mouth for another attempt to set the record straight, but, seeing the conviction of astonishment in his friend's eyes, no words would form. (From that moment on, any effort he made to correct the legend-size conclusion that he was master of vine *and* season was brushed aside by LaRue as mere modesty.)

"You know, Vish . . . ." Pausing, LaRue was suddenly quite serious. "I've coveted a lot that was yours before, but nothin' more than I covet your faith. Maybe if I had your faith . . . maybe I wouldn't a given up on my vineyards the last couple a years. Maybe I'd a seen a 'miracle' or two on my own land."

Poyāma looked around, silent, thoughtful. Finally turning back to his friend, he said, "I come back, and look . . . here you are working for help my land and build back my barn. Dis miracle is for we. You only need fait for share."

More reciprocal shoves and shoulder slaps demonstrated agreement.

"However it happened, miracle or genius, it happened practically over night," Sam said. "We had to round up help to handle all the work. It got to be such a spectacle of fun that folks just started showin' up from all over. I've met a lot a people." He looked at his wife, then back at Poyāma. "And made a lot a friends quicker 'n I ever dreamed possible."

LaRue stepped forward and placed a hand on Sam's shoulder. "And this fella . . . he can't be outworked. In fact, he reminds me of a maniacal Chilean man I know, a one-man labor force. Still, I defy even you, Vish, to keep up hammer and shovel with Sam for a day."

"No way! Dose day forget my knowing face and look for younger man like he for run a place like dis." Poyāma looked at Sam and raised his brows. "We talk later. Settle up for de mont you already work and look to de future."

He looked at LaRue. "It take me a long travel, but I come to decide you get it right."

"I got what right?"

"What you say ten year back when I leave you place upset."

"What was it?"

"'We all immigran here.'"

They grabbed hold of each other and exchanged hard pats on the shoulders.

"Who is that?" Ben asked his dad, pointing over to the boy standing beside a horse left to graze higher up the hill.

"O, I can' believe . . . ! How I leave you back like dat!" Poyāma scolded himself, whirling and running toward Malcolm. Taking him by the hand, they were quickly back with everyone else, the new Vishnu overwhelmed with warm introductions. He met more people in those welcoming moments than he had seen in the previous five years.

Poyāma looked at the young Willis couple and smiled. "Maybe I find you a place over dose hill we come from dat you can' believe. We go tomorrow for have a look. Den you and Malcolm have a talk. It belong for he."

Husband and wife looked at one another. Sam's face bore that serious expression connected to the fact that they had no money. "What can it hurt to have a look?" he said.

"Sounds fun," Anne added, as they both looked back at the enthusiastic salesman.

Suddenly, Anne looked over her shoulder, upset. "O, my goodness, I invited Gloria in to help me bake and left her in the house working alone."

"Yeah, and that was after she organized and instructed the vineyard crew, then spent the morning helping us raise those walls over there," Sam added. "Just point 'er in a direction and she'll get it done, whatever it is."

As Anne turned to head back to the house, Sam held onto his wife's hand. LaRue gave his returning neighbor an encouraging smack on the shoulder. It was not needed. Poyāma's heart was declaring the moment—the first time it had been in danger since the loss of his brother many years in the past. He was striding in the direction of the back porch of his house. Arriving at the open door, he stopped before leaning to look in. Gloria was also leaning, reaching into the oven.

"I never know dis place have a way for smell dis good," he said, stepping inside.

Gloria stood up, tipped the bread just removed from the oven in his direction and shrugged. "All credit goes to the bread."

"Can I show you someting?" Poyāma asked.

Gloria set the bread down but looked conflicted about leaving another loaf in the oven. The oven door was closed. "I like the beard," she said, as they walked outside.

Standing at the railing on the right side of the porch, Poyāma pointed down at the large stones beneath them. "I call dis Gloria Garden. I keep dis beautiful tend in you absence . . . for tink of you every day." Unsure how the idea of spiders as namesakes might be taken, he left it at that.

"It is beautiful," she said.

"Gloria, if I never have you by my side for wife, still I will never stop for cultivate dis love. And I continue for live and die a man I enjoy and strive for be. But if you see your way for become my bride, you make everyting sweeter . . . better . . . like de perfec wine I wait too long for tase."

Gloria was stunned by the boldness and spontaneity of the unforeseen proposal. Quickly, amazement at audacity was converting the initial jolt into offense. Poyāma, too, was surprised by what had been spoken by his own mouth. It was unplanned. And he too thought it needed some context.

"Do you remember de word what you speak . . . a maturity for what you heart will yearn?" For a moment they looked at one another as if traveling ten years into the past through one another's eyes, both enveloped by one memory. Gloria nodded.

"It finally come. Please . . . forgive me for how it take so long."

Gloria reached up and wiped tears from Poyāma's cheeks before addressing her own.

"However why, dat maturity for what you yearn have a very hard time for come to me. And I have a hard time getting found by it. But it finally come. You will see."

They stared long, this time finding the future in each other's eyes.

"Can I show *you* something?" Gloria asked. Turning and leading to the other side of the porch, she said, "You have a new corral."

Poyāma arrived at the rail beside her, eyes wide, mouth open. "But the same old horses," she proudly reported.

There, in a temporary corral off the western side of the front of his house were horses freed from the stable just before fire consumed it.

"How . . . what . . . I can' believe . . . ."

"All were gathered outside my door one morning."

They looked at one another. "You broter?" Poyama asked.

Gloria shook her head. "He says 'no.' But he did build the corral." Looking back out at the fine collection, she announced, "Twenty-four."

Several larger horses from Xerxe's side of the stable—those unable to stay with the charge of the initial group—were recognized. The rest of those before him were from the east corridor.

So, I lose nine dat go back in and stay wit de stable, Poyāma surmised after doing some silent math. He shook his head, lamenting. Spotting his Egyptian Arabian twins, he whispered, "DaKhla and Kharga. Now, Dat make me happy."

Gloria looked up at him. "The desert oases?"

With evident surprise, the insight was returned, "How you know Egyp so well?"

"Egyptian vineyards . . . ancient beginnings . . . are you kidding?"

Poyāma laughed. "Now, dat make me happy even more!"

Leaning against the porch railing, they talked of recent events until interrupted by the smell of burnt bread and smoke finding its way from the kitchen out of the house. Ignoring the words, "No problem, I have experience wit dis kind of ting," Gloria raced inside to make sure more *experience* was avoided.

A brief courtship was enough to convince Gloria that the man pursuing her was different than the one whose love had been so easily superseded by offence and success. Aided by Gloria's olfactory genius and lengthy discussions about the taste of wind, Poyāma made good on his promise to create Wind Wine, which became the vineyard's signature label, propelling their entire line of wines to a whole new level of popularity and broadened distribution. It was said that Vishnu Vineyards and wines had no rival for "rejoice."

Epilogue

Leaving the actual vineyard labor to Sam and his growing staff, Poyāma became Overseer in the higher sense exemplified by The House in the Casablanca Valley of his youth. This dispelled the longstanding notion that the owners of The House merely lorded over laborers employed to do all their work for them. In fact, Poyāma quickly came to appreciate the words servant and overseer as synonymous. It was the most demanding and most gratifying work he had ever done.

The adventures with Wind left a soulful imprint. Poyāma constantly sensed the silvery white movements as if they cast bright, fleeting shadows in the corridors of his mind. Generous actions resulted, as did a reputation for "the zeal of goodness."

LaRue found his real love to be horses and his ability to breed and train them quite exceptional. Once resolved to shift devotions toward raising horses, winemaking fell back rather naturally to a semi-serious hobby. LaRue Ranch was soon bustling to meet the demands of a loyal and discriminating clientele.

When the rumor mill leaked hints about a very special foal at the LaRue's, Poyāma questioned Richard, who postured clueless. Questions turned to objections of "some hush-hush mystery of de ranch." These always returned a shrug, which in turn inspired a scolding, like, "A man don' keep his friend always back wit secret . . . no way should a broter get treat like dat!" Such was generally followed by agreement—"I know, Vish . . . you're right . . ."—but never explanation.

On a crisp July dawn under a corrugated orange and violet sky, LaRue passed beneath the entry to Vishnu LaRue Vineyards, reigns in his left hand, reigns in his right. Seeing his friend scurrying about in the distance making final preparations for another long-planned adventure, he gave his horse a gentle nudge to pick up the pace. Soon, arriving at the staging sight, he dismounted. "For you," he said, and handed over the reigns to the tallest, most stately black stallion upon which Poyāma had ever laid his eyes. "I remembered our conversation about Xerxes' stud fees and after a long search found a fella in Georgia." He looked up at the horse. "Pure Fresian . . . the great-grandson of Xerxes."

With every first-hint of changing season came the stirring necessity for Poyāma to head off on an expedition. LaRue was first to be notified and proudly supplied "expedition worthy" steeds for the three or four others that always turned up, eager to go along. Malcolm was an automatic inclusion and they were joined by Gloria and Claudia every third adventure or so. Like Columbus sailing for India, many noteworthy discoveries were made and adventures had while attempting to find the great, raging river, but it was never located . . . at least, not by them. With every failed pursuit, LaRue indulged a playful conviction that the river and the stories surrounding it were fictional. They did find the fissure in the mountain above the LaRue ranch, but not the pistol or the pocket watch lost there. (A broken chain hung from an empty black holster on the wall in the Vishnu home, reminding its owner of experiences he knew to be real.) Most excursions turned up a "Malcolm" or two, welcomed along and almost always returning with the explorers to take up residence amid an equally welcoming community in and around the small town of Morisa in the vineyard rich valley of Yadkin.

Never did two in-laws drink longer or more deeply from the blessed wines of brotherhood, friendship and forgiveness. More than once, while riding side by side, Poyāma looked over at Richard and said, "Once in he life, if very lucky, a man find a friend like you. I tink God himself connec us."

The response was always the same. "Don't talk like that, Vish. Except for havin' to endure your tall tales of swollen rivers and your radiant horse friend, I was just beginnin' to respect you for your good judgment." For this, LaRue endured *more* previously unspoken details intended to validate the stories about the glorious white stallion, Wind. Those stories grew to encompass Poyāma's entire life, throughout which he came to believe he caught glimpses of Wind.

A different validation did come, in the form of respect, when Richard and Claudia LaRue accompanied Poyāma, Gloria and Malcolm on a trip to the Casablanca Valley of central Chile. Honor the Frenchman received from *French* wine masters at The House solely by association with his Creole speaking neighbor and friend proved humbling. He also gained a different opinion of the value of experimentation when learning of its significant influence on the French wine industry. LaRue returned home from Chile feeling more authentically "French" than ever before, and nobler in Poyāma's company than he could have otherwise imagined. Numerous subsequent trips were made.

The experimental motivations of the partners of The House initially led them to central Chile. As it turned out, Chilean conditions were uniquely retardant to the pestilential louse, phylloxera, a blight decimating European vineyards. Owners of French vineyards seeking a refuge to avert annihilation found The House well established in that land and instrumental in their transplant throughout its vine-friendly valleys. Decades of scientific research and experimentation at The House informed the work of other scientists in the United States and Europe, a process which LaRue followed closely, on occasion proving to be an important liaison. Such efforts lead to the solution saving Europe and the world from phylloxera: grafting susceptible rootstock to rootstock immune to the blight. Though his contribution was minute, Richard LaRue found personal reward in the redemption of his ancestral vineyards from ruin.

Sam and Anne did indeed fall in love with the little home Poyāma and Malcolm restored. By hard work and the help of solid employment, they paid a fair price for it. What went on inside the house prior to the restoration remained known only by the two renovators. Malcolm, Ben and Emily were as one another's shadows, riding their horses every chance they got over the hills separating their homes. Only a few times did they have a serious "fallin' out," as Malcolm called such things. In each case, he went silent and took to chopping wood. Soon, having come to some resolve by that curious means, he would head off to set things right and all would be back to normal.

On the first family visit to Chile, Malcolm hit it off with his new grandparents immediately, whom he took to calling "Papa-Vish" and "Ma-Māya." But his bond with Māya was by all counts something special. From then on Malcolm made annual trips to the Casablanca Valley, most accompanied and funded by Poyāma, some paid for with Māya's weaving income, and the rest paid for by Malcolm himself, using money received from the sale of his family homestead.

It was not until his third trip—the first one alone—that Māya felt compelled to ask why, of all the people she had known in her life, he loved and understood her so. After a minute or two of silence, he leaned close, looked her right in the eyes and said, "Ma-Māya, my mama was blind . . . and in his own way, Papa was too." From that moment, it never entered Māya's mind that Malcolm was any other than her own kin. Poyāma learned of the interaction through his father and was amazed at the boy's ability to keep such secrets. Malcolm never saw it as ability with secrecy, but incapability with certain subjects.

As she had done through the years, Māya sat once in awhile with subtle furrows of frustration upon her forehead, bothered, wanting to recall just some small piece of the inspiration for the name Poyāma. When finally exasperated, she would force her thoughts in another direction. Turning to her husband, Vishnu, she would say something about how pleased she was with Poyāma, with their daughter-in-law, Gloria, with their friends, Richard and Claudia LaRue, and with their treasured grandson, Malcolm. She would then express to him her thankfulness for their many years of "side-by-side." That was the closest she ever came to recalling the meaning.

For the rest of his days Poyāma made frequent treks up into the tall hills to the northeast. Alone, he sat remembering, always with the same anticipation of a glimpse of Wind, anticipation invariably ending in disappointment. And always, when he returned, disappointment melted away at the sight of his beloved Gloria and the sound of her voice.

Edwards Brothers Inc.
Ann Arbor MI. USA
September 25, 2017